Chris Curran was born in London but now lives in St Leonards-on-Sea near Hastings, on the south coast of England, in a house groaning with books. She left school at sixteen to work in the local library – her dream job then and now – and spent an idyllic few months reading her way around the shelves. Returning to full-time education, she gained her degree from Sussex University. Since then she has worked as an actress, script writer, copy editor and teacher, all the time looking forward to the day when she would see her own books gracing those library shelves.

Mindsight is her debut novel.

CHRIS CURRAN

Mindsight

KILLER READS

an imprint of HarperCollins*Publishers*
www.harpercollins.co.uk

Killer Reads
An imprint of HarperCollins*Publishers*
1 London Bridge Street
London SE1 9GF

www.harpercollins.co.uk

This paperback edition 2015
1

First published in Great Britain by
HarperCollins*Publishers* 2015

Copyright © Chris Curran 2015

Chris Curran asserts the moral right to
be identified as the author of this work

A catalogue record for this book is
available from the British Library

ISBN: 978-0-00-813273-6

Set in Minion by Born Group using Atomik ePublisher from Easypress

For Paul, with much love

Chapter One

The road twisted ahead, a blur of heat shimmering above it. I looked away, my eyes dazzled by the fields flashing past: bright green, pale green, dark green, brown, brown, acid yellow, and green again.

Alice changed gear into what must have been fifth, and I gripped the edge of my seat. 'OK, Clare? Won't be long now.' She reached across to flip open the glove compartment. 'There's some water in there.'

It was fizzy and tasted harsh, drying my mouth even more. I closed my eyes. And here it was again: that other road. A dark road, flickering with shadows of trees and cloud. Then the stab of light and the chaos of jolting, screeching, and skidding. *Oh, God.*

I jerked upright and saw we were approaching the turn off for Wadhurst. Something pulled hard on my insides and my foot pressed an imaginary brake. 'Alice, do you think …' My voice cracked.

She looked over at me and slowed the car, then pulled into a lay-by. Her blue eyes were clouded. 'We can't, Clare. I haven't told him it's today. And you said yourself it was better to wait. Get settled first.'

I nodded: she was right. She squeezed my hand, giving me a wobbly smile. 'OK?' I managed another nod, and Alice drove on, as I looked back down the road and that tug came again, so strong this time it felt like pain.

Another swig from the bottle; the gassy stuff stinging my throat. Alice twisted a dial and a draught of cold air blew into my face and around my ankles. 'Any better?' she asked.

'I'm sorry, can we stop again?'

She pulled into a pub car park and I got out, tugging at the jeans and shirt that clung too tight. Alice walked round to open the boot.

'Look, why don't you put on something cooler?'

All I wanted now was to get back to the safety of the car, away from the wide sky and the fields, but I pulled out the holdall and followed her. The toilets were just inside the main door, and Alice led me into the Ladies, leaning on a sink and talking to my reflection, her own distorted by the mirror.

'I'll leave you to it then.' She rubbed my back. 'I'll get us some lunch. You should eat something.'

The place was cool and clean, a bowl of potpourri between the two sinks, but as I rifled through my clothes I could smell the stench of prison on them: strong enough to overwhelm the faint scent of lavender. My face in the mirror was bleached stone beneath the dark curls, and the fluorescent light revealed lines around my eyes that I'd never noticed before. *Thirty-three wasn't that old, was it?* I pinched my cheeks, running my fingers through my hair.

Locked in a cubicle, I stripped off. The floor was cool under my bare feet, and I rested my head on the metal door. Then put on a thin blouse and cotton trousers.

I felt better for the change, but as I stood in front of the sinks again, staring at my white face, I couldn't imagine how I would get through the door. *Come on; come on, just do it.* A woman and child burst in, the little girl holding the door for me, and I found myself in the bar.

I stood, with the conspicuous holdall on the floor beside me, scanning the room. The worn floorboards stretched away to open French windows, a babble of voices echoing all around.

I couldn't see Alice.

'Don't look so worried, darling. If you can't find your friend, you can sit with me.'

I recognised that look. You get it even in prison. The one that imagines fucking you, making you squirm. I wanted to tell him what I was – to take that smirk off his face – but instead I clenched my teeth and headed for the French windows.

She was sitting by a stream, her blue dress hanging over the edge of her chair, pale legs stretched out before her, strappy sandals on her feet. I forced a smile as I sat and she motioned to the drinks.

'I got you still water.' She raised her own glass, full of white bubbles. 'Ordered us some sandwiches too.'

I took a sip, grateful for an excuse not to speak or to look at the girl who approached with two plates.

'Tuna, or cheese and tomato?'

Alice smiled at her, then back at me. 'We'll share shall we, Clare?'

For all the world as if we were friends out for a jaunt in the country. Two men glanced over at us as they brought their pints to the next table: the younger giving Alice's long legs an appreciative look up and down. She tucked them under her chair and his glance flickered to me, before returning to his drink.

We were nothing like sisters, of course, and I wondered if we even passed for friends.

Alice's blue dress was crisp and her blonde hair dropped like pale water to her shoulders. Looking at her, I couldn't help pulling at my creased trousers and moving my feet behind my holdall to hide my trainers.

She pushed some keys across the table at me. 'I hope the flat's OK. It was three months' rent in advance, so no need to worry about that for a bit.'

We ate for a while in silence, but I didn't have much appetite, and Alice soon stopped eating too. She looked into her glass, twisting it so the bubbles swirled and sparkled.

'I've mentioned you to a friend who owns a florist's shop near the flat. She might have some work for you, if you're interested. Just don't rush it.'

'Who is she?'

'Don't worry; it's no one you know. Stella's the sister of an old boyfriend.' She laughed. 'I realised I didn't like him much, but Stella and I hit it off and we've stayed in touch.'

'What did you tell her … about me I mean?'

'The truth – more or less.'

She would have done it perfectly. Even as a little girl, five years my junior, I remembered her watching my tantrums with puzzled eyes.

'Your little sister's nothing like you,' people would say and, depending on my mood, I might laugh and say it was just as well. In my darker moments, I would shout, 'She's not my real sister, that's why. I'm adopted. I'm not even English.' I told people my mother was a Romanian princess, knowing she must really have been a peasant who couldn't, or didn't want to, support a child.

'Oh look, aren't they lovely,' Alice said, as a flotilla of grey cygnets appeared around the bend in the stream and she began tearing pieces of crust from her sandwich and tossing them into the water. Soon the cygnets were jostling and squabbling for the bread, as the parent swans glided in, their wings arched behind them. 'That's a threat you know. They're warning us not to hurt their babies.' She cast a few more crumbs at the birds, as the parents' tiny black eyes watched.

I hoisted my bag onto my shoulder. 'Shall we go?' I wanted the journey over. I needed to be alone.

As we got closer to the sea, small grey clouds drifted across the sun, reminding me of the little cygnet siblings. Poor Alice, she had stuck by me through it all, and yet, I had never said more than the odd, gruff, thank you.

4

'You're still my sister, and I know how sorry you are for what happened,' was all she said, when I asked her why she was so good to me in spite of everything.

By the time we got to Hastings, and turned onto the seafront road, the sky had changed from blue to white, the water grey and almost still. There was some kind of hold up and the traffic stretched ahead, unmoving. The layer of cloud covering the sun had trapped the heat and stifled the breeze so it was hotter than ever. Alice tapped her nails on the steering wheel and opened the window to peer ahead.

'Oh God, what now?' She put both hands behind her neck, lifting the shimmer of hair away from her skin. 'At this rate it'll be rush hour before I get back on the A21.'

I wanted to shout that I couldn't stand sitting in this sweatbox any longer, that I needed to be alone and quiet, but, instead, I leaned back and closed my eyes.

A scream jolted me from my trance, and I stared up at the huge sky filled with a mass of whirling white. But it was just a flock of seagulls, their shrieks echoing against the thick roof of cloud as they fought over scraps of fish.

We'd reached the Old Town, huddled between two hills, and the gulls were circling over the boats drawn up on the shingle and the tall, black net huts where the fishermen stored their gear. Alice pulled into one of the narrow streets; the car slowed, this time, by holidaymakers sucking ices and eating chips from paper parcels.

'It's just up here, round the back of the church,' she said.

As the road became steeper, and the jumble of small, crooked houses and shops gave way to larger, Victorian villas, the tourists disappeared. Apart from the gulls, we could have been in any suburban street. Alice pulled into a parking bay, touching my arm as I undid my seatbelt. 'Careful, this is a rat run. They drive up and down here like maniacs.'

I got out slowly, my feet uncertain on the steep road. 'It's just here.' She pulled open a gate and shepherded me into the overgrown garden of a large house. Four bells flanked the blue door. 'Go on, your flat's number one. You've got half the ground floor.'

I fumbled at the lock until she took the key and slotted it in. The tiled hallway was cool; the doors to the two downstairs flats facing each other and between them a wide staircase leading to what Alice said were two more flats. My door was on the right, and Alice ushered me in and moved straight on to a swift guided tour.

In the bright living room, she said, 'There's only a small TV, but you won't mind that.' She looked at me and smiled. 'What?'

'It's just that, TV becomes so important when you're inside. But you're right; the last thing I want to do is sit in front of the box.' Even as I said it I wondered how true that was.

The sofa and two mismatched armchairs looked clean and comfortable but, seeing me look at them, Alice said, 'They're a bit shabby, but you can always brighten them up with cushions.'

She was trying so hard and part of me wanted to hug her and tell her how grateful I was. Another part longed for her to shut up and go away.

As I followed her into the kitchen, I saw the coffee maker next to the kettle. Alice must have noticed my stillness. She gripped my forearm. 'Oh, no, did I do wrong bringing it here? I thought you'd want it. I know how you love your strong coffee.'

It was from my old house. Alice had cleared the place when I asked her to sell it. I ran my fingers over the glass and touched the new packet of coffee she'd put beside it. I couldn't speak, but as I headed back to the living room I managed to smile.

She cleared her throat and walked over to a small table in the corner. 'I sorted out the new laptop for you, like I said. Set it up with broadband, email, and everything.' She picked up a little note-book. 'I've written all the details, your email address, passwords, and so on, in there so you should be ready to go.'

'Thank you. You didn't need to do all that,' I said.

She was smiling and holding up a white envelope. 'And there's this too.' I recognised the writing at once. 'Go on,' she said, 'it won't bite.'

The card had an old-fashioned photo on the front. Three little girls on a beach in white dresses and sun hats. The two bigger children had long dark curls and the smallest was an angelic blonde. Inside: *Welcome home, dearest Clare, with all our love from Emily and Matt. (Hope to see you soon!) XXXX*

As I closed the card I couldn't stop a sob bubbling up. Alice came behind me, resting her chin on my shoulder. 'Oh, Clare.' Her voice wobbled with tears, too. 'They're just like us.' That was how we had always been: Alice, and me, and our cousin Emily, who was like another sister.

I hadn't seen Emily, or her husband Matt, for more than three years.

Alice sighed and walked over to stand by the four large sash windows. 'I'm sorry the place smells musty.' She fiddled with the old-fashioned locks and managed to push up one of the sashes, catching her finger and letting out a muttered curse. 'It's a shame it's so cloudy: there's normally a wonderful sea view from this room.'

I peered out over the misted rooftops to the whiteness beyond – a couple of dark fishing boats, nosing close to shore, the only things to distinguish sea from sky. Alice perched on the arm of the sofa, sucking her torn finger.

'What do you think? Is it all right?'

I nodded, without turning, and she was suddenly behind me, so close the warmth coming from her brought a prickle of sweat to my spine. I inched away, but she put her hands on my elbows, giving them a gentle shake.

'You don't like it do you? And you'll be all alone here. I should have insisted you come to us, taken you straight home.'

The quiver in her voice brought a spurt of anger. It was too late to start on that again. In the old days I would have flared up at her, but not now.

'I'm fine, and the flat's lovely. Thanks for sorting it out.'

'I got some shopping for you – just the basics – but don't offer me coffee because …' glancing at her watch, 'I need to get off. Shall I ring you later?'

'Better leave it till tomorrow. I'm so tired I think I need to settle in then get to bed.'

She gestured to the telephone. 'I've put my mobile number, as well as the one for home, into your phone memory, so you don't need to call the house until you're ready.' After a moment's hesitation, she pulled me to her and whispered, 'It'll be all right.' But I couldn't speak and my arms hung heavy at my sides.

She stopped at the door and I forced a smile. 'Go on. I'm OK.'

The kitchen overlooked the front garden and I watched her go. She turned at the gate to wave, and I raised my hand, longing to call her back and ask her to take me home with her.

When I heard the car start up and drive away, I pulled down the kitchen blind, went back into the living room and shut the window to let silence fill the place. Then I sat on the sofa, leaning back and closing my eyes. *Deep breaths, one step at a time.*

In the bedroom, I unpacked the holdall, my clothes lost in the big wardrobe. My one precious possession – the photograph in its cheap plastic frame – I put on the bedside table, my fingers lingering for a moment over each glassy face.

Alice had made the bed, and I pulled off my clothes and crawled into the soft darkness, lying hunched with the effort of clamping my mind shut. I knew I deserved to feel the pain the oh-so-familiar thoughts and images would bring, but, for now, I would allow myself a few, blessed, moments of peace.

I woke to darkness, knowing I'd slept for hours. I didn't need a clock to tell me it was 3 a.m.: the time I'd woken every night for the past five years. Oddly enough, there was no confusion about where I was. The softness and the stretch of the bed around me, the silence and the feeling of space told me everything. I thought of my friend, Ruby, and longed to feel her warm, brown skin against mine; to tell her how frightened I was. But Ruby was still in prison, and I knew she'd only repeat the last thing she said to me: 'This is the first day of the rest of your life, girl. So, get out there and live it.'

The floorboards were cold under my feet as I fumbled for socks and a sweatshirt. I knew, if I turned on the lamp, I'd never be able to cross the huge space to the door, but there was enough grey light to lead me to the living room windows. As I looked out, I felt a shock of disorientation; it seemed the stars were below, and the dark sea above. Then I realised that, of course, there *were* no stars. The shining pinpoints were lights from the houses in the town below; the darkness, above and beyond, was the sky merging with the water. I recalled the milky emptiness I'd seen from the same window earlier and the phrase that had come to mind then – *the end of the world*. This was how ancient mapmakers thought of the Earth: a slab of land bustling with life, a strip of sea and then – nothing – just emptiness.

I leaned my forehead against the window and closed my eyes. If I could stay perfectly still, block out my thoughts again, I might be able to sleep when I got back to bed. But the chill glass, dripping condensation on my skin, brought me fully alert. I was shivering, rocking back and forth, and chanting the familiar, meaningless charm, 'Oh God, oh God, help me.' It brought no more comfort than my own clutching arms, or my head beating against the cold glass.

The darkness in my head flickered with images of flames, my ears echoed with screams, and I longed for Ruby to hold me and help me cry away the agony. 'That's it, baby,' she would say, 'you'll feel better soon.' And a storm of tears would exhaust me so much that I no longer felt anything. But now, alone, I couldn't cry, and I knew that all the tears and the therapy had just been another way to keep up the barricades.

I sometimes went to church services in the early days in prison, and the chaplain talked once about what he called *the dark night of the soul*. It seemed a good way to describe how I felt. But, later, I read another phrase that fitted better – *the torments of the damned*.

For I was certainly damned for what I'd done.

Chapter Two

The phone jolted me from sleep and I sat up, hugging my arms tight around my knees.

'Hello Clare, it's me. Are you there?'

I grabbed the handset. 'Alice, your name didn't register.'

'I'm ringing from the surgery. I can't talk long. Just wanted to check you were all right.'

'I'm fine. What time is it?'

'Half past eight. Try to get out for a bit today, won't you. A walk will do you good.'

'I should go and see your friend in the flower shop.'

'Don't rush it. I told Stella not to expect you immediately. Why not start by meeting your neighbours. The ones I talked to seemed lovely.'

In the end, I couldn't get myself through the door. Still wearing the musty T-shirt I'd slept in, I switched on the TV and curled on the sofa in front of it, dozing and waking, dozing and waking. According to the weather forecast, it was the hottest heatwave since 1976, and when I opened the windows, all that came in was steaming air and the screeches of the gulls. I made tea and toast I didn't finish, wanting only to sleep again.

Around four o'clock, I found myself staring at the phone. I picked it up, put it down, then tried again. At the third or fourth attempt I began to dial the number, but halfway through, I clicked to disconnect and threw the handset onto the other end of the sofa, as far from me as it would go. Then I dragged myself back to bed, pressing my face into the pillow. *You coward, you fucking coward.*

I didn't leave the flat for three days. When I wasn't huddled on the sofa or in bed, I was in the bathroom, standing under the shower, letting the water soak into me, through me, washing out the filth of five years.

Alice rang every morning, and on the second day I lied that I was going for a walk later on. Each afternoon, around four, I would sit and stare at the phone, my hands clammy, mouth dry. Once or twice I started to dial. Once, I even let it ring for half a second before clicking to disconnect, my whole body shaking.

On the fourth morning I made myself get up early, glad to see that, at last, the sun had disappeared and a light curtain of rain made the outdoors more kindly, easier to hide in. I knew I had to get out and I needed to find something decent to wear to visit the florist's. I'd been watching and listening for my neighbours; the flat across the hall from mine seemed to be occupied by a young woman with a small child. My kitchen overlooked the front garden and I saw them, through a gap in the blinds, leaving about 8.30 every morning, and coming back around half past five.

Today the woman looked back, fair hair flopping over her face, and I jumped away from the window. It was minutes before I caught my breath, but the silence and the empty front garden reassured me they were safely out of the way.

Alice had said one upstairs flat was empty, but I heard enough from directly above to guess someone was living there: someone who liked jazz and was often walking around in the early hours, but sometimes clumped down the stairs in the morning too.

I stood by my closed front door, listening, and checking my bag yet again. My keys, the most important things of all, were still there, nestled in an inside pocket.

11

I had the cash Alice had given me on the first day and there was a debit card too. She'd put £5,000 in the account and told me I could have more whenever I needed it. After all, she said, Dad would have wanted that. I wasn't so sure.

I was still inside, minutes later, with no idea what to do next: it had been so long since I'd been free to walk through a closed door. I made myself turn the knob and peep out. The hall was silent, and I stood for a moment, steadying my breath. A creak from somewhere above had me shutting the door again: leaning my head on it. *Come on, come on. Get on with it, you stupid cow.*

I forced myself through the hall, stumbling down the garden and out of the gate in one gasping rush. A car roared past, almost brushing me with its wing mirror, and I remembered Alice's warning about the traffic. There was no pavement here, so hugging the hedge, and unsure whether to look behind or ahead, I scurried down the hill.

The rain had stopped by the time I reached the safety of a narrow pavement and the sun was out again, already hot enough to send filaments of steam from the patches of water on the ground. I didn't dare go into any of the tiny shops in the Old Town, but it wasn't far to the modern shopping centre where I could be anonymous. It might have been a pleasant stroll, but I kept my head down, my whole body clenched against anyone coming too close. No one knew me here – one of the reasons, along with the cheap rents, I'd chosen Hastings for my bolthole – but I felt as conspicuous as if I wore a convict suit, complete with arrows. I couldn't forget the publicity around my trial – the photographers. I was even something of a minor celebrity in Holloway Prison at first, which certainly hadn't helped.

It was still early, so the shopping mall was almost deserted, but the colours were so bright, the floor so shiny, my eyes were dazzled. I stood still and began to take in the individual shops. Marks and Spencer was in front of me. Yes, that would do, it was big enough for me to pass unnoticed, and empty enough, at this hour, that I wouldn't have to queue. It would all be over in a few minutes – and then back home.

Inside, it seemed huge, the lights too brilliant. But it was quiet, just a few figures wandering at a safe distance. The rails of clothes, crowded together, gave some shelter and I walked through them, touching the soft cloth of shirts and trousers and avoiding the mirrors.

At last I spotted a few dresses. A blue one looked OK, not my size, but there was another in green that would have to do. Scrabbling with my bag and purse, I tried to replace the dress on the rack, but it didn't seem to fit. When I let go, it fell to the floor dislodging the blue one and a white cardigan. My breath caught in my throat as I tried to control the clothes, the hangers, my purse, and my bag, and the purse came open in my hand spilling coins onto the floor.

'That's all right, dear.' A waft of perfume as she picked up the bundle of clothes, shaking them and slotting them back in place, then crouched beside me. 'Can I help?'

'No.' I clutched the purse to my chest, knocking her hand away from the scatter of coins.

She flinched, her face flushing under the film of make-up.

I left her there, and the money where it lay, and looked for the exit. I couldn't think where all these people had come from. I pushed past a woman posing in front of a mirror with a frilly strip of something, and bumped into a pushchair. There were stacks of china and glittering glass around me, as I turned on the spot, terrified to move in case I broke something.

At last, I saw the doors and was able to get out. But the mall was crowded, now, and my ears throbbed with the clamour: squeals of laughter from a group of women, a screeching child in a pushchair, and behind it all the tinkle of piped music.

It was hot, so hot, and, head down to hide the tears that had begun to sting my eyes, I made for the main doors. As I reached them, a teenage boy charged through, bashing hard into my shoulder. The stab of pain brought me back to my senses and I made myself stand for a moment to get my bearings, then headed for the seafront.

On the promenade I stopped, leaned on the rails, and looked out over the calm water, slowing my breath to match each rhythmic sweep of waves back and forth. You're not in prison anymore, I told myself, and the woman was trying to help you. That's what people do outside. Five years of learning to fight, to meet aggression with aggression, to show everyone you're hard so they won't bully you. To make sure you never let anyone near your precious spends, or your few belongings. That was something I had to unlearn if I was to be fit for normal society.

Back at the house, I felt in my bag for the keys, my breath catching when I couldn't find them.

'Here, I've got mine out already, let me do it.' It was the young woman with her pushchair. The red-faced baby, head slumped, asleep.

'I'm Nicola, Nic, and you must be Alice's sister. It's Clare isn't it? She said you'd be moving in soon.' I managed a nod as she opened the door and together we dragged the pushchair inside.

'Honestly, the nursery phones me at work,' she said. '"Your Molly's been sick you need to come and get her." By the time I'm there she's playing and laughing with her little mates, but they still make me take her home. Any excuse.'

Her chatter helped to calm me and I found my keys easily enough.

'Let's have a coffee sometime,' she said, hauling the baby into her arms. The little girl was blonde, like her mother, her hair curling at the nape of her neck, chunky legs hanging down. So vulnerable.

In the flat, I made some tea, cradling the warm mug. Tea was Ruby's remedy. At one session in prison, the therapist, Mike, asked us to write and read out an account of our lowest moment. For Ruby it was when her pimp threatened her children if she didn't work that night. She stabbed him. 'But the kids are safe with my mum and they know I did it for them.' Mike sat po-faced, as the rest of us clapped.

I couldn't bring myself to read my account and Ruby told me I needed a cup of tea. I gave her the paper and afterwards there were tears in her eyes to match my own.

I killed my family. That was what I'd written. My father, my husband, and my darling son. And my darkest moment was when I finally had to admit I must have been to blame. I couldn't remember the crash and although some people thought that should be a comfort, Ruby realised it only added to the agony.

It was my cousin Emily's wedding day, in the Lake District. I'd never driven Dad's Mercedes before and I enjoyed the contrast of its smooth comfort to the bumps and grunts of my own rust bucket. But it was further than we'd realised, the roads narrow and winding, and we were only just in time at the small, stone church. It was next to the farm where the reception was to be held, overlooking one of the smaller lakes, and I remembered thinking how beautiful it was; the day one of those cloudless rarities so precious in that part of the world.

Dad sat next to me in the passenger seat and Steve was annoying me by tickling our giggling eight-year-old, Toby. I told my son to calm down; he was going to have to behave in the church. He answered in a voice bubbling with hysteria. 'Don't tell *me*, Mum. It's Dad's fault. Tell *him*.' And that's where the memories stopped.

At first I'd hoped, and dreaded, that I would recover the rest eventually, but only the odd flash returned. In hospital, Alice had tried to fill me in on the facts she knew and of course I'd heard plenty more during the trial, but nothing seemed to explain what had happened when I crashed the car on the way back that night, or how I managed to crawl free leaving the others to burn.

Or why my bloodstream had been full of amphetamines.

Chapter Three

Next day, I had to see my probation officer. The office was not far and I made sure I arrived early. I wasn't surprised to have to wait for what seemed ages on an uncomfortable plastic chair, but the woman who came to get me was brisk and smiling. 'Nice to meet you, Clare,' she said, leading me to a stuffy cupboard of an office and glancing at her watch as she closed the door. Apparently I could call her Sophie and she was sure we would get on well.

She had an open file on her desk. I looked away from it, didn't want to read anything about myself there.

'I'm going for a job interview later today,' I said, knowing that was what she wanted to hear. Her eyes strayed to the clock on the wall and she said we would need to meet weekly for a while, but that could probably be reduced soon.

'If you do get work, let me know and we can organise our meetings to suit your hours. But you must make sure you attend regularly.' She glanced at the file and her index finger grazed the top page. 'And of course you must stay clear of drugs,' She beamed up at me. 'But I know you'll do that, Clare.'

The room was suddenly silent and, although she continued to smile at me, all I could see was her finger still moving back and forth, no doubt tracing the words of my conviction: *causing death by careless driving under the influence of drugs*. I swallowed.

Careless had always seemed to me such a strange way to describe something so terrible.

Outside, I stood taking deep breaths of fresh air and longing to head back to the flat, but instead I forced myself to turn towards the shopping mall. I managed to find a dress and some sandals and at home I took a shower and put them on. I didn't dare look in a full length mirror, but they seemed to fit and made me feel fresh and clean. My hair stayed as unmanageable as ever, but after struggling with it for an hour I gave up and finally got myself out of the flat, my insides churning.

Bunches was on one of the narrow streets of the Old Town, just a stone's throw from the flat. I paced up and down, a few yards from the place, willing myself to go in. Once, I had my hand on the door but then turned away to study some second-hand books on a rack outside the neighbouring shop. Finally, I forced myself to go back, but I might have run away again had the door not opened and an elderly man stepped back to usher me in.

It was a tiny, old shop with a low ceiling and uneven, tiled floor. Tall vases and metal buckets stood near the walls, each one crammed with the flowers and greenery that filled the place with damp, peaty odours. A red-haired girl stood behind the counter. She looked up with a smile as the old-fashioned bell over the door jangled at my entry. 'Can I help you?'

I swallowed, tempted to walk out again. But thinking of my promise to Alice, I said, 'I'm looking for Mrs Lucas – Stella?'

She opened a door behind her and I glimpsed a small room, another door at the back open to the sunshine. More buckets of blooms crowded the floor and a long table was covered in loose flowers, ribbons, and coloured paper. 'Mum, someone to see you.'

An older and curvier version of the girl emerged, removing gardening gloves and pushing red curls back from her face. 'Hello. You wanted me?'

Once I'd introduced myself as Alice Frome's sister she was all smiles. 'Harriet, I'll be upstairs for a bit with Clare. Try not to disturb us, will you?' She ushered me through a side door and up a narrow staircase, explaining as we climbed that Harriet had been helping out since the last girl left but she was off to university in September. 'So there'll be a definite full-time vacancy, then. At the moment we need someone who can be flexible. It'll be at least three days a week but some odd mornings too, maybe.'

I'd hoped for more, but I was in no fit state to argue. By the time we reached the small room at the top of the stairs I was so nervous I could hardly breathe and I was grateful she went straight into the tiny kitchen. It was divided from the living room by a looped-back curtain, so she carried on talking as she made coffee. I had been dreading some kind of inquisition, but, clearly, Alice had done a good job of selling me. Stella already knew I'd worked in a couple of shops, *some years ago,* and after a few gentle questions about how I was getting on, *since you moved here,* she made it clear the job was mine if I wanted it.

'Sit, down, sit down,' she said, as she plonked two mugs onto the coffee table and settled on a worn leather chair, kicking off her gardening clogs and tucking her toes under her.

I perched on the squashy sofa opposite.

'So what about a trial period, and if we're both happy we can make it permanent and full-time in September?'

I would barely be earning enough to cover what I imagined would be my expenses till then, but I felt pathetically grateful to her for making everything so easy. I kept the mug close to my mouth to avoid doing more than answer her questions, but could swallow only a few sips.

She looked closely at me. 'Are you sure you'll be happy dealing with customers? Most of them are fine of course, but we do need to be tactful when it's a funeral or even a wedding. Emotions can run high at times like that.'

I made a supreme effort to smile, to seem normal. 'Yes, I'm looking forward to it.'

She nodded, and I sat back, exhausted.

18

'Of course. Fine, then.' She swallowed her coffee in a couple of gulps, thrust her feet back into the clogs and stood up. 'In fact, how about starting tomorrow?' She must have noticed my squirm of anxiety, because she smiled and added, 'You can come in for half a day, see how it suits you.'

Outside, I stood for a moment taking a deep breath. I glanced back through the window to see Stella, with her back to me, talking into the phone. For a moment I wondered if she was calling Alice to report on the interview, but I told myself not to be paranoid.

It was all I could do to get back to the flat. Although it was only mid-afternoon I stumbled to the bedroom and was asleep in minutes.

I'm in a cold room surrounded by flowers, trying to arrange them into wreaths, and I can hear crying nearby. My feet are bare on the tiled floor. I'm naked, too, under the rough dress. Of course I'm in the punishment block. And the flowers have disappeared. One of the screws, red hair tumbling over her face, looks in and tells me I'm no good to anyone. The room is full of smoke now, but the warder is holding me back so I can't get to the crying, and the fire alarm is ringing and ringing…

The phone had stopped before I got to it, but in my sleep I'd made a decision and one I knew I had to act on before I lost my nerve.

I chose Alice's home number instead of her mobile. As I heard the distant ringing, my hand moistened and my mouth went dry. A click signalled someone answering, and I dared not wait any longer. 'Alice? It's Clare. Is he there? Can I speak to him, please?'

A moment's silence. A breath. Then a voice with a heart-piercing adolescent wobble, 'Mum? Is that you?'

I hardly slept that night and by dawn I was sitting in front of the TV in my dressing gown. Inevitably, I dozed off and woke certain I was already late for work. I tore into the kitchen to check the clock, relieved to see I just had time to wash and dress. It didn't matter that it was too late for breakfast, because I couldn't have eaten anything. But my throat was bone dry, so I stuck my mouth under the tap and glugged down a few swallows of lukewarm water before setting off at a run.

Stella had told me to come round to the back door, and I found her unloading the van, too busy, thank God, to notice I was breathless. 'Oh, good, you're just in time,' she said, thrusting some trays of flowers at me.

Harriet was already in the shop and they both talked almost non-stop as we got ready to open. They rarely seemed to expect an answer from me, so I focused on following the torrent of instructions. At nine o'clock Stella opened the shop door. 'Harriet, sweetie, would you show Clare how we make up a simple bouquet.' She smiled at me. 'It's not difficult, but best if you have a bit of a practice before you do it for real.'

When the bell jangled half an hour later Harriet smiled at me. 'Over to you then – your first customers.'

The two women were poking at a large container of roses and, as I walked over, I forced a smile, very conscious of Harriet behind the counter. 'Can I help you?'

Without looking up, one of them began pulling roses from the vase and handing them to me. 'Yes, can you do these up with some greenery, love?' I knew my hands were shaking as I wrapped the bunch for her, but I managed to deal with the till without too much trouble.

'Just started have you, dear?' she said.

Harriet answered for me. 'This is Clare. She's taking over when I go to uni.' Obviously this was a regular, and they chatted for a few moments. I should have been relieved, but all the time I was aware of the woman's friend watching me.

'Local are you?' she asked.

I fiddled with the Sellotape dispenser, avoiding her eye. 'I've just moved here.' I could tell she wanted more, but her friend was already at the door. They stood outside for a moment, glancing back at us as they talked.

When Harriet went into the back room to sort some orders, I leaned on the counter, my legs almost too weak to support my weight. I asked myself why I'd agreed to a job like this, where I would be constantly on show. Stella was Alice's friend, of course, and they'd made it easy for me, but I wasn't at all sure I was going to cope.

I managed to deal with the next three or four customers and at last Stella shouted down that coffee was ready. Harriet ran up and brought down a mug. 'Go and have a sit down with yours, Clare. You deserve it.'

Stella was standing, draining her mug. 'Take your time,' she said. 'No rush.' I suspected she was going to get a progress report, but was just grateful to be able to lean back and close my eyes for a few moments; to give in to the thoughts I'd been fighting since yesterday.

A part of me was terrified about what I had to face that night, but another part was joyful. I had spoken to my son, and – the memory was a sliver of sunlight dancing with motes of something wonderful, something amazing, something I'd thought impossible – Tommy wanted to see me.

'Did Alice tell you I was out?' I'd said when I was able to speak, cursing myself for the crass remark.

'She said it was soon, but I worked that out anyway.' There was silence, as his unspoken question hung in the air. *Why didn't you come and see me right away?*

There was no point in making excuses, no point, either, in raking up the past. The conversation, if you could call it that, faltered to a halt and I asked to speak to Alice, to arrange for her to drive me over. 'That's OK, I can tell her,' he said, the edge to his voice suggesting he suspected I might try to get out of the arrangement.

Neither of us mentioned his dad, or his granddad. Or Toby – his twin – his other half.

Tommy had always been the more forceful, the more inde-pendent, of the twins even though he was the younger by half an hour. He hadn't been involved in the crash because he'd been invited to his best friend's birthday party the weekend of the wedding and he'd stayed over. Toby had been happy to come on his own: to have all our attention to himself for once.

After I was sentenced, Alice took Tommy on and brought him up: yet another thing I had to be grateful to her for. It was agony to lose him too, but at least I knew he was with someone who loved him almost as much as I did.

Down in the shop again, Stella said she needed Harriet to help in the back room. 'You'll be OK out here on your own, won't you, Clare?'

I was very aware of the sounds of clipping and muttering, the scrape of shifting stools and the occasional burst of running water. At least the shop was quiet, only two more customers buying flowers from the displays. Neither of them did more than glance at me and I began to tell myself that maybe it would be all right.

By quarter to one I was almost too drained to keep standing and I found myself looking at the clock every few seconds, sure it had stopped. Finally, it crept to one o'clock and, on the dot, Stella emerged. 'Right, I'm starving and we close for an hour now, so why don't you pop off?'

As I crossed to the other side of the counter, she was fiddling with her hair and frowning down at a small notebook. But, before I could escape, she spoke. 'Oh, Clare…' I looked into her button brown eyes. 'Now I know I said you could start properly next week, but …' I froze, '… I wonder if you could do tomorrow morning too. Saturdays are always busy and we've had a load of last minute orders.'

I managed to gasp out a, 'Yes, that's OK.'

'And if you can do Monday to Wednesday next week that would be wonderful.'

He must have been listening for the car because he was standing on the steps of Beldon House as we pulled into the driveway. I knew, of course, that he was thirteen now: I'd pored over each new set of photographs for hours. But the shock at his height and the sharp bones replacing the soft roundness in his face jolted through me all the same. His arm rose and then fell as I climbed from the car and he took a half step towards me. But the car door was comfortingly warm and I leant back against it smoothing my dress with damp hands.

A deep breath. 'Hello, Tommy.'

His eyes flickered away and his hands pulled at the sleeves of his sweatshirt, dragging them out of shape. It was a habit the twins had shared, and I swallowed, trying to move the huge lump blocking my throat. Then I pushed myself forward, hands stretched out.

On the step he was taller than me. 'It's lovely to see you.' *Stupid, stupid*. I didn't blame him for turning away without a word.

Head lowered, he led the way through the hall to the kitchen. As we'd approached the house it looked the same as always – the same as it had been when Alice and I grew up here. Inside, the hall with its black and white tiles certainly hadn't changed. Mum's favourite vase, a big copper thing filled today with sunflowers, still stood on the table by the stairs and Alice had put a photo of Mum and Dad next to it. But, as Tommy threw open the kitchen door, I saw that a huge and lovely space, with the sun streaming through open French windows, had replaced the clutter of little rooms I remembered. Tommy slumped down at the table twisting open a can of Coke and watching as a line of fizz foamed down the side.

Say something, do something for God's sake. I glanced round. 'Shall I make some tea, Alice?'

But she wasn't going to let me off that easily. 'No you sit and talk. I'll make it.'

I pulled out a chair next to my son. One large hand, his nails chewed like mine, traced the grain of the table while the other turned the can round and round making a series of wet, sticky circles on the wood. He muttered something to the tabletop.

'Sorry, Tommy. What did you say?'

'Tom – everyone calls me Tom now.'

'Oh yes, sorry, I should've remembered. You started putting Tom on your letters.'

We both watched the can as he turned and turned it again.

'Sorry… I'm sorry about not writing lately.' His ears and the side of his jaw had flushed pink and I realised he thought I was telling him off for neglecting me. My throat throbbed.

'That's OK. I expect you've been busy.' *This was hopeless, hopeless. Say something sensible you stupid fool.*

Alice sat opposite plonking two mugs and a biscuit tin with a floral lid on the table. 'Tell your mum about your music, Tom.'

His voice was so low I could only make out odd words. *Grades* and *examiners,* and soon he stopped speaking and went back to playing with the can.

'Would you like to be a musician?' I said it softly, and for the first time he met my eye, nodding, before looking down to crush the sides of the can with a crack.

'Tell you what. It's too nice to sit inside. Will you show me the garden?' I jumped up, hoping to make it impossible for him to refuse.

We left Alice in the kitchen and my tall son strode down the tiled path so quickly that, as I tried to match his pace, my skirt caught on the overhanging plants and a sweet herby smell filled the air. Alice had worked magic on the garden too; its flower-filled lushness bore little resemblance to the vast expanse of lawn bordered by huge woody shrubs that I recalled. He led me to the far end where a bench overlooked a vista of fields. The sun was hot once more and the fields flared with the painful yellow of oilseed rape, dotted here and there with a flush of poppies. It reminded me of a Van Gogh painting – too bright, too hectic.

I sat on the bench, but Tom stood by the low wall staring over the fields. His hair was a slightly darker blond than it had been when he was little. 'I'm sorry I stopped writing to you,' he said.

'Tom, it really is OK. You don't need to feel bad about anything.'

'I was mad at you.'

I gripped the bench, the rough wood biting into my palms. I wanted so much to help him. To tell him if he wanted to shout at me, to hit me, it was only his right.

'You lied about me not being allowed to come and see you in prison. Mark's dad's a solicitor and *he* said.'

How stupid we'd been. 'You see, Tom, I didn't want you to come there because Holloway's not a very nice place and ...'

'That's bollocks.' His voice broke and the word hung in the air. I think he was as shocked as I was. 'Sorry.' When he turned I could see his eyes were glassy, and I was beside him, my arms round him, rubbing his stiff back. He was too big and too bony, but then I felt him relax, his head resting on my shoulder as he muttered again, 'Sorry, sorry, Mum.'

I led him to the bench and made him sit. He scrubbed his face ferociously, as I patted his other forearm and echoed his throat clearing and sniffing with my own small cough. 'Tom.' I laid my hand over his larger one. 'You've got nothing, nothing at all, to say sorry to me for. I can't make it right again, I know, but please don't blame yourself for anything. All I want is for us to be friends.' Even as I said it I knew I'd got it all wrong. But what would have been right?

He looked up, and there in his clear grey eyes was my little lost Tommy. 'OK, and if it's all right with you, I want to live with you again. Alice says I can't, but you *are* my mum aren't you?' The words came out in a rush and I guessed he'd prepared them.

My own eyes filled with tears, but whether they were tears of joy at hearing the words I'd never dared hope he would say, or of pain that I couldn't take him home right now, I didn't know.

Don't lie to him again. 'Well... Alice does have custody you know.'

'Yes, but you're my mum.' His voice was hard.

'And there's nothing I want more than to have you with me all the time. But, you know, it's going to take me a while to get settled. I've already found a job so that's a good start. And, if it's all right with you I want to see you as often as I can, because we need to get to know each other properly again. So will you be patient for just a while longer?'

He jumped up and began pacing the little patio. I couldn't tell if he was angry, disappointed, excited, or just too full of life and energy to sit still.

When he turned to me, his eyes were shining. 'One thing, one thing I've been thinking, is that I could help you.'

'What do you mean, Tom?' I loved saying his name.

'You know, to show them they made a mistake; to show them it wasn't your fault.'

Chapter Four

Alice had roasted a chicken with all the trimmings and opened some wine. I knew she was trying to make this a celebration of sorts for my homecoming, but I couldn't force much down. My mind whirled with it all, but mostly with the idea that Tom still believed I was innocent. At the trial I'd pleaded not guilty, but in prison I finally had to accept what Mike and the others told me: that my amnesia was caused by my inability to face the reality of what I'd done. I'd tried to explain it to Tom in my letters, and I cursed myself for not making it clearer.

We didn't speak much, but he ate well. When he'd cleared his plate he pushed back his chair, looking at Alice. 'Got to do some homework,' he said.

As he thundered upstairs, Alice touched my hand. 'It's bound to be hard for him. Give him time.'

'He thinks there could be some way to prove I was innocent.'

She shook her head, and I followed her to the kitchen where she fiddled with a fancy-looking coffee machine. 'I was afraid of something like this.'

'What?'

'He spends a lot of time at his friend Mark's and, according to Mark's mum, the two of them have started watching that bloody programme about miscarriages of justice.'

I knew the one she meant; it was a favourite with some of the women inside. 'But you should have told him there was nothing like that with my case.'

'It wasn't so simple, Clare. I tried, but what could I say? If your letters didn't convince him how could I? I couldn't tell him about your past, the drugs, and everything, could I?'

'But you should have made him understand.'

'Look Clare, it's you who doesn't understand. You haven't lived with him all these years.' She slammed a brimming mug on the table so that coffee dripped down the yellow stripes on the china. 'He believes what he wants to believe. I tried to talk to him about it, but all he would ever say was, "My mum's a good driver and when they find out she'll come for me." Lately he just won't discuss it, not with me anyway.'

I sat down, gulping at the scalding coffee. 'I'm sorry. I know it hasn't been easy for you.'

She shook her head, looking suddenly very grey. 'Tom's a great kid and he deserves to know the truth. But that can only come from you.'

'But I can't remember, you know that. Just those few images I've told you about. I'm not even sure they're really memories. I've heard so much about what might have happened that I could have invented them to fit.'

Alice pushed her fingers through her hair. 'Well, tell him what you do know then.'

'Be completely honest, you mean?'

She nodded, taking my hand and gripping it hard. 'I'm sure most kids are wiser and more realistic than we imagine.' I put my hand over hers and looked into her blue eyes. They were shining with tears and for the first time in years she looked like my little sister again. 'Go on,' she said, 'speak to him now.' She sniffed and smiled and when I stood she kept hold of my hand for a moment.

I paused in the doorway of Tom's room. It was the one the twins had always slept in when they stayed here. His choice or Alice's,

I wondered? At least I was thankful it looked different from the room where I'd kissed my boys goodnight so many times.

It was large, like all the rooms in the house, and seemed larger with only one bed now instead of two. There was a distinct, though not unpleasant, tang in the air: a mixture of damp socks, orange peel, chocolate, and peppery sweat. The bed was rumpled, a shirt and a bath towel in the middle of the floor, but otherwise it was surprisingly tidy.

The mantelpiece and the shelf next to it held a row of metal trophies and the walls were decorated by several large posters – *The Hobbit*, *Hunger Games*, and a couple of footballers.

I noticed Tom's hair still stuck up at the back and his shoulders, bent over the keyboard as he tapped away, were surprisingly broad.

'Come in if you want,' he said, making me jump and slop coffee onto the pale hall carpet. I rubbed it in with the toe of my shoe.

'I'm just admiring your room.'

'Oh that's Martha, Mrs Cooper. She cleans up. But just in the week.' A glance back at the messy bed and the clothes on the floor. '*I'm* s'posed to do it at weekends.'

I stayed in the doorway, fingers pulling at the fabric of my dress. *Say something.* 'How's the homework going?' *Stupid, stupid idiot.*

Without looking at me he pushed at the chair next to him. 'Nearly done.'

I sat on the chair, put the coffee I couldn't drink on the floor and sat watching as he did something complicated with a spreadsheet. 'That looks impressive.'

He laughed. 'It's not really.' A glance at me. 'But thanks anyway, Mum.'

It was the name that did it, and I found myself burying my face in his hair, breathing in the musky boy smell, different to what I remembered, but not so different that I didn't know it for the scent of my child. He tolerated it for a bit then twisted very gently away. 'You all right?'

When I could speak I apologised. 'I'm silly I know, but it's just so nice to hear you call me Mum.'

'What do you expect me to call you?' A long pause, his face and neck mottling pink. 'Mum, do you – you know – often think about Tobe and Dad?'

'Of course I do, but sometimes it hurts too much.'

He looked at the floor, swinging his chair back and forth and chewing at his nails. 'You know the party? The one I went to? Toby could've come too.'

'But he didn't and there's nothing we can do to change that now.'

'But Daniel's mum wanted to ask him as well, and I said he wouldn't want to come.'

'Well that was probably right. He was excited about going to the Lake District on his own with the grown-ups. And Daniel was really *your* friend.' I fought to keep the tremors from my voice.

'But Daniel liked Toby a bit and he said his mum was going to ask Toby anyway, and I told him I wouldn't be his friend anymore if Toby came. And then I told Toby Daniel didn't like him.'

I laid my hand on his back. His guilt seemed so ridiculous compared to mine, but it was clearly a huge burden to him. 'Maybe it was a bit mean of you, but you weren't to know what would happen. And don't forget, Toby was sometimes nasty to you.' Thank goodness he was still looking down and couldn't see me shaking the hot tears from my eyes.

'Yeah, well, that was why really. I wanted to get back at him cos he took my Gameboy and broke it.'

'You were always breaking each other's things. What about the time when you had kites for Christmas and you lost yours up a tree that same day? And then Toby laughed at you, so you trod on his.'

'And when he kept stealing the batteries from my remote-control car, and I kept stealing them from the TV channel changer, and Dad went mad at us both, and you went mad at Dad?' We laughed at that, although the laughter was forced. Then he turned to face me. 'What about Dad? Only sometimes, when we were little, Tobe and me thought you might be going to get divorced.'

I told him this was probably because of what was happening to the parents of other kids they knew. 'Dad and I argued a bit, but all married couples do.' I'd promised myself I'd be honest with him, but it was going to be so difficult, when I often didn't know the truth myself.

I took a breath. 'Alice wants to take me back soon, but what about a quick walk?'

We didn't talk till we reached the little wood down the lane from the house. It was quiet and cool, the late sun sending delicate fingers of gold low through the trees.

'I remember coming here when I was small, usually when I'd done something wrong,' I said.

He scuffed his feet through the dry leaves and twigs covering the ground. 'I know. You used to bring us when we came to see Granddad. You were always telling us that.'

I bit my lip. Of course. What else had I made myself forget? Odd, disjointed memories came back: Toby dancing in the Indian headdress he'd been so proud of; Steve chasing two screaming five-year-olds with a discarded snakeskin; and little Tommy jumping out from behind a tree to shout *Boo* at us all so loudly it made Toby cry.

Tom's new, deep voice jolted me back. 'Me and Tobe used to think it was a forest. Used to pretend we were outlaws.'

The name hung in the air between us and I began kicking at the leaves, matching his rhythm.

A pheasant burst from a bush just ahead and we bumped shoulders as we stopped: me with a gasp and Tom with a gruff chuckle.

'Tom,' I said, when we were moving again. 'I've been thinking about what you said earlier.' I didn't look at him as we continued to scuff along together. 'You know I don't remember the accident: that I lost my memory?'

'Amnesia, yeah.'

'And you know why they put me in prison?'

31

He kicked hard at a pile of leaves making them rise into the air. 'Course I do.' His voice was curt. 'They said you took drugs – amphetamines.'

Don't treat him like a baby. 'Well, I pleaded not guilty at my trial because I didn't believe I could have done that.' His intake of breath told me he was about to speak, but I had to get this out. 'But you see, I had a lot of time to think in prison, and I came to realise I must have done it – somehow got hold of those pills and taken them. I don't know why I would have done it, but it means I *was* guilty.'

'But maybe you didn't want to take them. Someone could've put stuff in your drink. You know, at the wedding. I've been looking up amphetamines on the internet and it says they can be dissolved in liquid.'

I could have smiled if it hadn't hurt so much. 'But why would anyone want to do that?'

'Maybe it was a joke, or someone had it in for you or Dad – or for Granddad. He was important wasn't he?'

'Well, he ran a successful company, yes.'

''Cos I looked him up, and he's on Google. He was just the kind of guy people might have a grudge against. There was all that stuff with the arthritis drug too. It was in the papers.'

'You have been busy.'

His voice was stubborn. 'I want to help you.'

'I know and thank you.'

He stopped walking; his crossed arms and lowered head telling me I was doing it all wrong again. I looked up into the dark branches above us, knowing it had to be now, however badly I said it. 'What you don't know, Tom, is that before you were born, I was an addict for a while. When I was a teenager I got in with a bad crowd and thought taking drugs was cool. It isn't, it's stupid, and I managed to get off them. Then I met your dad and I was so happy I never thought about drugs again. You and Toby and Dad were my life. But maybe something happened the night of the

32

wedding to make me slip back into my old ways. I met addicts in prison who'd been clean for years, but who relapsed when things went wrong in their lives.'

He turned and crashed away, almost at a run.

'Tom. Wait. Please wait for me.'

A bramble twisted round my foot and leg as I tried to follow him, biting into my calf and making me stumble. I pulled at the wretched thing, cursing under my breath, aware he had stopped and was watching me. When I looked up again he was still there kicking at a tree trunk and staring down at its roots. I went to him, daring to touch his arm. He didn't push me away.

'I'm so sorry, Tom. I should have told you this before.'

His grey eyes were misted and he shook his head as he spoke. 'But why did you want to take drugs?'

What to say? 'You know I was adopted, don't you? Well my mum, your grandma, was ill. Not physically, but she had mental problems that made her depressed and unhappy. So she was often angry with me. It wasn't her fault, but I didn't understand that and so I ran away from home and met people who were very bad for me. That's not an excuse, Tom, and it made things worse not better. Which is what always happens with drugs.'

He leaned back against the tree, arms folded, and looking down at the crumbled soil as he stirred it with the toe of his trainer. The whole wood seemed to have gone silent.

'But, Tom, this doesn't mean I don't want to know exactly what happened that night. So will you give me some time to think about your ideas and to try to remember more?'

I almost said I needed to find out who could have supplied me with the stuff at the reception, but it was better if he didn't start thinking that way.

He nodded and I gestured with my head that we should start back. Then took a chance and put my arm through his. He tensed at my touch. *Careful, careful.* 'You *can* help me, Tom. Just give me time.'

33

'OK.'

Then we walked back together through the cool, silent wood while phantoms from the past played and laughed around us.

Back at the flat, as I lay in bed, I couldn't stop thinking about Tommy. My mind churned, veering from a kind of happiness to the sort of despair that makes you want to beat your head against a wall. And I did slam over and over into the pillow, pummelling it into a solid lump. I got up twice to use the toilet, then for water and finally to make a mug of tea that sat growing cold beside me as I stared up at the ceiling.

Night is the worst time in prison. That's when you hear the sobs and the groans, the shouts of, 'Shut up, you bitch, and let me sleep.' It's then you relive and regret, not in the therapy groups with a gentle voice saying you can rebuild your life. It's your own voice that curses you as a pariah; a leper who would be better off dead.

At first I tried to remember what happened that night; to piece together fragments that came to me, sometimes awake, sometimes in dreams. Some things were constant: the dark road, the grey shadows overhead, the flashing light, but were they memories, or just images patched together from what I'd been told? After a while it didn't matter because I didn't want to remember. But now maybe I would have to if that were the only way to help Tom. And if I didn't know why I'd done it, how could I be sure it wouldn't happen again? How could I trust myself to be a real mother once more?

Apart from those horrible fragments, my memory of the day ended hours before the accident. Emily and I were close in age and we'd always been good friends. In fact, because of the five years between me and Alice, I'd probably been closer to Emily when we were kids.

Her husband, Matt's, family owned a farm in Cumbria and the wedding was held there. Alice was a junior doctor in Newcastle, but we lived close to Dad in Kent. Most of the guests were planning to stay at a country house hotel and, when I said Steve and I couldn't possibly afford a place like that, Dad offered to treat us. I agreed, on condition he let me pay him back by doing all the driving.

I remembered the journey to the church along sunny, twisting lanes edged by glassy streams and brilliant fields. Then, like a TV with a faulty signal, the picture stuttered and disappeared to be replaced by flashes and bursts of noise.

As those images played over and over in my head I wanted only to push them away just as I'd always done over the past few years. But I couldn't let myself do that any more.

I got up and went into the living room where the card from Emily and Matt was still standing beside the laptop. I switched on, found Emily's email address in the notebook Alice had left for me, and sent a message. I kept it short, just telling Emily how pleased I was to get her card. I wouldn't blame her if she was still upset with me, but I'd love to see her. I gave her my home and mobile phone numbers, added three kisses, deleted two, and pressed send before I could change my mind.

Something woke me and I lay confused for a moment. Then a loud buzz came from the direction of the living room. I had no idea what it was and sat up in bed, switching on the light. Nearly 2 a.m. That metallic buzz again. *Oh, God,* it was my door buzzer. I clutched my dressing gown round me. Whoever it was couldn't get in; they were outside the big main door, not in the hall. In the living room I stood in the darkness, away from the grey rectangles of light from the windows. Another buzz. It must be one of the other tenants, who'd forgotten their key. On the next buzz I picked up the intercom phone, but didn't speak.

A rasping cough, then, 'Come on, open up. I know you're in there.'

I rammed the phone back on its holder, as if it was on fire, grabbed my mobile, and locked myself in the bathroom. Who could I ring? Certainly not the police, and Alice couldn't help. Instead, I huddled on the floor, my back against the bath, pulling my dressing gown close. I didn't dare turn on the light or go back to the bedroom in case he came round to my window.

Buzz, buzz, buzz, longer each time. They seemed to go on forever, but finally fell silent.

Who the hell was it? My case had made the papers, five years ago, mainly because of the recent scandal involving Dad's firm. During my trial I was presented as a druggie debutante, a spoiled little rich girl, too reckless even to care about her own child, and I'd received plenty of hate mail. What if someone was out to make good those threats? Or maybe a reporter was trying to track me down?

After a while, the silence let me slide back the lock and creep to the bedroom. I switched off the light and shivered under the duvet trying to relax, even to sleep.

But now there was another noise. Not a buzzing this time, but an insistent tap, tap, tap on my own front door.

Somehow he'd got into the hall.

Chapter Five

In the living room again, I told myself the door was double-locked and the chain was on. I was safe. And I knew how to look after myself: had to learn that in prison.

The tapping again. 'Clare, are you there? It's OK, he's gone. It's just me, Nic, from across the hall.'

I put my ear to the door. No sounds of movement or even breathing. I checked the chain and opened the door a crack. Just her, in a shiny blue dressing gown. Behind her the door to her own flat was half-open. She gave me a nervy smile, pulling her fingers through her untidy fair hair.

'Sorry about all that, Clare, it was my ex. He was so drunk he started ringing the wrong bell. I heard him shouting and realised what he'd done, but I didn't dare come out till he was gone.'

I leant one shoulder on the wall, trying to speak calmly. 'Is he dangerous?'

She looked down, kicking the door jamb with her slipper. 'Oh no, but I didn't want him waking Molly. And there would only have been an argument.'

I began to close the door, but Nicola held up her hand. 'Look, I won't get back to sleep for ages. What about coming over to mine for a drink?'

There was little chance of me sleeping either, but I shook my head. 'I've got work in the morning.'

'Come on, just one. I'm feeling really jittery. And I owe you one for putting up with him without calling the police.'

I didn't tell her there was no chance I'd ever do that, but I felt jittery too. It might do me good to relax for a bit and talk to someone who knew nothing about my past. I grabbed my keys from beside the door. 'OK.'

Nicola's flat was a messier mirror image of mine. She gestured to me to sit on the red sofa covered in crumpled cushions and called from the kitchen. 'White wine OK for you?'

'Thanks.'

She handed me a large glass filled to the top. The first sip made me feel calmer and I leaned back, while Nicola perched on the edge of the matching armchair. 'This is nice,' she said. 'I don't sleep well anyway, what with sharing the bedroom with Molly and worrying he might turn up in the middle of the night.' She must have seen something in my expression because she flushed and took a deep drink. 'Don't get me wrong, Clare, he really isn't violent, just a fucking nuisance – pardon my language.'

'Is he Molly's dad?'

'Yeah, and she loves him so much. Kids need their dads, don't they? So I can't cut him out of our lives altogether. It's just when he's had a skinful or been on the skunk or something stronger.'

I smiled and concentrated on my wine. I'd noticed the smell of hash when I came in, so wondered if he'd been here earlier, and come back after she'd thrown him out. Or had she been smoking too. It was none of my business of course, but I didn't want to be anywhere near people who might interest the police or cause my probation officer to have doubts.

Nicola was talking on about Molly, and the nursery, and about her own job at the council offices. 'Dead boring, but if they make me redundant I won't be able to stay here for long. What about you? You said you're at work in the morning.'

There was no way out of it. 'I'm part time at the florist's up the road.'

'That's nice. And I've met your sister, what about other family?'

I needed to shut this down and I was amazed to see I'd finished my wine. I faked a yawn. 'Sorry, Nicola. I'm really tired so I'd better try to get a few hours' sleep. Thanks for the drink.'

She followed me to the door. 'No, thank you, babe. Let's get together again soon, eh?' As I reached my door she stayed watching me then leaned out, pointing to a small table by the main door. 'Hey, I've just thought. Are you Clare Glazier?'

I swallowed, *oh God she'd guessed*, but before I could speak she'd picked up an envelope from the table. 'Mrs C Glazier,' she read. 'Sorry I put it there yesterday. It's where we leave the mail. Didn't realise that was your surname.' My smile must have made my feelings obvious. 'Good news?' Nic said.

'Yes, it's from an old friend.' I knew the distinctive hand at once and my heart lifted. Lorna – my godmother. Of course, I knew she'd be in touch.

I thanked Nicola and went back into the flat, ripping the envelope apart before I was even through the door. As always, the paper smelled of Lorna's perfume, mingled, it seemed to me, with a waft of fresh air from her garden. She was the only one, apart from Alice, I'd let visit me in prison. She was a real old-fashioned letter writer and I'd treasured every one of her notes and cards, as well as the long letters she sent when she knew I was in need of something more.

This was quite short, although set out as perfectly as ever and I smiled, remembering how she always insisted personal letters must be handwritten, never word processed, and there was no excuse for slapdash presentation even in a casual note.

Dearest Clare,

I'm so happy to know you're back in the land of the living with us and I can't wait to see you.

It's going to be difficult for you, I know that, but don't forget I'm here whenever you want to see me. I'm not too decrepit to

travel, so I can come to you, if that's what you would prefer.
Call me to arrange something soon, and remember there are
lots of people out here who are on your side.

With fondest love from,
Your fairy godmother, Lorna.

My parents were atheists so I didn't have a real godmother, but at eight years old, at a C. of E. school with a High Church ethos, I got religion. I never went so far as to demand to be baptised, but when I heard about godparents I nominated Lorna. It was her idea to call herself my *fairy* godmother.

Lorna worked with Dad. He called her his secretary, but she was much more than that. Mum was often ill, so Lorna organised much of our home life too. Next to my dad, she was the person I loved most in the world, and after the accident I knew, in spite of everything, she would stand by me.

When I ran away from home and was living rough I sometimes went to Lorna. She would let me have a bath while she washed and dried my clothes. Then she'd feed me and sometimes persuade me to stay the night.

As always her words came at just the right time, and she'd added her mobile number too, so I texted her straight away.

So good to hear from you. I'm fine. I'd love to see you soon.
Working this morning, but will give you a ring asap. XXXX

I switched on the TV, curled up on the sofa, and dozed till it was time to shower and dress for work.

I was swallowing some toast and coffee when the phone rang. I let the machine answer, expecting it to be Nicola for some reason.

'Clare, my love, I just got your text…'

I grabbed up the handset. 'Lorna, oh thank you for calling.' I explained I was working that morning and couldn't talk for long and, as usual she read my thoughts. 'But you'd like to see me. Well how about this afternoon? I'm free as a bird and I'd love a jaunt down to the seaside. I'll come on the train. Not sure about times, but I'll try to get there for about 1.30. Meet me at the station and I'll buy you lunch.'

Somehow, just the thought of seeing Lorna meant that, despite everything, I didn't find the morning too difficult. Stella and Harriet left me in charge of the shop, as they made up bouquets and Stella drove back and forth with deliveries. The open back door allowed splashes of sunlight to fall on the counter, and the warm breeze carried the scent of flowers and the murmur of their voices into the shop.

There were plenty of customers, but they all seemed so absorbed in their own business that they hardly seemed to notice me. I was very glad about that, and I had no time, either, to worry about making mistakes. The morning passed quickly and Stella seemed happy enough too, laughing that, if I could cope with a summer Saturday morning, then I could cope with anything.

Outside, as the sun shone down on me, I almost felt ordinary again: someone with a job, a home, and a friend to meet. Even the calling seagulls seemed tuneful, and I stood for a moment breathing deeply, my knees a little wobbly with something close to happiness.

Down at the seafront the water shone like crinkled foil. The clear air showed me Bexhill a few miles down the coast and, further away still, the white cliffs of Beachy Head near Eastbourne. I felt I could easily have walked there.

Lorna was standing outside the station. I hadn't seen her for a few months because she was having trouble with her knee and needed an operation. Knowing I'd soon be out, we'd agreed she wouldn't keep doing the journey to the prison, and I was shocked to see how much she had aged. She was as neat and elegant as ever, but although her eyebrows were still dark, her hair, twined into a gleaming knot, was streaked with grey. She patted it as she caught me looking. 'You have to stop dyeing it at some point, you know.'

'It suits you.'

She smiled; her face a spider's web of tiny lines. Though she was still slender, I noticed she breathed heavily as we wandered down to the Old Town. It was obviously not easy for her to walk, but she insisted she was fine. At the little tapas bar we chose for lunch she exclaimed, 'My goodness, Clare, it's so cheap! I hardly ever eat out in London anymore. All the places I used to love are out of my league now.'

Lorna ordered a bottle of wine and as I sipped I felt a shiver of anxiety. When I was living rough, I'd spent plenty of time out of it on cider or cheap vodka, but once I straightened myself out, got married and had the twins, I found it easy enough to drink sensibly. But I'd been happy then. There had been times in prison when I'd longed to get smashed out of my skull, to forget everything for an hour or so, and the way my life was at the moment I knew I should be careful – I'd drunk too much wine in the last day or so and enjoyed it too much.

Lorna nibbled an olive and looked at me with dark eyes that sparkled as brightly as ever. 'And how are you, sweetheart? You look thinner, but…' she held up a blue-veined hand, a large gold bangle encircling the elegant wrist, '…it suits you. Just don't go too far will you?'

'I won't.'

She smiled up at the waitress unloading the little dishes of food, then said a warm, 'Thank you'. Lorna always gave her full attention to anyone she was with, whether it was an important client of the firm or the scruffy little girl I had been. Now she turned the full beam onto me. 'So what do you think of your handsome son?' She forked a few slices of tomato and chorizo onto her plate and began peeling a prawn, leaving the words to do their work, but I was wise to her technique and in any case I didn't want to keep anything from her.

'Oh he's wonderful, and you were right all along. I should have let him visit me. I was so stupid.'

She smiled. 'I'm not going to argue with you there, but you've spent enough time letting past mistakes get in your way. I think you owe it to Tom to start afresh.'

'The problem is he doesn't want to believe I was to blame for the accident.'

'Don't forget, it took you a long time to come to terms with it, and Tom's still very young. You have to help him.'

'That's what Alice says, and I'm beginning to think the only way is to try to find out the whole, ugly truth myself.'

'Regain your memory, you mean?' She placed the piece of bread she had been eating, very carefully, on her plate, and looked at me. 'Is it possible after all this time?'

'Apparently it can happen. The doctors say this kind of amnesia is sometimes a way for the mind to protect itself from something traumatic – something that's too painful to face.'

'Do you have any memories at all?'

'I have dreams that seem to have something to do with it. A dark road and trees, a flash of light, clouds spinning, flames and… oh I don't know, it may all be something my mind has put together from what I've heard since.'

Lorna drank some wine, looking around the little restaurant at the rough white walls covered in Spanish-style plates and bright paintings. She turned back to me. 'So what are you going to do?'

'I think I have to go back to where it happened. To see if anything sparks.'

'And see Emily and Matt?'

'I'll have to. Although, it's not going to be easy to talk about the accident with them.'

She touched the coil of hair at the nape of her neck. 'You do realise that delving into the past may only mean more pain and guilt?'

I couldn't answer.

Lorna wiped her hands and scrunched up her napkin. 'Come on, I'll pay for this if you make me coffee at your flat.'

We walked slowly, without talking. Lorna was limping quite badly, although she said she was fine. I could only hear those words of hers: *more pain and guilt,* over and over in my head. That was what I feared so much; that I would find out something even worse than I knew already. Not just that I had taken the speed deliberately, but that I had wanted to harm my family. If I had, then that would be the end. I could never try to be a real mother to Tommy again if I knew he might not be safe with me. And I couldn't bear to live if he had to know that.

'And what about Alice? How's it going with her?' Lorna asked.

I pointed to a bench and Lorna headed towards it. 'Yes, let's sit for a minute. This wretched knee.' I was aware of her twisting to face me. 'So, you and Alice? Are you getting on all right?'

I looked down, fiddling with a loose thread on my skirt. 'She's been wonderful, as always.'

'But…?' The hint of a smile in her voice.

'I'm being my usual surly self. I'm so grateful for all she's done, but I can't seem to show it when we're together.'

'Your son's been living with her all these years. That's something to do with it, surely?'

'I suppose so, but I've no right to resent her. I mean she gave up her chance of getting on in her career to make a home for him. And her boyfriends never seem to last long, do they? It can't be easy to develop a relationship with a child in the picture. Someone else's child.'

Lorna rubbed her leg and stretched it out in front of her, giving me that sweet smile of hers. 'I remember how Alice worshipped you when you were kids and she still thinks the world of you, that's obvious. Yes, she's given up some things, but I know she loves Tom very much and after what happened – losing her father and Toby, and you too, in a way – I think it's helped her to have Tom to focus on. He's been good for her.'

By the time we reached the flat it had clouded over but was still warm, and I opened a window to let in the breeze. We sat at the table, looking over the sea that gleamed silver under the clouds, the odd ripple and tinge of green like the tarnish on an antique mirror. Lorna sighed. 'This is beautiful, Clare. Alice did well finding this place. I could sit here all day.'

'Trouble is, I can't afford it.'

'What about the money from the sale of your house?'

'That's still in the bank. I asked Alice to use it for Tom, but she refused so I'm going to put it towards a place for the two of us, for when he comes back to live with me. But prices have gone up so much and our house was still mortgaged and I need to save every penny I can.'

She shifted and winced, then opened her bag to find some painkillers, swallowing down a couple with a gulp of coffee. 'But Robert left you both well provided for, surely?'

'I can't keep using his money. Alice wants me to, but…'

'But what?

'As I've tried to tell her, I'm not entitled to it after what I did. And anyway, she was our parents' only real child and if she'd been born earlier they would probably never have adopted me.'

'Clare, I'm sure that's not true. And Alice is right, your father would be furious if he thought you'd rejected your inheritance.'

I stood and turned away, a lump choking at my throat. 'Lorna, I killed him.'

The table creaked as she leant on it, pushing to her feet. She turned me to towards her, gripping my hands and moving them up and down to emphasise her words. 'Now look, I knew Robert. You were the apple of his eye and he loved you as much, if not more than, Alice. He'd have hated you to ruin your own life with regrets.'

'I gave him nothing but trouble, you know that.'

'He was well aware that you had a hard time from your mother and, although I shouldn't speak ill of the dead, they both bore a lot of responsibility for your problems.'

'That doesn't excuse what I did.'

'He would have forgiven you even that, because he would know, as I do, that you've punished yourself enough.' She sighed and released me, picking up her bag to pull out a tissue. 'Now, will you call me a taxi, I don't think this knee will cope with any more walking today.'

At the door I clung to her, breathing in her familiar scent. She pulled back and looked into my eyes. 'When are you coming to visit me?'

'Soon.'

'I shall hold you to that. Then we can really talk.'

Chapter Six

Once I was alone in the quiet flat again, I thought about Lorna. She had been kind, but she couldn't really help me. It was the same in prison when she used to tell me I should let Tommy visit, and I knew she was right, but I just couldn't do it.

Oh, I kidded myself I was thinking of what was best for him. Ruby saw her kids, but there were plenty, like me, who persuaded themselves they wanted to spare their children: to save them the heartache of being separated again and again, blah de blah. The truth was, we were ashamed to face those clear eyes, the inevitable questions.

I had to face them now if I ever wanted Tommy back with me; to be a real mother to him. I picked up the phone: desperate just to hear his voice again.

Alice answered and I asked, 'Is he all right? Do you think it went OK yesterday?'

I heard sounds, as if she was moving to another room or closing a door. 'He's been very quiet since, but apart from that… What about you?'

'I'm all right, better, I think. I've emailed Emily, just to say hello.'

'That's good, I know she really wants to see you.' Now her voice came from a distance, calling to Tom. 'Yes it is. Come and speak to her.' Then close to the phone again, very gently. 'Here he is.'

Silence. I tried to speak but my throat had dried so much it came out on a cough. 'OK, Tom?'

'Yeah.'

Keep it light. 'What are you up to?'

'Nothing much.'

This was awful. 'I was hoping to get over again tomorrow,' I said. 'It's Sunday, so we'll have a bit more time together.'

'Oh, no, I've got a table tennis tournament all day tomorrow and I'm going to Mark's after, for tea, so I won't be back till late.'

'Oh… Fine. Of course… '

'Sorry.'

'That's OK, don't worry about it.' The silence stretched between us. 'Well… good luck… hope it goes well.'

'Thanks.' I heard his breath, loud and fast in my ear, but he said nothing more and I couldn't manage anything either. I asked to talk to Alice again.

'I'll get her. Bye.' The phone clunked down, as if he'd dropped it, and I heard his footsteps, a mumble of voices, then the sharp crack of his laugh followed by a chuckle from Alice.

'I *am* sorry, Clare. I didn't know about the table tennis, or the tea for that matter,' she said when she came on. 'I try to keep track of dates, but he's getting worse and worse at letting me know.'

'It's fine. I can't expect him to put everything on hold for me.'

'Why don't you come over anyway and have lunch with me? Or I could check what he's got on Monday and Tuesday and we can arrange something then.'

I promised to ring her the next day and said some kind of goodbye. Then I sat holding the silent phone, rocking back and forth as I bit the inside of my mouth, hoping the physical pain might somehow help. I had no idea what I'd expected, but at least I'd hoped to see him soon. Hoped he would want to see me.

What bothered me was the way he seemed so remote. And the way he'd laughed with Alice. So different from our few stumbling words.

Of course, it was bound to be awkward at first, and I should have planned what to say more carefully – I promised myself I would do that next time. And I couldn't put the blame on Alice or anyone else. It was my own fault, all of it. How stupid I'd been to ban him from visiting me.

Some of the women in prison were honest and admitted they'd never wanted kids in the first place and the one good thing about doing time was that it freed them from those clinging bundles of dependency. Most were like me, lying to themselves. I told myself it was better if he got on with his own life and forgot about me. But the truth was that seeing my child would have been unbearable because it would have reminded me of all the ways I'd hurt him.

I decided to write to Ruby. She'd told me not to, told me to put prison and everything to do with it behind me, but I knew she would be happy to hear from me. And she was the only person I could tell everything.

But when I'd finished pouring it all out onto the page, I realised I couldn't send a letter like this. The screws would read it before Ruby and I imagined that big bitch Maureen having a good laugh at my pathetic ramblings. I tore the paper into tiny pieces and scattered them on the table, pressing my fists against my temples as I muttered curses to myself, to the bastard screws, and even to the crumpled sea for lying there so grey and sluggish.

Unbelievable as it seemed, I wanted nothing more at that moment than to be back in prison, with Mike to tell me to put the past behind me, and Ruby to cheer me on when I began to hope I might have some kind of future outside.

It had been terrible in the early days. I was sure I was innocent and could only grieve for the family I had lost and obsess over the agony of separation from Tommy. The one thing that kept me going then was believing my appeal must succeed and I would soon be back with him. But even before the appeal failed I realised I had to be guilty, and for a long time after that I could hardly imagine how to carry on living. Didn't want to go on.

I was never sure when things changed, but one day I found myself talking to Ruby, and later to Alice and Lorna, about seeing Tommy again and trying to be a mother to him once more. I had been so determined to make it work that I remembered a few days when I had felt so hopeful it was almost like happiness. If I could hear Ruby's voice again, maybe I could recapture that sense of hope.

In the end, I wrote her a short note, saying I just wanted to make sure she still had my address and phone number. I would buy a phone card and slip that into the envelope hoping she would understand it as a plea to call me.

But almost as if I'd actually spoken to her, I could hear what she would say. It was no good dwelling on how badly I'd dealt with things in the past. I had to give Tom what he needed now and that meant taking his questions seriously, and trying to find some answers, no matter how difficult it was for me. It would mean probing into things people would rather forget. And, above all, trying to force my own stubborn brain to reveal what it was hiding. It would hurt, I knew that, it might even turn Tom against me, but it was the very least I owed him.

I would have to start with Emily and Matt. And the place where it happened. I hadn't seen Matt since that night. But Emily was there through most of the trial, spoke up as a witness for my defence, although she didn't know much, and then sat and watched, smiling and nodding encouragement at me. Later, she came to see me regularly in prison until I refused her visits.

'I don't know how you bear it,' was what she'd said, oh so kindly, the last time she came. And I looked up to see myself, tiny and far away, reflected in her eyes – a specimen behind glass. It was the word *bear* that did it, and I knew she didn't mean, how did I endure the loss, or stand the grief, but how did I bear the burden of my guilt. That was when I told her I didn't want to see her again; that was in the days before I knew I was guilty.

After the way I'd treated her, I could hardly blame her if she didn't want to see me. And even if she did, how would she and

Matt feel when I started asking questions about that night? I thought how dreadful every wedding anniversary must be for her and how the strands of my guilt entangled all the people I loved.

God knows how I could raise it with either of them, but they were the only ones who knew everyone at the wedding and I needed to ask if they had any idea of who might have given me the pills. If I could find that out, maybe I could also discover why I'd wanted them.

The sessions with Mike in prison had shown me how easily it could happen. There were others, like me, who claimed to have been clean for months, or years, but always there was a trigger to send them back to the vodka, the speed or the smack. Ruby's man came home from wherever he'd been, beat her and gave her heroin to cheer her up. Jo had her kids taken away, and Lillian's husband left her. They all agreed, though, that torturing yourself over the whys and wherefores was a waste of time.

I'd accepted it then. It seemed to make sense. But I knew now there was no way I could even think about *rebuilding my life* before I found out why I'd destroyed it.

And I had to show Tom I was taking his theories seriously. Lorna could help me with how Dad had handled the drug scandal, and if there had been any unpleasantness. Matt had worked for the company too, as a chemist, and it was just possible he could shed light on the way the labs worked; might even have known the doctor who wrote the report that caused all the trouble.

My mind was buzzing with so many thoughts I could feel a headache brewing and nothing seemed to make sense anymore. I needed to get out of the flat, to walk until I was tired enough to stop thinking for a while. Long walks were one of the things I missed most when I was inside, and another reason I'd chosen Hastings was because I knew there would be hills to tire me, sea views to soothe me, and long stretches of countryside to exhaust me. It was too late to go far, so a fast tramp up the nearest hill would have to do.

The clouds had lifted again to make a beautiful evening, the sun still high in the sky, the sea calm, and I clamped down on my thoughts and concentrated on putting one foot in front of another. Turning towards the town, I found a convenience store open and bought a phone card, slipped it in with the note for Ruby, and posted it. Then I headed sharp uphill between the jumbled old cottages, along one of the steep cobbled alleyways the locals call twittens.

Before I'd gone far, the alley turned into a flight of almost vertical steps and I was grateful for the handrail, but, all the same, by the time I reached the top my calves were aching and my chest was tight. The climb had left me hot and sticky, but up here a cool breeze blew across the wide stretch of grass, and I was glad to find an empty bench.

To my right was the ruin of William the Conqueror's castle. Ahead, beyond the grassy cliff-edge, the sea was dotted, even at this hour, with small, dark boats. Coloured lights twinkled over the little funfair and amusement arcades, and a miniature train slid silently along beside the beach. To the left was the other hill, the East Hill, where the wooden carriage of a funicular lift hauled itself to the top. And, huddled between the two hills, the clustered houses, cafés and pubs of the Old Town bustled with activity.

Even up here the grass was heaving with life. A dog bouncing after a stick, a group of teenagers grabbing and squealing at each other, families with children, and a few elderly couples, arms linked as they strolled along. As I watched, a woman left the café that stood near the cliff-edge and began to lock the door, looking back to the road behind her to wave a beefy arm at a passing car.

I was close to them all, but felt as distant as if I was behind glass. Were they all as carefree as they looked? The two girls, one skinny, one plump, their pretty faces contorted as they zigzagged across the grass, taunting a couple of boys; the young couple, her arm round his waist, his hand tucked into the back pocket of her jeans; the little family, Mum with a baby in a buggy, and Dad pushing a little boy over the lumpy grass as he strained pink-faced on a bike with two wobbly trainer wheels.

Did we look like that, not so long ago, Steve and I, with our twins? And *were* we happy? I had thought so, but now I wasn't sure. I always told Steve he saved me because I realised I was love-able, despite everything.

I met him shortly after Mum died and I'd cleaned up my act. I was doing a temp job at Dad's firm, mostly helping Lorna in the office. A few of the guys had slimed round me once they knew who I was, but Steve was different. He was working for Dad, too, as a freelance gardener. I thought he was absolutely gorgeous; tall, blond, and with a kind of gangly grace that turned my insides liquid. I started eating my lunch on a bench outside and one day Steve asked if he could join me. And that was it.

When I became pregnant I thought nothing could make me go back to my old ways: to the drugs or drink. So what happened?

Although I hadn't been able to stop thinking, the walk and the fresh air had done something positive and I came down almost at a run. I was suddenly very hungry, and giving silent thanks to Alice for stocking the freezer with ready meals. But as I came in sight of the flat I saw a tall man turning away from the front door. I slowed my steps. If it was Nic's ex I didn't want to meet him, and even if it was the mysterious upstairs tenant, I wasn't keen on a conversation right now.

I took out my mobile phone, pretending an interest in it, to avoid looking at him. But he had stopped at the garden gate and was staring along the road at me and after a minute or two I had no option but to raise my eyes.

It was Matt, Emily's Matt. He looked a little older and rather more solid, but it was unmistakably him.

The shock of seeing him here made me step back and the hedge of the house I was passing pressed into my back. He was coming towards me, his hands outstretched, but all I could do was stare.

'Clare, I thought I'd missed you.'

His arms were round me, my face pressed into his crisp blue shirt. He was very warm, but smelled only of citrusy aftershave. When he pulled away he held me at arms' length, nodding and smiling.

'You look great.'

'You too.' It was true. The weight gain suited him and with a tan and designer sunglasses he looked really good. 'But what are you doing here?' I cringed at how that sounded, but he laughed, threading his arm through mine and walking us back to the house.

'Came to see you, of course. And I've been hanging about for half an hour, so I hope you're going to ask me in.'

'I'm sorry, that sounded awful. I was just so surprised to see you.'

At the front door of the house, he leaned against the wall as I fished out my key. 'I've just come back through the Tunnel – conference in Le Touquet – so I was almost passing,' he said. 'Emily phoned to tell me you'd emailed and she's desperate to know how you are and made me promise to persuade you to come visit us soon.'

It was just as well that, as I let us into the flat, he walked straight into the living room and over to the windows, and he couldn't see me scrub at my eyes, because if he'd opened his arms to me again, I would probably have sobbed on his chest.

He was looking out of the window, swapping his sunglasses for an ordinary pair as he did so.

'Hey, nice view. Must make a change from what you're used to.'

I laughed, 'You could say that.'

He turned, pulling a face. 'Sorry, but you know me, not the most tactful of men.'

'It's fine, I'd rather keep it out in the open.' It was true. I certainly didn't want to talk about prison with strangers, but it was a relief to be with people who knew. And I'd always liked Matt. There was a warmth about him, a sense of reliability that had something to do with his size, but was more about his personality. Now he sprawled on the sofa, seeming to fill the room, and looking more like the Matt I was used to in his dark-rimmed spectacles. I headed for the kitchen. 'Coffee?'

A chuckle. 'If you don't mind I'd rather have tea. If I remember right, your coffee is strong enough to stand a spoon in.'

'Actually, after the dishwater I've been drinking for five years, I'm making it a lot weaker. Still, tea it is.'

When I brought the tea and sat in the armchair opposite, Matt leaned over and touched my knee, with a big friendly hand. 'It really is good to see you looking so well, Clare, and Emily can't wait for you to come and stay with us in Cumbria.'

'Well, I've got a job.' He put down his mug, a broad smile on his face, but I shook my head. 'Only in a flower shop, working for a friend of Alice, but it's good to be back in the working world. I'm still part-time, though, so I should have a few days free soon.'

I knew Emily was finally pregnant after years of trying, IVF and so on, and we talked about that for a bit. The baby was due in a few weeks and Emily had stopped work and was staying at their house in the Lake District all the time. Matt still had to be in London and was using their flat there. 'So poor Em gets lonely. I'm working extra at the moment to have more space when the sprog appears. In fact I've got some meetings in town tomorrow.'

'On a Sunday?'

'Well since the Yanks took over the firm, it's breakfast meetings, late night conference calls, you name it. To be honest, I can't wait to get out, but they're cutting the chemistry departments in the universities and there's a glut of people like me looking for a change.' He ran his hand through his dark blond hair, looking more like his old scruffy self by the minute. 'Still you don't want to know about all that. How you are, really? How are things with Tom?'

I took a breath, better to start as I meant to go on. 'It's early days, but so far so good. There is one problem, though, Matt. He's convinced himself I wasn't to blame for the accident. Wants me to look into the whole thing again.'

He rubbed his hands over his face. 'Blimey, that's a bummer. So what have you said?'

'That I'll try to find out what I can.'

He drained his mug. 'Look, I should be going. Only stopped to deliver the message. If I remember, it's a long and winding road from here to London. Just tell me you'll definitely visit us soon and my job here is done.'

'I promise, but why don't you stay for something to eat?'

He stood up. 'Better not, I have some work to do before these meetings tomorrow.'

I couldn't let it end there. 'I wanted to ask you a couple of things. To help Tom.'

His spectacle case had slid down the side of the sofa and he bent to fumble for it. 'What's that?'

'Well, I've always wondered about who could have supplied me with the speed. It must have been someone at the wedding, you see.' It was difficult to talk to him while he was pulling out the case, then opening it and rubbing at the sunglass lenses, and I was very aware I was holding him up. 'You and Emily knew everyone there, so I wanted to know if there was anyone you could think of?'

He'd put the sunglasses on again and was looking more like the stylish guy I'd seen outside the house. 'It's a long while ago, Clare, and if any of our friends did have a habit we didn't know about it. And to be frank I wouldn't want to give you their names if I did. Can you imagine how they'd feel if you turned up asking questions like that? And the chances of them telling you if they did supply you are zilch I'd say. Besides it was more likely someone from the catering company.' He leaned close and kissed me, his cheek just a little stubbly. 'Let it drop, sweetheart. Tom'll forget about it once he gets used to you being around and starts enjoying having a mum again.'

After I'd seen him out I closed my front door and leaned my head against it. I'd made a complete hash of that and I knew I should have waited until I'd thought out what to say more carefully.

I microwaved a pasta meal and ate it at the kitchen table, wondering how I'd got myself into this when I should be focusing on making a new life for Tom and me.

The day, and the sleepless night before it, had drained me completely and I wasn't even tempted to turn on the TV. Instead, I threw off my clothes, pulled the curtains to shut out the glow of fading sunlight and climbed into bed.

The pillow was smooth and cool but I was wide awake again, my mind racing. I turned on the bedside light and picked up the photo frame. Steve and my boys smiled at me. The eight-year-old Tommy in the picture was still more real to me than the awkward teenager I was trying to get to know. And Toby – the gap where he'd just lost a tooth making his grin cheekier than ever. My dear little boy would never be a teenager, never grow up, because of me and I could never look at his face without that agonised throb. 'I'm sorry, Toby,' I whispered.

My husband was standing behind the boys, smiling his wide, white smile. One hand was on Toby's shoulder, the other pushing strands of fair hair away from his own face. Little Tommy leaned back against him. 'Oh, Steve…'

I smoothed their dear faces with a fingertip, then pressed the photo to my chest. But it was only plastic and glass and it gave no comfort.

Chapter Seven

It must have been close to midnight when the phone rang. Still half asleep I grabbed it. 'Alice?' There was some noise in the background, but no one spoke and then the line went dead. I lay down, but couldn't rest. What if Alice was calling from a hospital to tell me Tom was ill or hurt? I groped for my mobile and texted her.

Did you ring me? Is everything OK?

Her reply came through almost at once.

Didn't ring, all's well here. I'm in bed but call if you need to talk XXX.

I sent back:

Thanks I'm fine – goodnight XXX

I slept well for once and woke on Sunday knowing I'd dreamed of my family. They had been happy dreams: the kind of dreams I'd had in the early days after the accident – the cruellest ones of all. In the first waking moments you lie warm and comfortable, knowing everything is all right, everyone is alive and well.

It takes a few minutes to remember that the happy dreams are the fantasy and it's the nightmare that's real.

The weather had taken a turn for the worse and as I lay listening to the rain I felt the loneliness twist inside me, worse even than it had been in the first days in prison when I was in too much shock to feel anything.

My mood today reminded me more of when I was a teenager. By the time I was fourteen I was barely speaking to Mum or Dad and no one at school seemed to like me. Emily was miles away and Alice was too young to confide in. I knew I was adopted, my Romanian birth mother hadn't wanted me, and I was pretty sure my adoptive parents wished they had never taken me on either. I spent whole days lying in bed paralysed with misery. When I did get up I would wander the streets alone, walking myself into exhaustion.

It was on one of these tramps when I took shelter from a chill drizzle in a bus shelter. Although it was close to Beldon House, I couldn't face going home to Mum's silences and pursed lips. Out in the country like this, with no bus due for an hour or more, the last thing I expected was for anyone to join me, but the girl who did looked around my age and was so chatty it took only minutes to feel we were friends.

She offered me a drink. It was vodka, and I'd never had more than a sip or two of wine before, but although it tasted like sour fire and made me gasp and cough, I kept pace with her as we passed the bottle back and forth. Her name was Lizzie, and she had dyed yellow hair and eyelashes heavy with black mascara. Her nails were bitten to the quick, there were scars on her thin pale arms, and I thought she was the most glamorous creature I'd ever seen. She told me she had run away from three foster homes and now she was looking out for herself. She'd been staying with some friends in the village, but was having to move on. 'They got fed up with me. People usually do,' she said, with a throaty laugh. We swapped mobile numbers and when she got on the bus I longed to go with her.

I didn't dare that time, but after the next row at home I met up with Lizzie in Tonbridge and stayed the night at the squat where she was living. I went home, very defiant, late next evening, opening the front door to be met by Dad in the hall. He looked so angry I was terrified but hid it with a toss of the head as I pushed past him, heading for the stairs.

He grabbed my arm, 'Oh no you don't, young lady. I want an explanation.'

He was a big man with a loud voice, but he had never raised his hand to me or to Alice. I could see, though, that he was tempted to hit me when I curled my lips and met his eyes.

'What?'

He took an enormous breath. 'I suppose you realise we had to call the police? You've made your mother ill and Alice hasn't stopped crying. We thought you'd had an accident or been abducted.'

I pulled my arm away. 'Well I'm back now, so you can all relax.' Then I headed upstairs with a look I hoped was loaded with contempt.

I expected him to follow me, but he didn't and he was at work when I got up next day. Mum was ill in bed and Alice was at school. No one seemed to care what I did. So I packed a rucksack and walked out. The first of many times.

It didn't take long to lose touch with Lizzie, but by then I'd met Gaz. I kidded myself it was love and we headed for London. Gaz disappeared after a couple of weeks and I went home for a bit, but the pattern was set. Gradually, I was staying away for longer and longer, moving from squat to squat, sometimes sleeping in parks or even shop doorways. It's amazing where you can sleep if you're drunk or wasted enough.

I got picked up by the police and taken home a few times, but left again after a couple of days. My parents must have squared it somehow with school. Maybe they just carried on paying the fees and everyone agreed it was easier that way. I never went back to school.

The only thing I ever felt guilty about in those days was leaving Alice, and even now I felt a twinge when I recalled looking up one day, as I was shambling up the driveway, to see her little face at her bedroom window. Her mouth was moving and she was trying to push up the wooden sash so that I could hear her. But she couldn't manage it and that image of her tearful face as she tried to call me back stayed with me until the downers I'd pinched from Mum's room began to take the edge off everything.

The phone rang: Alice's number. I took a swallow from the water beside my bed, but my voice must still have sounded croaky because Tom said, 'You all right, Mum?'

'I'm fine. I thought you were out all day today.'

'I will be in an hour. Just wanted to speak to you before I went.'

I held the phone to my lips for a moment unable to speak. 'Well, it's lovely to hear your voice.'

'I'm sorry about yesterday, Mum. Alice said you might have been upset. I thought I told her about the table tennis and everything, but I must have forgot.'

'Don't worry. I can't expect you to rearrange your life to suit me. Now off you go and win that tournament and I'll be over to see you tomorrow or Tuesday – OK?'

Alice came on then to ask about last night's call. 'It was nothing,' I said. 'Just a cold call, but it was so late I got worried.'

'Do you want to come over for lunch?'

'If you don't mind, I won't. I'm really tired. It was a bit of a day yesterday.'

She had to go then because Tom was there, asking if she knew where he'd put his table tennis bat and did he have any clean shorts. It was just as well because I couldn't face talking about Matt's visit until I'd thought about it myself.

I switched on the laptop, almost expecting an email from Emily, but my inbox stayed empty. I had her number in the notebook Alice had left for me, so I picked up the phone to call her, but somehow I couldn't do it and phoned Lorna instead. There was no reply, but I left a message to tell her I wasn't working on Friday and could come to her then.

After that I stood eating some toast and staring from the window at the rain, the grey clouds, and the empty sea. I knew I should clean the place and do some washing for next week, but instead I watched TV and tried to read.

Finally, I forced myself to put a few things in the washing machine and push the Hoover round the flat. At least it seemed to give me an appetite, but looking in the freezer I knew I couldn't face more microwaved food. It was five o'clock and too late, on a Sunday, to go to a supermarket.

There was a convenience store not far away, but when I got outside the sun had come out and I found myself heading past the shop, following the smell of fish and chips to the corner of the High Street. When I saw the queue I stopped, ready to turn back to the flat and another frozen ready meal, but I took a breath and forced myself to stand behind the man on the end.

As the queue moved forward, and nobody paid me any attention, I felt myself begin to relax. And, when I asked for a pickled onion from the huge jar on the counter, I was even able to laugh with a woman behind me when she said, rather me than her, she couldn't stand the things.

As I was pushing my way out I felt a tug on my arm. 'Hi, babe. How's it going?'

'Oh hello, Nicola. Fine, yes, I'm fine.'

The slim, dark-haired man was obviously with her and I took a step back, although he didn't look like the aggressive character I'd imagined buzzing on my door bell the other night.

Nicola's hand remained on my arm and at the same time I felt something clutch my knee. The little girl, Molly, was standing, clinging to her mother's leg and using mine for extra support. Her sticky smile said she wasn't going to let go without a struggle.

'She likes you, Clare. You'll not get away now.' Nicola turned to the man. 'Kieran, this is Clare who I was telling you about.'

He smiled and held out his hand. 'Hello, Clare, nice to meet you. I'm your upstairs neighbour.' So it wasn't the ex. Kieran's hand was warm and dry and I tried to return his smile.

Molly was moving restlessly, giving high-pitched little screams, each one greeted by heavy sighs from the man serving the chips.

'Clare, you wouldn't be a darling and take her outside for a minute would you?' Without waiting for my answer, Nicola peeled the little hand from her own leg and turned the child towards me. 'Go on, darlin', go with Clare.'

By now Molly had her hands raised to me, and I had no option but to push my packet of food under my arm and haul her up. She was warm and smelled of sweets, and when she put her arms around my neck and rested her little head on my shoulder something inside me began to ache.

They'd parked the pushchair outside, and Molly clambered from my arms and into it, grabbing a bottle from the seat as she did so and sucking away, her eyes closed with satisfaction. I stood watching her.

Kieran took charge of the pushchair and led the way, stowing their food in a bag hanging from the back and Nicola threaded her arm through mine. 'This is nice. We can all eat at mine. Kieran's bought us a bottle, but I've got another couple in the fridge.'

'I'm sorry. That would be lovely, but I can't, I've got an urgent phone call to make.' It was a lame excuse, but I couldn't face the thought of socialising, especially with someone as pushy as Nicola. And had I imagined it, or had Kieran's eyes lingered on me just a fraction too long? I knew it was unlikely anyone would recognise me from newspaper pictures of five years ago, but I made sure to lower my head and let my hair fall across my face as we said goodbye.

Inside, the phone was flashing with a message:

Hi, Clare, it's me, Emily. I was hoping I'd catch you. Matt says you look great, but he couldn't get a definite date for a visit out of you. Please, please try to come soon. Once the baby arrives I expect it will be hell here for a bit, so get up here before and we can have time to chat without interruptions. Sorry… rambling… ring me.

It was so lovely to hear her voice that I played the message three times, picking at the fish and chips straight from the bag. When the phone rang I grabbed it, but there was only silence – another cold call. This time I was glad of the interruption because it stopped me dithering. I called Emily's number. She burst straight into talk. 'Oh, Clare, it's wonderful to hear your voice again.'

'I was just thinking that about yours.' It was so easy to talk to her, as if the years of silence between us had faded away.

'So when can you come up?'

'I'm not sure when I'm working, but I could probably get away for a couple of days next week or the one after. This is so good of you, Em…' That wretched lump was choking my voice again.

Emily sounded tearful too. 'Don't say that. I'm not being good. I've missed you so much. Oh damn these hormones. I never used to cry, remember?'

I took a wobbling breath. 'Of course, you were the hard one. And I can stay in a B&B, you know. You don't want guests when you must be so tired.'

Emily coughed and her voice steadied. 'Rubbish, you're staying here. But look, we're not doing very well at this so why don't we say you'll let me know as soon as you can? Just give me a few hours' warning.'

I didn't think I would sleep that night, but I must have dozed because I was woken by the phone. The handset by the bed said the number was unavailable, and I'd asked Alice always to leave a message, so I ignored it.

After that, I seemed to hear every sound. The creak of a door and muffled voices from the main hall had me tensing, wondering if Nic's ex might cause trouble again. A few minutes later I heard footsteps on the stairs and then the faint strains of jazz from above:

Kieran arriving home I guessed. I didn't mind the jazz; it was soft enough to be soothing, as was the patter of rain on the windows.

Next time the phone rang it woke me from dreams of fire and flashing light. I couldn't stop myself from checking the caller, but, of course, there was that word *unavailable* again. It was a word I was beginning to hate. Afterwards, I lay, eyes wide, ears still hearing those shrill sounds piercing the silence, until, at last, I fell back into fevered dreams.

Walking along the deserted streets I shivered, whether from cold or tiredness I wasn't sure. Ragged clouds sped across the sky but there was little rain, just a damp haze with the odd flurry of big drops blown from trees and shop awnings. It was some time before 7 a.m. and I felt as if I'd hardly slept. Needed to wake myself properly before work.

The beach was empty, even of gulls; the water slapping and sucking on the grey shingle. I closed my mind and set off towards the pier, walking as quickly as I could against the pull and slide of the pebbles. As I concentrated on the effort of walking, I could feel my jangled nerves easing a little but the rain became steadier and the wind increased, the water dripping down my neck and wet tendrils of hair sticking to my face, making me clench my teeth and huddle into my thin mac.

They were working to rebuild the pier and there were barriers on the beach, so I turned to go back. But the wind and rain hit me with much greater force. I spotted a shabby café with a sign saying it was open for breakfast but hesitated at the door, thinking maybe I should just try to get a bus home.

'Hello, Clare. Didn't take you for an early riser. Here, let me.' I turned to see Kieran behind me. He reached over my head and pushed open the door. Although I wanted to turn and run, I could see no option but to walk to the counter with him. He smiled down at me, making me even more conscious of my wet hair and pallid face. 'You sit down and I'll get them. What do you want?'

I ignored my growling stomach. 'Oh just a coffee, please.' The ridiculous thought crossed my mind that Nicola had sent him to follow me, but I was grateful when he came back to the table with our drinks and a couple of muffins.

'If you don't want it I'll eat yours, but you look starved to me.'

I took off my mac, very aware of my damp T-shirt and the heat that throbbed in my cheeks. He smiled. His eyes were an unusual shade, greenish brown, under very dark brows and his chin was grey with the shadow of stubble. He stood to take off his jacket, hanging it over the back of his chair. I concentrated on the muffin.

'So you were hungry after all. Sure you don't want mine?' he said.

I shook my head with a laugh.

'And you look tired. Didn't sleep well?'

'No.'

'Join the club.'

He was smiling, waiting for me to say something. 'It's the light mornings, I suppose.' *That's good, keep going.* 'It'll be better later on.'

'Hey, don't wish the good weather away. I'd rather not sleep than go back to winter.'

His laugh was infectious and the man behind the counter joined in.

'Too right, mate, our summers are short enough as it is.'

Kieran looked at me, his face serious. 'You will tell me if I make too much noise over your head, won't you. I sometimes forget that other people are asleep. And I do love to listen to Billie Holliday and Peggy Lee when I'm awake in the night.'

'I've heard your jazz playing now and then, but it doesn't bother me. I like it.' I finished my coffee and began struggling back into my wet raincoat. He stood to help me, and I found myself staring at the slightly frayed denim cuff of his shirt and his very brown hand. 'I've got to be at work in an hour. Better get going,' I said.

He was slipping his jacket on, too: I wasn't getting away that easily.

The rain had stopped and the promenade was beginning to get busy with joggers, walkers, and cyclists. We walked for a while in silence, then he laughed as he took my arm to help me avoid a boy cycling on the pavement. 'Nicola's a great girl isn't she? I'd say she's one of the nicest, most genuine, people I've ever met.' Another little laugh. 'Mind you, I was annoyed she got to meet you first, because I felt as if I already knew you.'

They talk about your blood freezing, and I knew at that moment what it meant. The world shuddered as I remembered the photographers outside court, the grainy snapshots in the tabloids. *What Price Three Lives?* was one of the headlines.

Two gulls landed on the path to tear at a discarded doughnut. A small dog skittered past and somehow my legs continued to carry me onwards. I couldn't have spoken even if I wanted to and I very much didn't want to. Finally, what he was saying began to penetrate, to take on a different meaning and the world began turning once more.

'The landlord's a friend of mine. He asked me to look after the keys to your place and show people round, and I may say I recommended you over one or two others. Of course, the blonde girl, your sister, was pretty convincing about what a great tenant you'd be.'

I breathed again. No doubt he'd been looking forward to a glamorous Alice lookalike moving in. The scruffy brunette must have been a real let-down.

We got back just as Nicola was pushing Molly's buggy through the gate. She raised her eyebrows. 'Hey, you two, you're not getting together behind my back, are you?'

Kieran grinned and ruffled Molly's hair, then planted a kiss on Nicola's cheek. 'Hello, Molly, morning Nic.' Then he held the gate wide for me. I scuttled through, pulling out my key as quickly as I could.

As she walked away Nicola was laughing. She called back, 'Watch him, Clare, he's dangerous.'

Chapter Eight

Work was difficult. The rain had brought no real break in the heat. If anything it was hotter than ever and the shop felt like a greenhouse: the windows misty with steam, air heavy with the composty smells of greenery and earth. I was so exhausted it took all my efforts to concentrate on serving customers and I was very aware of Stella shooting me some concerned glances. I told myself I'd better make an effort to look brighter tomorrow.

Back in the flat I kicked off my shoes and stood barefoot on the cool tiles in the kitchen. I poured a glass of water and added ice to it. Then let the water run over my wrists and forearms.

My shirt was sticking to me so I pulled it out from the waistband of my trousers, undid the buttons, and flapped the cloth in the air.

It was when I was rubbing the cold glass over my cheeks and neck that I heard the knocking.

It wasn't coming from the front door, but from the bedroom. A light rhythmic sound: wood against wood. A half-closed door hitting the frame, again and again.

As I went towards the bedroom I heard something else, something different. Not rhythmic this time, but more like fabric brushing against the wall or floor. I pictured someone sliding behind the door or under the bed, alerted by the noise I'd been making.

I pulled my shirt together, and looked back towards my little hallway. Should I run over to Nicola or upstairs to ask Kieran to come down? But they might want to call the police and I couldn't have that.

I grabbed the heavy lamp that stood next to the sofa and crept to the door, pushing it open hard. It slammed against the wall – no one hiding there. The room looked just like I'd left it this morning: the rumpled bed, the T-shirt I'd slept in on the floor, one drawer half-open.

Then that sound came again and my breath stalled.

A curtain flapped away from the window, sweeping across the wall: the same sound. And no one was there. I lowered the lamp.

But the window was open: surely not wide enough for anyone to get in or out because the sash was fitted with metal pegs to limit the level it could be raised. An arm could come through to steal something, or even drop something inside. I wasn't sure if it was the breeze flipping the curtains back and forth that made me shiver or the thought of that arm. And, although there had been plenty of hot nights recently, I didn't remember ever opening, or even unlocking, the window in here.

I made sure it was closed tight and secured. Then looked inside the wardrobe, under the bed, and behind the door again, as if I might have missed something.

I checked every drawer and surface, then did the same for the whole flat. Nothing was missing and I didn't think anything had been moved. Could I have opened that window and forgotten about it?

In the kitchen I went to the fridge, but closed it right away. Before I could think about cooking or eating I needed to feel safe. I tried all the other windows, secured them again, and made sure the front door was double locked.

For once, I was very glad to think of Nicola and Kieran close by.

*

The weather was more pleasant next day and in the evening I waited outside the flat for Alice's car. Tom was in the passenger seat and, as she pulled up, he jumped out, without a word, to move to the back and I turned to thank him. He was fiddling with his seatbelt and didn't look at me.

Alice turned the car jerkily, bumping hard against the kerb. 'Right let's get going. I've left the food in the oven. Tom decided to come just as I was about to leave, then kept me waiting for ten minutes while he got ready.' There was a heavy silence from the back seat suggesting the aftermath of an argument.

I waited till Alice's attention was on the road before I dared to look back and give my son a smile that I hoped told him I was glad he'd come, without undermining her authority. The last thing I wanted was to cause friction between them. Tom flushed and looked away from me, pulled out his phone and began playing with it. I searched for something to say to Alice. 'I've had more of those late night phone calls.'

'Oh dear,' she said. 'I'm sure it's nothing to worry about, but who have you given the number to? '

'Lorna and Stella, that's all.'

'The letting agency has it, of course, but… oh, and girl opposite, what's her name?'

'Nicola?'

'Yes, she said she was friendly with the woman who lived there before, so she'll probably have it, but she'd hardly be calling you late at night, would she?'

Remembering Nicola's problems with her ex and our early morning drinking session I wasn't so sure. I'd have to ask her.

Alice said, 'You're sure there's no one else? '

Of course, there was Ruby as well, but I wasn't going to mention her. I knew what Alice would think. She probably hoped I'd cut all ties with my life inside. Which was, after all, what Ruby had told me to do. And I'd made enemies there. So if anyone was trying to rattle me it was most likely one of them.

Alice drove well, but she was clearly in a hurry and I was unnerved by the speed with which she took the country roads. I would always be an anxious passenger I supposed, and I couldn't imagine ever getting behind a wheel again myself.

When we pulled up at the house she jumped out of the car and went straight inside, calling behind her. 'Don't disappear upstairs again, Tom, supper's ready.'

I put my arm around his waist as we headed in together and whispered. 'It's good to see you. How did the table tennis go?'

He moved away. 'OK.' Then looked back at me as he hopped up the steps into the hall, his eyes brightening. 'I won all my matches and so did Mark. We're gonna be in the semi-finals.'

In the kitchen, Alice was dishing up what looked like a very good fish pie, although she said it was probably overcooked. 'There's some Muscadet in the fridge, Clare, will you open it?'

She poured two large glasses of wine, but I forced myself to drink slowly. Alice and I talked about the weather and my job, while Tom ate steadily.

'I'm hoping to go up to London to see Lorna on Friday,' I said.

Alice was picking at her food, but was on her second glass of wine. 'That's good. You should be getting out and about rather than sitting in the flat.'

Tom's plate was soon clean and when he jumped up; she looked hard at him, until he muttered a surly, 'Is it OK if I go?'

Alice nodded, her glance telling me to keep out of it. We sat for a moment in silence, then she turned to me. 'On the subject of getting out and about, I forgot to mention, we always have a barbecue for my partners in the practice and a few other friends at this time of year. I arranged it for this Saturday before I knew when you'd be out, but you must come.'

'Oh, I'm not sure.'

'Come on, Tom'll be upset if you don't and it's only a few people. Tom's friend Mark and his parents will be there and I know he'd love you to meet them. Most of them know about

71

you, but don't worry no one will mention anything. Then I thought you could stay the night and we'd have a quiet Sunday just the three of us.'

There was no way I could refuse. 'I'll come on the train, shall I?'

'Well, I thought I'd ask Stella. You know her, so that will make things easier for you, and she can give you a lift.'

She stood and began collecting dishes. I followed her into the kitchen, loading the dishwasher as she rinsed plates.

'No, Clare.' The edge on her voice almost made me drop the glass I was holding. 'They're crystal. The dishwasher will ruin them.' She was behind me, her hands on my hips to move me out of the way.

'Sorry.' I took the glass to the sink.

'Just leave it… I mean… it's fine, I'll do it.' With an obvious effort she softened her tone. 'Why don't you pour some coffee and take it into the garden.'

I didn't trust myself to speak but, as I reached the French windows, I raised the mugs to her and she nodded with a tight smile. 'Thanks, nearly done.'

Outside, I was glad to see the large glass-topped table already had a set of coasters on it. It would be just my luck to annoy her again by damaging it with the hot mugs.

I leant back on the cushions of the lounger and let the silence and the warm evening air wash over me. In my mind's eye, the flowers, the pots of herbs, and the little paths crisscrossing the garden disappeared, replaced by a smooth carpet of grass stretching away in neat lines. When we were kids there were hardly any flowers, just a few shrubs and the two tall trees at the end. Mr Hobbs came from the village to keep it tidy, but that was all.

And yet I loved it and so did Alice. It was where we spent most of our time when we weren't at school. Where we could run, and scream, and scramble up the trees before collapsing in their shade. Me more often than not with a book, and Alice with her dolls or the toy ponies she collected.

One day from that time sprang to mind and I could almost feel Alice's long hair tickling my chin as I held the back of her bike, pushing her along the path that ran beside the wall.

'Don't let go. Please Clare, don't let go.'

'I won't, I promise,' I said. But when I felt her begin to balance and push forward on her own, I did release her, running along behind, urging her on.

As she neared the end of the path, I stood, hot and sweaty from the effort and the excitement, knowing she'd be all right. But Mum opened the kitchen window, her voice shrill.

'Alice, be careful.'

Alice turned to look at her, hit the wall, and tumbled off. The bike fell on top of her, and Mum was out, pushing me away and gathering Alice into her arms. I watched them, knowing that, as usual, I'd mucked it up, and all too aware of my clumsy eleven-year-old bulk and the new, disgusting, smell of my sweat.

Two scraped knees were the only damage and Alice, despite her smudged face, wasn't crying as Mum helped her to her feet. She gave us her prettiest smile, and said, 'I'm all right.'

But Mum turned to me, her face twisted. 'You never think do you, Clare? She's just a baby and she could have been seriously hurt. Now go to your room and try to grow up a bit.' I stared at her, fighting back the tears. 'Don't you look at me like that, young lady.' She pursed her lips and wrinkled her nose. 'Get upstairs now, and before you do anything else you need to take a shower.'

Her eyes were slivers of blue glass and at that moment I hated her. She had never hit me, but her terrible stares and the silences that followed were punishment enough in those days. The days before I taught myself not to care.

As I stalked towards the house, Alice ran after me and threw her soft little arms around me. 'I love you, Clare,' she said.

Our mother pulled her away, in a waft of delicate perfume. 'Clare's very naughty,' she said. 'And you're being naughty too now. You're both making Mummy unhappy.'

Later, I heard Mum crying in her room and I looked out of my bedroom window. Alice was sitting under a tree, with her toys, singing to herself. When she saw me she came over. 'Don't be sad, Clare,' she called. 'Mummy's upset 'cos I told her she was mean to you, but I don't care, you're my best friend.'

I couldn't remember what happened after that. It might have blown over after a couple of hours, or a couple of days, of heavy silence or it could have been the start of one of Mum's breakdowns.

When the grown up Alice sat beside me, she was smiling, a guarded smile, head on one side. 'What?'

'I was just thinking about playing here when we were little. You were so sweet.' She laughed and I dared to ask, 'What's wrong?'

'Oh... nothing.'

'Alice...?'

She brushed her hair away from her face, glancing up at the window above, her voice low. 'I've been having trouble with Tom, that's all.'

A surge of feeling, I couldn't put a name to, caught at my breath. 'What happened?'

She took a sip from her mug then leaned back into the cushions, stretching out her legs and kicking off her sandals. 'Oh the usual. I'm sure it's mostly normal teenage rebelliousness but of course the situation doesn't help.'

'Me being back you mean?'

She nodded. 'We knew it wouldn't be easy. Today it was just something and nothing. He decided to come with me at the last minute and then wasn't ready, but he's been difficult for a while.' She looked at me. 'What did you say to him the other day?'

'I told him about my past and that ex-addicts can never be really sure they're cured.'

'Did that satisfy him?'

I shook my head. 'Not really. He's got the idea someone might have wanted to harm Dad because of the Briomab drug scandal.'

She gave a small snort. 'Oh my God, not a conspiracy theory.'

A flash of resentment. *Couldn't she see how important it was not to make light of Tom's suggestions?* I took a deep breath, trying to keep my voice even. 'I have to take his ideas seriously, Alice.'

When she didn't speak I picked up my coffee mug and drank a long drink. I didn't want to argue with her, but I remembered how determined Tommy had always been and I was sure I was right in this. Alice shifted in her seat. 'So what are you going to do?'

'Talk to Matt and to Lorna first of all.'

'Just be careful, will you. You're both under enormous strain.' She glanced up at the house again. 'He still feels guilty because he wasn't there and you must be finding things so difficult too.' She laid her hand on my arm. 'But I'll help all I can, of course.'

She looked close to tears and I put my hand over hers. 'I'm sorry. You're getting all the flak and it's not fair.'

'I'll cope. Just do me a favour and try to enjoy your time together rather than focusing too much on the past. That's the best way you can help Tom, in my opinion.'

I smiled at her. 'OK, doc, as long as you try to enjoy yourself a bit more too. Which reminds me, what about that latest man of yours – Duncan – how are things with him?'

'I told you he wanted to go back to Australia eventually,' she said. 'Well he did – a few months ago.'

'Oh, Alice, you didn't tell me. Did he ask you to go with him?'

Her hand clenched under mine. 'Yes, or to follow him out later, but I said no because it wouldn't be fair to keep him hanging on indefinitely.'

'And you said no because …' I jerked my head towards the house.

She looked at me, her blue eyes bright. 'I didn't want to go.' Her voice dropped to a whisper. 'Yes, it was partly Tom, of course, but … I just didn't want to go – couldn't have felt that much for Duncan after all I suppose.'

I knew she had been thinking of me as well as Tom. I squeezed her hand, but could only swallow on the words I should have said.

There was a sound overhead and we looked up. Tom was at an open window. 'Come up, Mum. I want to show you something.'

Alice smiled and picked up her mug. 'Go on, I'm OK.'

Upstairs, Tom was hunched over the computer again. He turned to me with gleaming eyes. 'Look at all this stuff about Granddad.'

There were loads of references to Dad and to his company: Parnell Pharmaceuticals. Most of them related to the suspicions that some data about a new arthritis drug had been falsified. I knew all this, of course, – the drug was implicated in making certain forms of cancer more aggressive. There were pay-outs, but it was never proved that the company had done anything wrong.

'Yes, it was a horrible time for Granddad. He wasn't involved with the testing data, but he felt bad, even though we still don't know if the medicine was to blame or if any of the data was faked.'

'It's worth looking into though, Mum. It says here that the directors got threats.' I bit my lip. If only his theory could be remotely possible. 'If they wanted to drug you then they must have had someone at the reception. We should check everyone, even the catering people.' His face was very pink and I could feel the heat coming from him. I wanted so much to hug him, but this wasn't the time. He had to know I was listening and he was helping me.

'You're doing brilliantly, Tom. And I'm going to Emily's soon so I'll find out anything I can from her and from Matt. I did ask Matt about people at the reception, but he couldn't tell me anything.'

'He worked for Granddad's firm as well, didn't he? Even before it was taken over.'

'Yes, although I don't think he was very important when Granddad was alive. So he might not know much about the ins and outs of the scandal.' I squeezed his forearm. 'But don't worry, I'll speak to him about it. And to Lorna.'

Before I left I looked into the spare bedroom, where Alice had stored some furniture from the little house Steve and I used to live in with the twins. It was a bit shabby, but we loved it. Dad had

76

given us some money for the deposit when we got married, but we wouldn't take anything else from him: both of us too proud. After I stopped thinking I was innocent and accepted my sentence, I asked Alice to arrange its sale. I knew I could never go back there.

She and Lorna had cleared the house, using their own judgment about what to save and what to get rid of, because I was in no state to think about it, and Lorna told me they'd filled a suitcase with personal stuff. It was probably just the kind of thing I needed to help kick-start my memory.

When Alice saw me carrying it downstairs she raised her eyebrows. 'Are you sure you want to take that now?'

'I've got to start somewhere.'

She insisted on paying for a taxi to take me home. 'I've had a drink and Tom should be in bed, but I don't want you hanging about for trains, especially with that heavy case.' I could see she thought it was a bad idea to take it.

Tom hauled the case out to the taxi, and I kissed him goodbye, holding him until he moved away, and wishing I could say something that would make everything all right. He stood waving as we drove away, and I kissed my fingers at him, the pain in my throat almost unbearable.

At the flat, the driver offered to take the suitcase in for me, but I couldn't face the thought of anyone else touching it. 'It's fine, not that heavy,' I said.

Although I was right, and I could carry it perfectly well, my arm was quivering by the time I got inside. Not because of the weight, but from the fear of what it might hold. I knew I wouldn't sleep if I looked in it tonight, so I pushed it into a corner of the living room. How I was ever going to face it I didn't know.

Chapter Nine

The case was the first thing I saw when I got in from work next day, but I told myself I should have something to eat and drink before tackling it. Usually I made do with a microwave meal or something simple like beans on toast, but this evening I felt the need to cook properly. So I mixed an omelette, chopping some herbs, grating cheese, and making a salad and doing it all with fierce concentration.

But once I'd dished up I could only play with the food. I swallowed some coffee and forced myself to pull the suitcase into the centre of the room and to kneel beside it.

The phone rang and I grabbed at it, not caring if it was a call centre of even a heavy breather. It was Lorna.

'Hello, Clare, my love,' she said. 'I'm sorry I missed you the other day. You asked about coming on Friday and of course that'll be fine with me. I'll look forward to it. We can have a nice long chat then.'

'Yes, please. I really need to see you, Lorna.'

'That doesn't sound so good. Are you all right?'

'I honestly don't know. Things that used to make sense just don't seem to anymore. And I've promised to look into stuff for Tom that's bound to upset people.'

'Is there anything I can do?'

'One of Tom's ideas is that someone might have had it in for Dad. You know all that fuss about the arthritis drug, how unpleasant did it actually get?'

'Well, your father was very upset about it, and when they thought it would go to court he was anxious.'

'I think Tom was wondering about threats, or anything like that.'

'Oh no. At least not that I know of. We did have the representative of the families' group into the office several times, but I don't know the details of what they discussed.'

'Except, there was a fairly big pay-out to some of the families and others got nothing, which must have caused a lot of resentment.'

She seemed almost annoyed now. 'But that was among the families themselves, Clare. It didn't affect us. And Tom's just a young boy. Surely you don't give the idea any credence?'

This was pointless. 'No, I suppose not. But I can't ignore it. I have to show him I'm taking him seriously. I promised I'd talk to Matt too. Do you think he might know anything?'

'Well, your dad liked Matt and always said he had a future, so they may have talked. Robert loved going to the labs and he was at his most comfortable there. I think Matt reminded him of himself as a young chemist.'

'And Matt must have worked with Dr Penrose.'

Penrose was the man they'd called the whistle-blower. He claimed that at least one of the tests he'd done on the drug, Briomab, showed possibly dangerous side effects. Said certain results had been deleted from the final report.

Lorna sighed. 'Of course, although Matt wouldn't have been involved with the research or the report.'

'What happened to Penrose?'

'I think he died a couple of years ago.' There was a pause, although I could tell she hadn't finished. 'I know this is important to you, Clare, but remember, Emily is pregnant and they've waited a long time for that to happen. So do go easy on them, won't you?'

My silence spoke for me.

'Oh dear, now I've upset you and that's the last thing I want to do. We need to talk face to face, so I'll ring off now.'

'OK, see you Friday.'

'Just remember, Clare. I'm on your side.'

There was nothing for it but to kneel by the suitcase. It was a big fabric thing that looked as if it had never been used for travelling. I guessed Alice had bought it specially. And, – oh God would there never be an end to these moments when a tiny lost memory would swoop in to skewer me – I'd packed our only case for the wedding. Because we hadn't had time to go to the hotel beforehand, it had been in the boot of the burning car that night. And now I saw, not Steve or Toby, but Tommy, his little rucksack bulging on his back, as he waved goodbye from Daniel's doorstep.

Gritting my teeth, and telling myself to get on with it, I unzipped and flipped back the lid. The first thing I saw, right on top – Alice, don't make it easy for me, will you – was a pale blue photo album: Toby and Tommy's baby book. Very carefully, making sure it didn't flip open, that no loose picture should slip out, I placed it on the floor, my fingers trailing over the cover. I let my hand rest on it for a long moment, but knew I mustn't open it yet. If I looked at it now, even held it for too long, I was finished.

Right at the bottom of the case I could see some white fabric wrapped in plastic: my wedding dress. What was I going to do with that? Hang it in my wardrobe, here, just as it had hung in our house? Hide it away and never look at it again, or get rid of it? I put my hand inside the plastic. The material didn't feel silky, as I remembered it, but somehow thickened, as if shrouded in a layer of dust.

Until I held my babies for the first time, I thought I could never be happier than on my wedding day. Steve was perfect and I was already pregnant.

It was a small wedding, Steve and I insisted on that, but as I got out of the car at the little hotel and stood in the sunshine holding Dad's arm, the babies kicked inside me for the first time, and it was so wonderful I determined to treasure the memory forever. After the accident, I forced it into the corner of my mind I kept shuttered and bolted. But I had to start bringing those memories into the light again and to look at them without flinching. So I let my thoughts run on.

Steve had been shocked at first; it was too early for him to start a family because his garden design business was just taking off. He'd been thinking of hiring an assistant, but that had to be put on hold, and as the news sank in he said we would make it work and it would be wonderful. By our wedding day I knew he was as excited as I was.

Eventually, even Dad came round to the idea of us marrying, and he and Alice both adored my boys when they arrived. Dad said they made him feel young again.

I pushed the dress back into its plastic cover, but as I did so, I saw Emily in her wedding dress, twirling in front of me, looking pretty with a coronet of red flowers in her dark hair. My heart gave one huge beat, high up in my chest, and for a second, I thought it was a lost memory of that day.

But no, a couple of weeks before I'd gone up for her hen weekend and she'd been excited to show me the dress. I bit my lip hard: it wasn't going to be as easy as that.

There were two other photo albums close to the top of the case and I would have to look at those later on. Just underneath them was a cardboard folder full of documents. Alice must have collected them from various drawers where Steve and I had stuffed them. I knew she and Lorna had gone through everything they thought was important, so this could wait.

It was when I peered into a small carrier bag to find two little pairs of shoes – the twins' very first – that I had to stop. I took them out and laid them side by side on the carpet. Toby's were red and Tommy's blue: we never dressed them alike, they weren't identical anyway, but Steve and I agreed we must always encourage them to be individuals.

I picked up Tommy's pair and kissed the grubby leather, breathing in the musty smell and pressing them to my chest as I swayed back and forth on my knees. Then I put them gently back into the bag. Toby's little shoes felt different somehow, older, more fragile, as if they might shatter like glass at my touch. I was afraid to squeeze them, but I held them to my cheek and to my lips, kissing them again and again.

And from somewhere deep, deep, inside I felt that familiar earthquake as my chest heaved and I choked on the huge sobs that tore out of me. This wasn't crying: it was more like some kind of brutal assault by my own body.

'Oh, Toby, Toby my baby, I'm so, so, sorry.'

How long I knelt there, heaving and choking, I couldn't have said, but at last I came back to myself. My face felt sore, my eyes sticky. I dabbed at the baby shoes with a tissue and placed them beside their brother's in the carrier bag. Then I took the bag and the photo albums to the bedroom and laid them carefully in an empty drawer.

The phone shrilled through the silence and I grabbed it: had to stop that noise. 'Hello,' Nothing. As I put down the handset it rang again: a withheld number. This time I didn't speak and heard a tiny click before the dialling tone kicked in. Of course it was just a call centre trying to sell something, but all the same it made me look round to make sure all the windows were closed.

Back in the living room, I started piling things into the case again. I couldn't face any more tonight.

A knock on the door. I stood behind it, listening.

'Hiya, Clare, are you in? It's me, Nic.'

I rubbed my face; it must be obvious I'd been crying.

Another tap, 'Clare?'

She had to know I was in so I opened up. 'Hello, Nic. Did you just ring me?'

She laughed. 'I'm not that lazy.'

'And you haven't rung me late at night anytime, have you?'

'Not me, babe. You should report it if you've been getting nuisance calls.' Her smile was very sweet and I felt bad about being suspicious.

She took a step forward. 'Just thought you might like a coffee. I've got some nice biscuits too. Molly's asleep, so we can have a proper chat. I did all the talking last time.' Her big grey eyes were shiny, but I could see she was probably lonely.

'That would be lovely, but I'm not feeling too well. I'm going straight to bed.'

'Oh, I thought you looked a bit peaky, what's wrong?'

'A cold coming on, I think. Don't want to give it to Molly.'

'Lemsip's what you need.' She turned towards her own door. 'I've got some you can have.'

'It's fine. I bought a packet on the way home.'

'Oh, OK, you get to bed then. Maybe later in the week for that coffee, eh?'

I closed the door. Poor thing, she was only trying to be friendly, but the idea of sitting over there was too much for me right now. And if I'd let her in, what would she have made of the open case and the evidence of my past scattered around it?

I pushed the case back into the corner of the room. What I'd said to Nicola wasn't so far from the truth. I felt awful. I stood by the window, staring at the sea, still and pale today under a bright evening sun that hung in the sky like a ball of fire.

I begged my brain to come to life. Eyes closed, I tried to conjure up those images I sometimes saw: the dark twisting road, the trees and clouds overhead. But it was no good, behind my lids the sun turned everything red. I pressed my fingers to my eyes to make them as dark as my memories. But still nothing came, not even the disjointed glimpses I'd seen before. It was hopeless and I let my eyes fly open again, so fast that the sunlight made me blink.

And something stirred.

It was nothing like the way they show it in films about amnesia. This was more like that feeling when you're searching for a word you know very well, but can't quite bring to mind. An itch in the back of your brain as intolerable as nails on a blackboard, or the screech of an old gate closing.

On the other side of the gate stood a Clare who knew the truth.

I reached and reached for it, desperate to stop it swinging shut, and finally touched it, my eyes squeezed tight again with the effort. It slowed, and for a millisecond the screeching was stilled.

Then my mind flinched back: *more pain and guilt*. And whatever I had known for that brief moment was gone.

I was very tired when we closed the shop on Thursday, but I knew there was next to nothing in the fridge so I had to force myself to shop for food. As I stopped at the gate with my two bags of groceries, I wanted nothing more than a cool shower.

'Hey, look who's here.'

Nicola and Kieran were sitting at a white plastic table that had suddenly appeared amongst the overgrown greenery of the garden, a wine bottle in front of them. Molly played on a blanket with a mess of plastic toys. Kieran jumped up, and before I could protest had taken my bags from me.

'Let's put these things away and you can join us. It's too nice to sit indoors.'

I allowed him to take the bags through the front door then insisted he go back out while I put away my groceries. I took my time, but decided there was nothing for it but to give in to the inevitable. And I had to get used to socialising with people.

It wasn't so bad. Nic had a fund of funny stories about Molly and seemed able to talk non-stop without taking a breath. When she paused to open a packet of chocolate buttons and hand them to Molly on her blanket, she said, 'Come on Kieran, Clare wants to know about you too.'

He was a photographer doing a lot of advertising work and told us about a recent shoot with some child models and their ghastly parents. Nicola put her hand on his arm. 'But he's being modest as per usual. You should see the pictures in his flat. They're wonderful. He's having an exhibition and they're going into a book.'

Kieran laughed and shook his head. 'Clare doesn't want to know about that.'

'Oh yes she does. Clare, you must get him to show you. Which reminds me, Kieran, don't you owe me a meal?'

'Yes, I'm sorry,' he said, smiling and raising his dark brows at me. 'I've got a lot on at the moment, but you'll both be invited as soon as I have a free evening.'

At least I wasn't going to be cornered into agreeing to anything here and now, and the little smile Kieran gave me when Nic went to collect a ball Molly had thrown into the bushes suggested he intended to let me off the hook.

They both evidently knew Bunches and it was enough that I was able to talk about Stella and Harriet for a few minutes. 'No Dad there either?' Nic said.

'No, but Stella and her daughter are very close.'

'There's hope for us all then,' she said, refilling our glasses before I could stop her. She laughed as I began to protest, saying, 'Go on, let yourself go. There's another bottle in the fridge. In fact, Kieran, if you've got my key on you, can you go and get it? I'm knackered from running after her ladyship.'

He pulled some keys from his pocket and rattled them at her. 'I knew there was a reason you wanted me to look after your spare.'

When he was inside, Nic leaned towards me, speaking softly. 'So what do you think of Kieran, eh? Bit of all right isn't he?'

'He seems very nice.'

'Well he likes you. I can tell by the way he looks at you. And before you got here just now he was asking about you.'

Chapter Ten

Back in the flat, the suitcase was still lying in the corner, still open, and I knew I needed to check through it once more. There was a CD down the side of the case, and when I pulled it out I remembered what it was: photos I'd taken at Emily's hen weekend. Apart from the pictures of the wedding itself these were the closest in time to the accident.

I slipped the disc into the laptop and here was Emily, in a silly little veil and tiara, with Alice and myself, all gurning for the camera, drinks raised high. It was the last time we three were out together – all so carefree.

It was hard to look through, but I forced myself to go slowly: to try to put myself back in those moments, to go behind the smiles and recall how it had really been. My trousers were too tight, I remembered and I had been uncomfortable lolling on the leather sofa in the cocktail bar. And I'd been worried about Alice because she looked so tired, working long hours in A&E at the hospital and obviously finding it difficult.

I clicked onto a photo of Emily, sitting on her own at the table in the restaurant where we'd eaten. She seemed unaware of the camera, looking at something or someone in the distance, and her expression was almost unhappy.

Something else I'd forgotten was that she'd told me the night before how difficult things had been with Matt for a few weeks.

'It's not us, Clare, it's work, but it's affecting us.'

'What's wrong?'

'All this trouble with the Briomab fiasco.'

'I didn't know he had anything to do with that, and anyway it's all sorted now, surely.'

She'd laughed then and put it down to pre-wedding jitters from both of them. But now I had to wonder. And was it something I could ask her about?

Right at the bottom of the case was a scrapbook I'd kept as a kid. I couldn't see how it could help, but maybe going right back might jolt my memory into action.

Sitting on the sofa, I flipped through it. The early pages made me smile, they were filled with pictures cut from magazines, cute kittens and rabbits mostly. I'd forgotten how much I longed for a pet when I was about ten. After that there were dried flowers and grasses squashed under messy strips of Sellotape. Then some rubbings of stones and shells in different coloured crayons that represented the extent of my artistic phase. A few cuttings of pop stars came next and then – ah this was better – some photos.

I must have taken them with my first real camera. Lots of snaps from the Christmas when it was one of my presents. A couple of pages of Alice at various times, clearly enjoying the attention. Then a few of Mum and Dad on what looked like birthdays. Finally, a couple of Lorna. How lovely she was then and how I adored her: the fairy godmother nickname was never really a joke to me.

Here she was in our sunny garden, sitting with Dad, plates and drinks on the table. It must have been one of those times when Mum was in hospital and Lorna came round to cook for us.

And, as I looked, I understood the meaning of that expression about scales falling from your eyes. It was so clear from the way they sat, his hand across the back of her chair, her smiling up at him. Why had I never suspected?

Lorna had always been far more than Dad's secretary, even more than just a family friend, but I'd always thought of her as *my* special person. I looked at the photo again – maybe I was wrong, what could you really tell from one picture? And she had been there for me when I needed her. If she really had loved Dad, could she have been so good to me when she knew I'd killed him?

All of us – me, Alice and Emily – had worked at the office with Lorna at various times as teenagers. So, of course, she was at Emily's wedding, and even though she wasn't called to give evidence, she came to the trial every day. Looking at her now, so elegant, I thought again how dreadful she must have found it when she visited me in prison.

Being searched, sitting in those bleak rooms, on scratched plastic chairs, and trying to keep chatting when I was so often surly and ungrateful. More than once she had to watch as a fight broke out. And then there was the time, as she was about to leave, when the warders wrestled a prisoner to the ground in front of her. I was being taken out, but I could still remember Lorna's look of horror as she saw the woman's mouth forced open to get at the drugs her boyfriend had passed her in his goodbye kiss.

I told her several times she shouldn't keep coming, but it was Lorna, along with Alice, and later Ruby, who helped me to stay sane – to carry on living.

Lorna lived just off Kensington High Street, and as I stood waiting for her to open the door, I reminded myself again of how wonderful she had been to me all those years ago. What the neighbours must have thought about a bedraggled teenager, smelling of vodka and worse, even daring to enter their street, let alone being welcomed inside one of the neat mews houses, I could hardly bear to think now.

Those days, when she let me have a warm bath, dress in clean clothes, and fill up on proper food, were what I credited afterwards with keeping me in touch with the normal world. Allowing me to see it might be possible to become part of that world again one day.

But more important than all the comforts was the knowledge that at least one person still thought I was worth something – still loved me, whatever state I was in. But now I wondered if she really did care for me, or if I was just another way to keep close to my dad.

When she opened the door she held me for a long moment. I let my hands rest on her shoulders. Even now I hoped she'd tell me I was wrong, there had been no affair. But would I believe her if she did?

She walked heavily as she led me into her small living room. Of course her knee was bad, but she also seemed depressed. 'There's hot coffee in the kitchen, but I'll leave you to bring it in, if you don't mind. Thank goodness it's not much longer till they fix me up.' She patted her leg and lowered herself into a pale leather armchair. It was placed so she could look through the length of the room to the French windows and beyond to her lovely courtyard garden.

The tiny kitchen gleamed. There were pots of herbs on the window sill: basil, parsley and thyme, and the coffee percolator sent out fragrant steam. The oven was warm, obviously cooking our lunch. It smelled good and a bottle of red wine stood next to the coffee mugs, but when I went to the fridge for milk, I noticed how empty it was. A bowl of salad, a pork chop in its Sainsbury's tray, a small wedge of stilton, some yogurts and a bag of grapes – the fridge of a single woman, and possibly a lonely one.

I put the tray of coffee on the low table and sat on the sofa, glad of the chance to fuss with the cups and milk. 'You've done a lot with the place.' I waved my hand to take in the vase of lilies; the fitted bookcases; the gleaming parquet flooring.

'Well, your father left me some money, so I was able to buy it, after all those years of being a tenant, and I've really enjoyed making it my own.'

This was the moment to ask her about their relationship, but I found I didn't want to. It was so good to be with Lorna, in the way we'd always been. When I didn't speak she murmured, 'He was very generous.'

I sipped my coffee, my throat so dry it seemed to have closed up. Lorna shifted forward on her seat. 'I've worried so much about you all these years, you know – even though I suppose I had no right.'

I couldn't stop my chin from wobbling, and set my cup on the coffee table, looking down and rubbing my eyes. Lorna pulled herself from her armchair and sat beside me, taking my hands.

'Things are bound to be difficult for you for a while. You just need to take it slowly, one step at a time.'

We were quiet for a bit and I leaned back into the cushions and closed my eyes. She stroked my hand, her voice soft. 'I'm really not sure it's a good idea for you to start stirring up the past again. It's bound to upset you. Couldn't you just forget it, and get on with the here and now?'

I wanted nothing more, at that moment, than to say yes, but it was too late. I had to face it. I sat up, pulled my hand away, and moved to leave a gap between us, twisting to look at her. 'No, I can't. I owe it to Tom and to myself. It is difficult because I'm discovering things I wasn't prepared for. That even people I loved and trusted completely may have deceived me.' My heart was beating wildly. What if I was wrong?

'Are you talking about Steve?'

'What?'

'Didn't you say the police thought you took the drugs because you found out something about him that night? That something was wrong with your marriage?'

'Yes, they did, but that's not what I mean.' I stood and went to the French windows. In the courtyard a robin perched on a stone bench pecking at something, his bright eyes watching out for trespassers on his patch. I took another breath and turned to her. 'You were Dad's mistress, weren't you?'

One of her thin hands, shaking now, reached out towards me, but I leaned back against the window. 'Oh, Clare,' she said.

We stared at each other. Her dark eyes were shadowed but steady, and I looked away first. 'So, all those years, when I thought …?'

I walked back towards her, unable to stand still. 'All the attention you gave me was just to keep close to Dad.'

'No, no. You can't believe that. I loved you. I still do.'

I was almost glad to see the tears in her eyes. 'Well you had a strange way of showing it.'

She was fumbling for a tissue and I turned away again. There was so much I wanted to say, but now it seemed pointless.

After a while I heard her blowing her nose, and as the robin flew onto the branch of a tree, head dipping up and down as he continued his fierce surveillance, she spoke. 'How long have you known?'

'I found an old photo of you and Dad and it was so obvious I can't think why I never guessed. You covered it up very well, or maybe I just didn't want to see.'

'It was wrong, I knew that and Robert did too. But Elizabeth wasn't easy to live with and yet he couldn't leave her. She was so unstable there was no telling what she might have done. He certainly couldn't leave you and Alice with her and he knew she would try to keep you from him if they'd separated. '

'So, when Mum died, why didn't he marry you?' I looked at her and saw her eyes cloud again.

'It was more or less over by then. We waited too long, I suppose, or maybe Robert realised marriage wasn't really for him after all.'

Obviously the decisions had all been on Dad's side. 'Still,' I said, 'you got this house.' It was vicious, and when her hand went to her mouth, I hated myself.

She didn't speak for a moment, then looked up at me, her eyes brimming. 'Please, Clare, come and sit by me.' And when she patted the cushion next to her I did as she asked.

She reached over and touched my hand. I let it rest and met her eye, fighting to hold back my own tears as she spoke. 'You have every right to be angry with me, but please believe I always loved you. Probably more than I loved your father. But I loved him too and I'm not ashamed of that. I just wish there had been some way to be more honest with you.' I shook my head and folded

91

my arms across my middle like an angry child as she went on. 'If you can't forgive me I do understand, but, believe it or not, I'm glad you know. I hated all the lying and, however you feel about me, I shall still go on loving you.'

I couldn't bring myself to stay for lunch because I knew I'd handled it badly with Lorna and I was afraid of making it worse. Now I sat huddled in the corner of the train carriage, wishing I'd used the journey here to plan what to say to her. Instead I'd spent the time imagining all the other passengers were watching me and worrying about how I would cope with the busy London station and the crowds outside. Why, oh why, had I been so pathetic?

As we pulled out of Charing Cross, and passed over the river, I stared at the London Eye, my thoughts echoing its endless slow turning. For the first time in my life I felt sorry for Mum. If she guessed, and I suspected she did, it must have been awful for her. Not only having Lorna invading her home, but hearing me prattling on about her all the time.

I suddenly recalled, very clearly, one incident from when I was seven or so. A friend's mother had brought me home from school and I ran into the kitchen – which was much smaller in those days. Alice was in her high chair chewing on a piece of toast and she raised her hands to me in delight. 'Care, Care,' she crowed, unable to get her baby tongue around the *l* in my name.

I had laboured for weeks at school on a piece of sewing, rows of coloured cross stitches on a strip of cloth. A bookmark I called it, and after I had leaned in for a Marmite-sticky kiss, I began waving it in front of Alice's face.

Mum turned from whatever she had been doing at the sink, and placed a drink and a plate of toast in front of me. 'Don't torment her, Clare. What is that anyway?' She held out her hand and I gave her the sewing.

I had intended the bookmark as a present for her, but now I saw the stitches were clumsy and the edges of the cloth too frayed and, before she could criticise, I blurted out, 'It's for Lorna. I made it for Lorna.'

Her, 'Oh,' as she handed it back and turned away again struck me silent, and Alice began to cry.

When I opened the main door of the flats the hall was gloomy. I didn't bother to turn on the light, but as I stepped inside a sudden movement made me gasp and jump back. Then I saw it was just Nic, already in her dressing gown. And as my eyes got used to the lack of light, I saw Kieran too, in shirt and trousers, but without shoes. They were standing at the bottom of the stairs.

'Oh, Clare, you gave me a fright,' Nic said, moving back to her own doorway.

Kieran started up the stairs. 'Well, goodnight both of you.'

As I began to open my own door, Nic laughed. 'Thank goodness for neighbours, eh? I'm forever running out of milk.' It crossed my mind that she didn't have any milk with her. But perhaps she'd already put it indoors. It was none of my business, but for some reason it disturbed me.

Back in the flat, I phoned Alice. 'Tom's already in bed, you know,' she said.

'It's all right; I need to talk to you.'

When I told her about Lorna and Dad, she laughed. 'But surely you realised that was the score? It must have gone on for years.'

'So when did you find out?'

'For sure, just before Dad died. But before that, when I worked at the office, it was pretty obvious people there knew something.'

'But how did you know for sure?'

'Oh, it must have been the last time I was back home before he died. Yes, it was, because I was collecting some stuff I wanted to wear for the wedding. Lorna arrived one morning while I was still in bed and I heard them arguing. Can't remember exactly what they said, but it was obvious they'd had a long relationship.'

'Did you say anything to Dad?'

'Oh, no, I kept my head down, waited till she'd gone.'

'Why didn't you tell me?'

'There was no point. It was obviously over. And you adored Lorna. So why upset you?'

'But weren't you upset?'

'I suppose so, but it's not as if we really imagined he was faithful to Mum, did we?'

It was strange, but I'd never thought about it. 'I suppose not, but this was Lorna.'

There was a sound as if she was sitting down. 'Well, that's why I didn't tell you. I was never as close to her as you were, so it didn't really hurt me. And I had so much else going on at the time. I was exhausted from being on call at the hospital, and Dad and I had already had a couple of arguments about that. You know what he was like. He couldn't understand weakness. Always thought everyone else should be as confident and energetic as he was.'

'Do you think Mum knew about him and Lorna?'

'Probably, and that did make me sad for her. But you have to feel sorry for Lorna too. By the time I worked at the office, Mum had been dead for quite a while and it must have been clear to Lorna she wasn't going to get Dad to marry her. That would have been hard after waiting all those years.'

'So, did he have someone else by then?'

'He never seemed short of female company, let's put it like that. The second summer I was there, a redhead used to pick him up now and then in a sports car. You could see old Lorna wasn't too pleased. But she did all right out of it in the end.'

'I suppose so. He left her enough to buy her house.'

Alice laughed again. 'And quite right too. I think that was where he used to spend most of those weekends when he claimed to be working away. It was their little love nest.'

On Saturday morning, Stella said she was looking forward to the barbecue. 'If it's not too busy, we'll let Harriet take over this afternoon, give us both time to get ready.' She was in and out with deliveries, or on the phone with various anxious brides and how I managed to keep serving, and smiling, I wasn't sure. There had been no late-night phone calls, but I'd slept no better.

Lorna, my beloved fairy godmother, had been my father's mistress for God knows how long. They had cheated Mum and deceived everyone for all those years when I thought Lorna was the most wonderful person in the world. If I looked at it coldly it was understandable. Mum wasn't easy to live with, even when she was well, and all her hospitalisations must have been even harder on Dad than they were on us. And he had so much charm that Lorna probably didn't stand a chance.

I couldn't blame Alice for not telling me because she didn't know for sure until just before the accident. Last night she had seemed to find it almost funny and I knew my reaction was mostly to do with the fear that Lorna's affection for me might have been faked just to stay close to Dad. But that was ridiculous. So much of what she'd done for me, even before he died, was nothing to do with him.

Stella told me to go home at one o'clock, saying she'd pick me up later. I knew I might have to ask her in, so I looked round the living room. The suitcase was still hulking in the corner and I didn't want Stella to notice it, so I dragged it to the bedroom and shoved it under the bed. I tidied the place quickly, then had a long shower, washed my hair, and put on the new dress, and ironed a skirt and top for Sunday.

It was then I noticed the phone flashing. My stomach quivered as I clicked to listen to the message, even though I knew it would probably just be silence again.

'Hey there, you dirty stop out. How's things? I'm glad you're not there because I'm hoping you're out on the razzle. Make sure you have some for me, won't you.'

Oh Ruby: her voice cracked something inside.

Chapter Eleven

I played the message over and over and after what seemed hours, but was probably only minutes. I got myself to the bathroom and tried to repair my face. I longed to be able to call Ruby back, to speak to her now, but you can't ring prisoners unless they've managed to get hold of an illicit mobile.

When the main door to the house buzzed, I couldn't for a moment think what it was. Then I remembered – Stella – and the barbecue – all those people. But there was no way to get out of it.

When we were in the van, Stella said, 'It's lovely for me to get out on a Saturday night. These past few years it's been difficult with just Harriet and me. She keeps telling me I'll need to be a lot more sociable when she's gone.'

Apparently Harriet's dad had died fairly young, six or seven years before. 'Cancer it was, very sudden …' I think we were both grateful for the noisy van engine at that moment, and I guessed she realised losing a husband was a topic we should avoid. So when she asked if I minded if she put on the radio, I was only too happy.

We could smell the barbecue as we pulled into the drive. I held up my bag and gestured that I would take that inside first and Stella reached behind her and handed me a big bunch of white roses. 'Will you give these to Alice then please, and I'll go straight round the back.

The front door was unlocked, and I dropped my bag in the hall with the flowers on top and went into the small downstairs cloakroom. As I ran cold water over my hands, I checked the mirror, hoping I looked calmer than I felt.

In the hall again I stood for a moment, breathing deeply. On the table by the stairs, next to Mum's favourite vase, Mum and Dad smiled out of a polished brass photo frame, as if waiting for me to make a fool of myself.

'Come on, you'll be all right. They're all harmless.' I jumped and Alice put an arm round my waist, bringing with her a waft of perfume and onions.

I tried to laugh and handed her the flowers. 'These are from Stella.'

'Lovely. Bring Mum's vase will you. I hate to see it empty.'

It was an ornate thing in shining copper and it had stood in the same place for as long as I could remember. As I filled it with cold water I felt for the dent I'd made when I knocked it over rushing in from school one day. I'd picked it up straightaway, and tidied everything, or so I thought, but some of the flower heads were hanging loose and the floor was still wet. Mum guessed and was angry with me, but she never noticed the dent, and I remembered that as a small triumph.

Stella's roses looked lovely and when Alice had filled the vase she took me outside.

The others were scattered across the patio so it was less intimidating than it might have been. Alice put her arm around me again. 'Everyone, this is my sister, Clare. Clare, that's David, the top dog at our GP practice, doing the manly thing with the burgers.'

The large man at the barbecue gave me a broad smile and a, 'Ho there, hope you're hungry,' as he waved a pair of tongs at me.

Next to him stood a younger, rather good-looking man, who also waved. 'Nice to meet you, Clare, I'm Gavin,' he said, his glance at Alice betraying he might be more than just a friend.

A chunky little woman with a grey bob was apparently David's wife, Josie. A younger couple, her dark and pretty, him tall and fair, were Lesley and James, Mark's parents. They also smiled and waved, but looked at me with rather too much interest – Lesley scanning my dress and shoes before turning on a bright beam with a flash of white teeth.

I was saved from having to do more than echo their hellos by Tom bounding up with a stocky brown-haired boy. 'Mum, this is Mark.' Mark looked at me with even more obvious curiosity than his parents, but I liked his smile when it came.

'Hello, Mark. Nice to meet you.'

'Hi, Mrs Glazier. Tom's told me all about you.' He reddened slightly and glanced at Tom, but my son was chattering on, asking me what I wanted to eat and the moment passed. None of the adults had reacted to him calling me Mum so it seemed they knew the basics of our situation at least, which was a relief.

The time passed bearably enough with much general chatter that allowed me just to nod and smile. I tried to keep standing, to avoid being cornered by anyone, but after I'd chewed down most of a burger and had a couple of drinks, I felt so tired I had to sit on a garden chair, unable to stop a sigh of relief, and Mark's dad plonked himself next to me.

'Busy week?'

'No, well, yes I suppose so.'

'Stella tells me you work with her. Flower shop. That must be fun.'

'Yes, I enjoy it.' *Go away, leave me alone.*

He took a swig from a very full tumbler of red wine, obviously not his first. 'So Hastings, eh. I've always thought it's a bit – you know – there. What's your opinion?'

Since I had no idea what *a bit you know* meant I could only smile and say I liked it. Luckily, this seemed to bore him so much he hauled himself up and wandered onto the grass, where Tom and Mark were kicking a ball back and forth. He grabbed his son in a headlock, stumbling and almost pulling them both down. The poor boy struggled free, looking over at the rest of us, beet red.

'Daaad, leave off, it's not funny.'

I caught Tom's eye and smiled as he raised his brows and grimaced. He picked up his can of drink, and came over.

'All right, Mum?'

'I'm fine. This is nice.'

He asked if I wanted anything more to eat and when I said, no, took himself off to the barbecue.

Alice sat on the lounger next to me. 'I'm absolutely exhausted. You look done in too, but it's been all right, hasn't it?'

'Yes, I've enjoyed it.'

She laughed. 'You always were a bad liar, but you've made a hit with my friends, you know. And it's so good for Tom to see you as part of our normal lives.' She leaned towards me, speaking softly. 'He seems to be more settled lately. I think he's begun to accept things as they are.'

I looked over at him, handing Stella a drink then turning to say something to Mark's mum. 'You've done a wonderful job with him and I'm sorry I've been so ungrateful over the years.'

She waved her hand at me. 'I knew how depressed you were. I mean who wouldn't be in a place like that.'

I swallowed a gulp of my wine, leaned back, and closed my eyes. 'I know you think I should let the past be, but I can't. If Tom seems happy to forget about it for now that's great, but it won't last. Eventually he'll start asking those questions again and I must have some real answers for him when he does. And I've realised I need answers for myself too.' It was only as I said this that I saw how true it was.

Alice sighed and picked up her drink. When I looked at her she was rolling the cold glass over her cheek, her eyes closed. 'Maybe you'll get some answers when you go up to Cumbria,' she said, pressing the glass against her forehead. Then she opened her eyes and turned to me. 'You have told your probation officer about that, haven't you?'

'Of course. She's pleased I'm getting back in touch with relatives. She calls it *building bridges* and *reconnecting with my support systems*.'

Alice touched the arm of my chair. 'Just be careful, will you.' She raised her voice gesturing to the rest of the guests. 'Everyone seems to have enjoyed themselves anyway.'

I made my voice cheerful. 'Gavin seems nice.'

'Yes he is, but it's all right, he won't be here tomorrow. We, well, we're not serious.' She sipped her drink and looked down the garden. 'Do you remember Dad's attempts at barbecues?'

Of course I did. They were my idea, when I came back to live here after Mum's death. A way for the three of us to be together.

'He was hopeless,' I said, with a laugh.

'Yes, but I really enjoyed them.'

'Me too.'

By the time Mum died I was living in a squat in Battersea, out of it most of the time, and using anything I could get my hands on. Dad managed to track me down, probably with help from Lorna, to beg me to come to the funeral. He was a big bear of a man, not fat, but heavy, with thick grey hair the barber could never quite tame. He always dressed well, but somehow, even in a Saville Row suit, he never looked anything but relaxed. On that day, though, his hands were clenched on his knees as he crouched in a battered armchair. He looked smaller somehow, dwarfed by the chair. He moved a crushed beer can from behind him on the seat, but hardly seemed to notice it, or the stained and broken floorboards, the old mattress in the corner, or any of the other mess – even the smell.

He was always such a forceful character, but he didn't get angry with me that day, even when I shouted that Mum would prefer it if I stayed away. I reminded him that the last time I'd come home she had accused me of stealing one of her rings, and I remembered how indignantly I said this, very prim in the knowledge of my innocence. And conveniently ignoring the fact I *had* pinched twenty quid from his wallet, and a handful of Valium from her dressing table.

'It's been hardest on Alice, you know,' he said. 'With your mother ill so much in the last couple of years and me away a lot of the time. No kind of life for a youngster.'

I think I got up and walked away – shakily, no doubt – at that point, and said none of it was my fault.

'But Alice has always idolised you. So if you came back home, I know it would help her.'

I told him, more or less, to get lost. I couldn't help myself, let alone anyone else. But something changed that day, and a month or so later I did go back, determined to start afresh.

Alice was still talking. 'He couldn't do anything simply, could he? Everyone else had burgers and sausages, but he had to go in for whole trout and stuff like that.'

'Stuff we wouldn't eat, yeah. Still, *I* made sure we had the basics.'

It didn't last long: only one summer, but in its own way it was magical. The three of us became like a real family. We steered clear of talking about Mum, about anything that mattered, and maybe that was why it worked.

Alice touched my knee. 'Do you remember those steaks he cooked? When I had my friends from school over? '

He had tried out some kind of fancy sauce – very hot. 'And that poor boy was the only one who would eat it,' I said, 'and he turned puce after a few mouthfuls?'

'He was my first boyfriend. I was so embarrassed. But Dad was too obtuse to realise.' She looked at me with her little sister smile, the one I'd almost forgotten. 'But you took Adrian inside and made him sit down with a glass of water. He never said anything, but I know he was really grateful to you. So was I.'

Our eyes met, hers almost violet in the gathering dark, and when she spoke again there was a quiver in her voice. 'Those were good times.'

All I could do was nod. I almost said I wished those days could have lasted longer, but soon after that I got pregnant and, looking at Tom now, I certainly couldn't wish that away.

She followed my gaze and, after a moment, said, 'Tom's got exams next week, so I think maybe we should let him concentrate on them. He needs to do well if he's to have a good choice for GCSE.'

101

Another of those rushes of feeling that I knew I mustn't show. I swallowed and fought to speak gently. 'Don't you want me to see him?'

'Well, you'll have all day tomorrow, and then I thought maybe he could spend the whole of next Sunday at your place. It's Mark's birthday on Saturday so they're going bowling, but I'll bring him over on Sunday morning then make myself scarce. Let you have some time: just the two of you.'

That night, sleeping, or rather, not sleeping, in my old room, I knew why I had refused to come back to live here, even for a while, when I got out. Although Alice had transformed the house, it still held too many memories. A few, like the barbecues, were good, but it was the others that clamoured at me. The ones with Mum. I adored Dad, even when we argued, and I loved Lorna, but it was Mum whose approval I craved, maybe because I never got it.

Of course, I'd been a difficult child, but Dad made excuses for me. He had found me in a Romanian orphanage at the age of eleven months and I'd always pictured myself clutching a dirty blanket and staring glassy-eyed through the bars of a cot. I was lucky; Dad was the managing director of a large multi-national, so he must have used his clout to get me out quickly.

Apparently the doctors had told Mum she would be unlikely to have a child of her own, but how Dad could have imagined she might be satisfied with a raging bundle of suspect foreign genes was beyond me. And four years later the miracle happened and she brought a replica of her own blonde beauty into the world. One of my first memories was of Mum in the hospital bed, tiny Alice in her arms. Dad carried me and I carried a bunch of flowers as big as myself. Mum was sitting propped up, her hair untidy for once, looking down at the baby, and ignoring our noisy arrival.

I'd practised saying, 'Well done, Mummy,' but I was dumbfounded by the glazed happiness in the eyes she raised to us; a happiness quickly replaced by the look I was used to.

'Hello, Clare, darling. Do mind baby with those flowers. Put them over there will you, Robert?' I had scribed my name laboriously on the card, and I tried to pull it from the bouquet as he took it from me, desperate for Mummy to admire my writing. 'Oh look what she's doing Robert. Put her down. She's big enough to stand on her own two feet anyway. Clare, be good, or you won't see Alice.'

I wanted to stamp and scream until she looked at the card, but Daddy had made it clear only good girls were allowed in hospitals, so I stood in surly silence. 'Now we don't want any sulks do we?' Mummy was firm, her eyes blue crystals. 'You're not jealous of Alice are you?"

I had no idea how to reply to this, but a shake of the head seemed to satisfy her, and I was allowed to come close enough to peer at the little, crumpled face, to feel the warmth radiating from the shawl, and to smell for the first time that unique baby smell.

I don't think I *was* ever jealous of Alice herself, and I soon realised that, in any case, Daddy still loved me best. I even remembered explaining to Alice, as we sat in the garden one sunny afternoon, that Daddy was mine and Mummy was hers. We had been allowed to have sandwiches under the tree and Alice, a chubby five or six-year-old, a daisy chain we'd made together twined in her white-blonde hair, chewed slowly as she listened. Her eyes, bright blue in the sunlight, grew larger as I spoke, but she nodded, already understanding exactly what I meant.

The irony was that Alice probably killed our mother as surely as I killed Dad. Mum suffered what I now realised was severe post-natal depression and was never well again and, although she managed to survive for another fourteen years, she was in and out of hospital all the time. She killed herself when I was nineteen.

Thinking back, I wondered how reliable my memory of that first hospital visit really was. It seemed very detailed and vivid for the recollections of a five-year-old and I wondered if it was really a composite of all the others during my childhood. There were so many times when I woke in the morning, or came home from school, to find Mum gone. Dad always said it was just a precaution, but it would sometimes be weeks before we were allowed to visit her and even longer until she came home.

It was shortly after Alice's birth that our parents told me about my adoption. They had chosen me because my own mother was dead and Mummy and Daddy thought they couldn't have babies. It was meant, I suppose, to reassure me, but I recall being terrified that if I was naughty – and I often was – they might one day decide that now they had Alice they no longer needed me. It didn't help that my mass of dark hair and olive skin marked me out as such an obvious cuckoo in the nest.

Tom woke me with a cup of tea in the morning, saying Alice had gone to the supermarket. I was amazed to see it was close to 11 o'clock: I had slept after all. Tom sat on the end of my bed as I drank the tea.

'So,' I said. 'You've got exams coming up?'

'Yeah, worse luck.'

'Alice suggested you spend all of next Sunday with me in Hastings. There's a lot to do: amusement arcades, the Smugglers' Caves, Sea Life Centre, whatever you fancy.' He didn't answer. 'Only if you want of course.'

He shifted from foot to foot. 'That'd be cool, yeah. It's a whole week away though.'

I grabbed my dressing gown from the end of the bed and pulled it on to give myself time to think, but I'd promised myself I'd be honest with him. 'I know and I'd love to see you before that, but your exams are important, so why not concentrate on them and look forward to the weekend?'

'I could come over on the train after school one day.'

'I'd love that, but I'm working Monday and Tuesday, and on Wednesday I'm hoping to go and see Emily.' I didn't say that I couldn't interfere with Alice's decisions, but I could see he wasn't happy and he left the room without a word. That familiar ache throbbed inside. I hated to see his disappointment.

I took my time getting dressed, but he wasn't hiding away as I'd expected. Instead, I found him tucking into a bowl of cereal in the kitchen. He was studying some papers and I took a chance and spoke as if I hadn't noticed his anger. 'Revising on a Sunday? You are good.'

'No, it's more stuff about Granddad and some ideas Mark and I had about things you can try to find out.' I poured myself some Rice Krispies still standing up and looking out of the window. I wasn't hungry, but it was something to do, to hide how disturbed I was. He was obviously obsessing about this.

I tried to keep my voice casual. 'Tom, don't let this stuff get in the way of school work, will you? When I ran away from home I thought education didn't matter and it wasn't until I married your dad that I realised I how ignorant I was. I was lucky. I could do some studying part-time then, and later on in prison too, but I still missed out and I don't want you to do that.'

He smiled, still leafing through the pages. 'It's cool, Mum, don't worry. I like school.' He pulled out a piece of paper. 'This bit says Granddad made up a report, told lies. It was in the news.'

'There was a lot of stuff in the papers that wasn't true, you know, always is.' I sat opposite him at the table and pulled a sheet towards me.

'That's important, Mum. We need to find out about him, Dr Penrose, the whistle-blower. It says here he's dead, but there must be people around who knew him.'

'You're right but, Tom, I'm serious, please don't let it get in the way of your exams.' I heard Alice's car pull into the driveway. 'And let's talk about it when we're on our own, shall we? We don't want to upset Alice.'

He piled his papers into a cardboard folder. 'Right. I'll hide this.'

As he ran upstairs I felt a twinge. It wasn't right to encourage him to keep secrets from Alice, but she seemed so happy that – how had she phrased it – he'd *begun to accept things as they are.* So maybe it was best to keep quiet about it for now.

Chapter Twelve

'I think getting away from your flat and meeting a few people, has done you good,' Alice said, as she drove me back. 'You certainly look better than you did when you arrived last night.'

She needed to go back right away, because we'd left Tom getting ready for bed, so I gave her a quick kiss and jumped out of the car.

The house was very quiet and dark and I had to switch on the light in the main hall before I could open my own door.

But even as I stepped inside I knew something was wrong.

The little hallway was unbelievably hot. Of course, I'd made sure all the windows were locked before I left, and it had been warm today, but as well as the temperature, there was an insistent sound — a kind of whispering — that went on and on.

I stood looking at the living room door, afraid to touch it, feeling something ice cold shifting inside me even though my hands were damp from the steamy heat.

What if the place was on fire? I knew I shouldn't open the door, but I was already turning the handle, my mouth shut tight to stop myself taking a breath.

A gust of smoke came out at me. The whole room was filled with it. A thick, hot fog.

But, even as I slammed the door again, my mind whirred, trying to make sense, and the sound became recognisable. The shower. I'd left the shower on and this was steam, not smoke.

I dropped my bag and went in. The bathroom door was half open and the steam had filled the living room. Everything was dripping. I turned off the shower, unlocked and threw open the bathroom window, then all four windows in the living room.

I had used the shower on Saturday, but surely I wouldn't have left it turned on?

As wafts of night air spread through the flat I shivered, the moisture chilling on my skin. I closed and locked all the windows tight, checked each one twice, then double-locked the front door. After that I dragged off my damp clothes, pulled on some old pyjamas, and crawled under the duvet.

I am in a dark place, very hot and very scared. There's noise and heat all around me. I want to run away, but I can't move. Then I realise the noise is the roar of flames and I'm surrounded by fire. Outside, in the darkness, a woman stands looking at me. I try to scream at her to help me: I need to get to my boys. But my voice won't come. The woman is my mum and she just stands there even though she must see how desperate I am. When I look again I see it isn't Mum, but Lorna and she has turned and is walking away.

When I woke, the place still smelled damp, but I didn't dare leave any windows open, and before I left for work I checked the shower and all the taps, made sure the cooker, the kettle, and the iron were turned off, and tried all the windows again.

The shop was surprisingly busy for a Monday, Stella had loads of orders to catch up on and I helped her when I wasn't serving. Just before five o'clock I went into the back room. She glanced at her watch as she twisted yellow ribbons around a posy of tiny rose buds. 'Oh lord is that the time? You should be locking up and getting home.'

'Can I do anything before I go?'

'I'd love a cup of tea, if you've got time.'

I heard the shop bell ring as I carried her tea down and called out, 'Just one minute please.'

'It's OK, we're not customers.' I recognised Kieran's voice at once and felt the flush rise from my chest to my neck and up into my cheeks. But when I saw he wasn't alone, the flush drained away as my knees threatened to give. I could still hear Kieran's voice, but all I could see was his companion, looking at me with a sheepish grin.

'Hi there, Clare,' said Kieran. 'I found this young man hanging about in our garden. Says he's come to see his mum.'

Tom was still in his crumpled school uniform and carrying a bulging rucksack. The sight of him sent a thrill through me. He'd come to see me on his own; had really wanted to spend time with me. But after the thrill came a tremor of anxiety. Did Alice know about this?

Kieran gave a little wave and clanged out of the door. I wondered for a second what he was thinking. But that didn't matter. What mattered was Tom leaning on the counter obviously feeling awkward.

'This is a lovely surprise. I didn't expect to see you today. How did you get here?' I said.

His flush and the way he looked down at his feet made it clear I'd got it wrong again. 'I came on the train. Lots of kids from school do it every day.'

'Come on then, you haven't seen inside the flat yet.' This time it was OK. He grinned and shrugged his rucksack tighter on his shoulders as I grabbed my bag from under the counter and called a goodbye to Stella.

Walking to the flat, I couldn't speak. Tom was silent too, stomping ahead, his rucksack bouncing on his back. It felt unreal and yet so right to be walking home with my son and I was so proud of him I almost wanted to shout out to the people we passed that I was his mum.

But when we were in the house and I was unlocking my door, I knew I had to say something. 'So Alice is all right with this is she?'

His pause told me all I needed. 'She's got late surgery and I'm supposed to be revising at Mark's, so she won't worry. I told Mark where I am, and if she rings him he'll tell her I'm OK and I'm coming back on the train. I checked and they run till about midnight.'

As we came into the living room he headed for the windows. 'Wow, Mum, this is cool. You've got a sea view.'

'It's good isn't it? Have a look round the rest.'

I needed a moment to think because I realised I had no idea what kind of freedoms were appropriate for a boy of his age, but I certainly wasn't going to take any chances with his safety. In the kitchen I made myself some coffee, poured a glass of milk for Tom and opened a packet of biscuits.

When he came in he took a biscuit and gulped some of the milk, saying, 'Thanks, Mum.' Then grabbed his rucksack from the living room, put it on the table, and began to unzip it.

I pulled out a chair and pointed to the other one. 'Look, sit down for a minute, Tom.' When he'd done so and was looking at me, still holding his bag, I said, 'You shouldn't have come without talking to Alice you know. What if I'd been away?'

'You told me you were at work today.' He smiled. 'And Alice might have said I couldn't come.'

I tried to make my voice firm. 'If she did, it would have been for a good reason. You know that. Now I'd better ring her at work to let her know you're OK.'

'But I came to show you these, before you go to Emily and Matt's.' He pulled the cardboard folder I'd seen yesterday from his rucksack and sorted through the papers, his face animated again. 'This is what Mark and I have done.' He unfolded a sheet of A3 and pressed it flat on the coffee table.

It was a kind of printed flow chart about the accident. I saw the names of some of the people at the wedding with arrows pointing to a series of rectangles: one headed *possible suspects*.

'I've said why any of them might have been involved on the back.' He turned the sheet over. This time the names were listed in pen, each one followed by comments on Tom's theories. His handwriting was small and neat. I pointed to the names *Emily and Matt* and the words beside it: *Matt worked with Granddad (or jealousy)*. 'What does this mean?'

'Well, Matt could have had something to do with the scandal and Granddad found out about it.'

'And the *jealousy*?'

'That was Mark's idea. He says jealousy's a big motive.' He shifted awkwardly. 'So maybe Emily thought Matt liked you, or she liked Dad.'

'Oh, Tom, you don't think that, do you? You know Emily. And what's this about Lorna?'

He covered her name, but I'd already spotted: *for money*. He turned the paper over. 'I know, I know … but you have to put in everything.' He pointed to another box next to Emily and Matt's names: *waiters and others*. 'Like I said, you should ask her about the people who catered for the wedding.'

I tried to lighten the atmosphere. 'You sure that won't make her realise we're on to her?'

But he wasn't having any of it. '*Mum* – this is serious.'

Looking into his eager face, I felt that familiar lump in my throat again. 'I'm sorry, this is all really clever, but I need to look at it carefully. And I've had some thoughts too. First, though, I need to ring Alice.'

He followed me into the living room. 'Mum, I've just thought, why don't I stay the night? I can go straight to school from here in the morning.'

I longed to agree but it would have been too much like rewarding him for deceiving Alice. 'I want you to start staying here of course, but I'll need to get a put-you-up or something first. And we must talk to Alice about it beforehand.'

I couldn't get through to the surgery, so I rang Alice's mobile, not surprised to get no reply there either, but at least I was able to leave a message.

'Hi, it's Clare. Look, Tom has turned up here. I had no idea he was coming, but don't worry, I'll bring him back on the train as soon as I've given him something to eat. I'm sorry about this and I have explained to him that he should have asked you first...'

I threw down the phone as Tom hurtled past me, slamming the door behind him. But the front door of the house defeated him and he was scrabbling to open it when I got to him.

'Tom, what's the matter?'

He was pressed against the door, his shoulders heaving, and I could just make out the words. 'I'm going. You don't want me here, so I'm going.' His voice, gruff and wobbling with tears, echoed in the large space and I was ashamed to feel embarrassed in case Nic or Kieran could hear.

'It's not that. Come inside and we can talk.'

'No. If you don't want me, I'm going.'

'I never said I didn't want you. It's lovely to see you, but you should have told us first.'

'You said, and Alice said, I could see you when I wanted.'

'But we need to know where you are – to make sure you're safe.'

His teeth were gritted. 'You don't fucking want me. Nor does she, and you're both liars.'

I rubbed his back, as if soothing a baby, and felt him jolt and choke on a sob. I was fighting to hold back my own tears. 'Please, Tom, come back inside.'

After a long minute he turned, shrugging me off, and went into the flat, throwing himself on the sofa, his face turned away. I sat on the coffee table facing him, but when I put my hands on his knees he moved sharply sideways, elbows on one arm of the sofa, his fists clenched at his mouth as if to hold back the words he was frightened he might say.

After a couple of minutes I moved to sit beside him and he didn't pull away when I touched his shoulder. 'The truth is, Alice and I both love you to bits, you must know that. It's just that things aren't easy for any of us right now.'

'Alice said you don't want me back.'

'Surely not. Didn't she just say we needed to give it time?'

'Well … yes. Sort of.'

Careful, careful. 'And that's the truth.'

'But nobody asked me.'

I had no answer to that one. 'I know and it's not fair. None of this is fair on you, but please try to be patient.' Though he didn't speak I took the fact that he crossed his arms over his chest and leaned back into the cushions as a good sign and dared to press on. 'You must be starving and I know I am. So let's get a takeaway shall we?'

I found a couple of menus someone had left in the hallway. 'Go on, you choose, and we'll share it,' I said.

He picked a meat feast pizza, which came with a large bottle of Coke, and some ice cream and I phoned in the order, while he looked through his papers again.

'Now let's see what else you and Mark have discovered.'

He pulled some other pages from the folder and I could see he'd printed out various reports on the accident and my trial. It was horrible seeing it all again: those nightmarish pictures and the terrible words, and to think about him reading it. 'Oh, Tom, I wish you hadn't.'

'What?'

'These things, I hate to think of you reading them.'

'It's all right. Well, all right now, I mean. I saw it all ages ago so I'm used to it.'

A vision of little Tommy reading about his brother and father's deaths and the dreadful things that were said about me made my insides twist and my throat ache. I put my arms around him. 'You are so brave. I don't deserve you.' It took all my effort to force down the sobs that threatened to burst out. I couldn't lose it like that in front of him.

After a while he pulled away, his face very pink. 'All right?'

I dragged a tissue from my sleeve, rubbed my eyes, and tried to smile. Then gestured to the papers. 'I'm OK. So what else is there?'

'Just that you need to talk to the two witnesses when you go to Cumbria.' He pointed to a couple of highlighted areas. "*David Hillier, 64, and motor cyclist Jacob Downes, 18*". It says Mr Hillier was a well-respected local head teacher who lived in the village near the accident spot.'

He was right. If I wanted to find out more, even to recover my memory, the two people who were there just after the crash were the ones most likely to help. And of course I remembered them both. Mr Hillier, dignified and articulate in his smart suit, who gave me a sad and kindly smile as he finished his evidence. And the boy, Jacob Downes, in a leather jacket and jeans with lank hair he kept pushing back and letting fall forward again. His answers were so mumbled the judge had to ask him to repeat himself several times.

If Mr Hillier was still living in the same village it should be easy enough to trace him, at least. Bramstone was a tiny place, more hamlet than a village.

The food arrived quickly, but as I brought in the boxes I heard Tom talking. Alice had rung while I was in the hall. 'There's no need. I might as well sleep here tonight.' He looked up as I came in. 'She wants to speak to you.'

'All right. The food's on the table in the kitchen, so just get stuck in.'

Alice was clearly annoyed. 'What's going on? I only rang to say I'll be there in an hour or so to pick him up and he tells me he wants to stay the night. Was that your idea?'

I lowered my voice. 'No, but you must be tired after work so why not leave him. I'll sleep on the sofa. I'll see he does his homework and I can put his clothes through the wash for tomorrow. In the morning I'll walk him to the station and make sure he gets the right train.'

She sighed. 'I'm sorry, but I can't agree to him staying with you yet. We'll have to wait and see how things go before that happens.'

This time I couldn't keep the anger from my voice, although I managed to speak quietly: Tom mustn't hear us arguing. 'So you think he's not safe with me?'

'That's not the point. Tom is your son, I'm well aware of that, but he's my responsibility and has been for the past five years. I don't think you realise how vulnerable he is.'

'What does that mean?' It came out too loud, but my quick glance at Tom told me I'd got away with it, he was eating a big slice of pizza his eyes on something he was reading. *Be careful.*

'Look, I don't want to get into this now. I'll be over in an hour or so.' There was a short silence before the dialling tone cut in, and I stood gripping the phone as if it were a living thing I could punish for its unfairness.

Chapter Thirteen

She was right, of course. When I finally gave up trying to sleep, just after 2 a.m., I'd been through it over and over: my anger at her for her tight-lipped refusal to come into the flat as she told him to hurry up and go to the car; my own uselessness.

What kind of a mother was I to let him off so lightly: not to make it clearer he'd done wrong? For God's sake, I hadn't even thought to tell him he should never have talked to Kieran, a stranger, and wandered off with him, just because he claimed to be my neighbour. At least Alice didn't know about that and – pathetic creature that I was – I had no intention of telling her.

Huddled in jogging bottoms and socks I switched on the laptop, not surprised to find an email from her:

Clare,

I'm sorry if I seemed overbearing tonight, but I was really upset. Please don't think I want to keep Tom away from you, but we've got to go about this very carefully. (It's what we agreed before you came out, remember). It's not been easy all these years and of course he is sometimes rebellious with me, so we have to make sure he doesn't think he can use you to help defy me.

I've grounded him for the rest of the week and told him he'd better keep to that if he wants to see Mark on Saturday and you on Sunday. You can call or email him of course, but please, please back me up on this.

Alice.

We *had* agreed to take it slowly and I knew she had Tom's interests at heart and replied, of course, I would back her up. I told her I was hoping to visit to Emily and Matt anyway. I didn't mention Tom's outburst, ignoring the small voice that said I should.

As I closed down the laptop I noticed Tom's folder sitting on the coffee table. I put it in the drawer with the stuff from the suitcase. Then I crawled back to bed, certain I wouldn't sleep.

I was woken what seemed minutes later by the phone. As I snatched it up I saw the caller identification: *unavailable*, but I clicked to answer anyway. I was fed up with this. 'Hello, hello, who is that? Only breathing. 'Hello, who's there?' Still those rasping breaths. 'If you're too pathetic to speak then you can fuck off, you bastard.' I shouted.

The line clicked dead.

I lay awake, knowing I probably shouldn't have spoken, but glad I had. I learned in prison that you have to stand up to bullies. And I was sure this wasn't just some call centre, mistaking the time. It felt personal. Could it be someone I'd annoyed in prison? There had been a few of those, including one or two of the screws.

Or someone who'd followed my trial and knew I was out; someone who thought my sentence was too light?

None of it seemed to make sense, but I couldn't stop thinking about the other things that had happened: the shower, that open window I was sure I'd closed. Surely they couldn't be connected?

When I finally slept, my dreams were full of sound; ringing phones that turned into ambulance sirens. Screaming that went on and on amid the roar of flames. But along with the sound there was, as always, light. Lights spinning on the roofs of ambulances or beaming from headlights. Light that seared my eyes as it flashed out of the darkness.

Stella was out most of the morning, organising the flowers for a couple of weddings, and I was glad to be on my own. Selfishly, I was glad that the weather was cool today, with dark clouds threatening rain. At lunchtime I called Emily to ask if I could come and see her tomorrow or the day after. She was out, but I left a message and she texted back after ten minutes:

Come tomorrow PLEASE. Can't wait any longer XXX

By the time Stella got back the shop was quiet and I insisted she have a rest upstairs. I promised to call if I needed her, and she took me at my word.

By five-ish, with only a single customer in the past hour, and the rain steady enough to deter casual shoppers, the effects of another disturbed night had begun to bite with a vengeance. I called Stella to say I was locking up, and I left without waiting for a reply, dashing down the street with my cardigan over my head. Even so, by the time I stood shivering at the main door, my feet were cold and slimy in their sandals, my trousers clinging like wet leaves to my legs.

I'd just got the key into the lock when pounding feet behind me told me it was too late.

'Hello, Kieran. Can't stop. I'm soaked.'

As I stood at my own door however, he touched my shoulder. 'You've got some post.' He handed me a letter from the hall table. It was from Lorna.

'Thanks.' I began opening my door, but Kieran was not moving.

'I'll give you a chance to get changed and see you shortly. Just want a quick word.' He was heading upstairs before I could say anything.

I threw the letter onto the sofa and grabbed a towel from the bathroom, rubbing my hair and stripping off my clothes. But as soon as I'd dressed again in jeans and T-shirt I had to open it.

Dearest Clare,

I am very sorry that finding out about myself and your father has upset you so much. There were many, many times in the past when I thought of telling you the truth, but it wasn't only my secret. Robert would never have forgiven me for speaking about it when he was alive. I expect he'd have called it the revenge of a woman scorned, and maybe it would have been. Later, when he was dead, you had so many other things to cope with that I honestly didn't think it was important.

These must sound like pathetic excuses, so I won't say anymore. Except, and this is what I desperately want you to believe, Clare, I do love you and I want to help you in any way I can.

Please, my dearest girl, forgive me and call me when you feel able to talk.

Your very loving fairy godmother,
Lorna

I crunched the paper against my chest, thinking of all the other letters Lorna had sent me over the years and how much they had meant to me. Without her, there were times when my life would have been unbearable. I wanted nothing more than to ring her right now, but I wasn't ready yet, scared I'd say the wrong thing and upset her.

The silence all around me felt like a malevolent presence, filling every corner of the flat. Outside my double-locked windows there was only the grey of the silent rain and sea. Inside, it was chill and comfortless, and I wondered why I'd ever thought of this place as a refuge.

Maybe that was why, when Kieran knocked, I didn't make an excuse and get rid of him as I'd planned, but offered him coffee. The flat seemed just a bit more homely with him sitting at the kitchen table, mug in hand, smiling at me.

'I've come to apologise,' he said. 'Just hadn't thought how wrong it was to bring Tom to the shop like that. I could see you were furious and I don't blame you. I suppose people like me, without kids, are a bit thick about the stranger danger thing.'

I didn't tell him it hadn't occurred to me either, until later, and what he'd interpreted as fury was really shock that he and Tom had met, that I would have to give him an explanation. 'You probably wonder why my son isn't living with me.'

'Clare, it's none of my business.'

'I'm a widow you see and, well, it's taken me a long while to get over it. I was living away and it just seemed easier if he stayed with my sister.'

It all sounded very hollow to my ears, but, as he said, it was nothing to do with him and there was no reason to care what he thought.

He flashed me a smile. 'Of course, the problem wouldn't have arisen if we'd got to know each other better. Now how about fixing that, and letting me apologise properly by taking you for a meal?'

I told myself it was because I was too tired to argue that I followed him so meekly a few hundred yards to a pub he claimed did great food. The place was small, dark, and nearly empty. Kieran had insisted on buying the drinks and I asked for tonic water because it was important to keep my wits about me.

I knew I needed to get him talking about himself, to avoid any questions about my life and my strange mothering style, so I launched in right away. 'You're not local are you? Your name's Irish, but your accent sounds as if it's from the north of England.'

It was clumsy, but he didn't seem to notice. 'I'm from Lancaster, but my mother's family do have some Irish blood, I think. At least, they're Catholic, which usually means they came over during the potato famine.' I sipped my drink and sat back, hoping my smiles and nods would encourage him to keep talking. 'But Dad was from India by way of Kenya, so the black hair isn't Celtic and the tan doesn't come off in the winter. By rights, too, I think they should have spelt the name K-I-R-A-N.'

The bar man brought our food and for a moment there was silence, but I spoke before he could start to question me. 'So Catholic and, what, Sikh? That must have made an interesting mix.'

'Hindu – no turbans or gurus – but they were both pretty flexible in their approach to religion. They only had two kids, and Dad enjoyed a nice roast on Sundays and the odd pint. And, in fact, I've always thought the religions are rather alike: all the little figures of Hindu gods and the Catholic statues of saints, the shrines, the candles, the flowers.'

'So you're not religious yourself?'

'How did you guess? If I had to choose it would be Hinduism. Much more relaxed about sex, for instance. Some of the stories about Krishna are pretty racy.'

I knew I was blushing, and I could have sworn he noticed and had enjoyed making it happen. I looked down at my plate and forced in a mouthful of food, all too aware he was still looking at me with a slight smile. This was where the questions would come, and I braced myself to take care. But he let me off lightly. 'How's the food. Was I right about it?'

It was some kind of casserole, but I could hardly taste it. I nodded and gulped some of my drink. 'Yes it's very good. So Nic said you're a photographer. Do you do a lot of advertising work?'

'Just enough to keep the wolf from the door. The truth is I'm down here recovering from a bit of a breakdown. I got to thirty and decided I should try to earn bit more, you know, become a respectable member of society.'

So he was probably about my age. *Why the hell was I thinking that?* I felt a flush rise in my cheeks again as if he could read my thoughts and forced myself to listen to what he was saying.

' … foolishly got into the management side and found boardroom politics were just too cut-throat for me, couldn't cope.' The greenish eyes were suddenly intent. 'Maybe I shouldn't be telling you this.'

'A breakdown's nothing to be ashamed of.' I felt oddly flattered by his confession.

'It wasn't very dramatic anyway. Just couldn't get out of bed in the morning, but it lasted for days. Then, when I finally got in the car to go to work, I found myself driving down here instead and never went back.'

'Will you eventually, do you think?'

'Oh, no. I'm poorer, but so much happier. I only work free-lance for a few agencies, where I have friends. Apart from that I'm hawking my own stuff around the galleries and trying to do a book.'

'I used to love taking photos.' I could have bitten my tongue.

'And what about now?'

'Oh, I don't anymore.'

'Not even of your son?'

I think I blustered something about that not counting, but it didn't convince even me. I stood up, saying I needed the loo, knocking into the table and managing to spill the dregs of my drink in the process.

In the toilet, I washed my hands and stared into the mirror. My face was flushed and there were shadows under my eyes, but I looked OK; the turmoil inside certainly didn't show. I had been tempted, just then, to start talking about Tom and I knew I mustn't do that because it would inevitably lead to more – to Toby and Steve and God knows what else.

Kieran had bought more drinks when I got back to the table. 'I really ought to go. I've got a long journey in the morning.' *Why did you say that, you idiot.*

'Oh, where to?'

'Cumbria, visiting my cousin.'

'Oh, my neck of the woods. It's gorgeous up there when the sun shines, isn't it.'

I nodded, sipping my drink and hoping to shut down the conversation.

He did it for me, talking about how helpful Nic had been since he moved in. 'She's local, so anything you want to know she's your girl.'

Our glasses were empty and I pulled on my jacket. 'Yes, she seems like a lovely person.'

Thank goodness he was quiet as we walked home. I didn't want to talk, but the thought of my bleak flat slowed my steps. It was dry now, and the hint of a rainbow glimmered on and off amongst the clouds, but the street was still slicked shiny with moisture. As we approached the house, I realised I must say something.

'Thank you for the meal. I was much too tired to cook.'

'Still haven't been sleeping well?'

Damn, damn. When did I tell him that? 'Not brilliantly, no.'

'It's these short nights. You should put up heavy curtains. I replaced mine as soon as I moved in.'

I didn't say I had no trouble sleeping in the daytime; in fact I struggled to keep awake. With his own history of mental problems he would know what that meant.

When we got to our front door, I had my keys ready and unlocked it before he had time to take charge, but at my own flat, I felt his hands on my shoulders, turning me to face him; those green-flecked eyes staring down at me. And I could do nothing.

'Clare, I won't be so crude as to ask to come in for coffee, because we both know that's not what I want.' I could feel the warmth through his shirt and was suddenly tempted to lay my head against his chest. 'But may I do this?' He clearly didn't expect a reply and I couldn't have given one anyway. Instead I raised my face and we kissed. It was a long kiss, gentle and warm.

Then he pulled back and looked into my eyes. I knew I should say something, move away, but it was Kieran who did so in the end. 'Thank you Clare. Goodnight.'

I watched him head up to his flat, but twisted quickly away when he reached the turn in the stairs.

Chapter Fourteen

When I came to after the accident I knew my name, but little else. I opened my eyes to a vase of red flowers, a fly buzzing at the window, a pale light, and someone coughing nearby.

I think I croaked something, and a curt voice told me, 'You've been in an accident. Lie still and rest. Doctor will be in to see you soon.'

I thought, of course, that it was just me. Didn't even remember Toby, and Steve, and Dad. Everything hurt, and my head felt as if it was full of something soft and jelly-like that, if I moved too quickly, might seep out of my ears and eyes. So I lay still, trying not to think like that, not to think at all: to cling on to life and sanity.

Because I wanted to live then, even though I knew nothing except I was Clare, and this was a cool bed in a hospital room, with red flowers on a bedside table, a fly buzzing, a pale, painful light, and someone coughing – no, crying – nearby.

Then came the moment when I heard a child laugh and thought – *Toby and Tommy.* Just like that I remembered I had two sons. *And Steve.* I knew I hadn't seen them and I couldn't think why. Was I too ill, too horrible to look at?

The next day I was more clear-headed, and I knew something was very wrong. I asked again and again, and finally the nurse, who'd been ignoring me as she pulled the sheets tight and pushed and dragged at my pillow, sighed. 'Your sister will be here later.

She'll talk to you then I expect.' And I thought, *well then, it must be all right, or she wouldn't be so sharp with me.*

Later, in prison, when I first understood and accepted my guilt, I felt so bloated and swollen with it that I thought there would be no room inside me for anything else. But I was wrong. First, there was Ruby, bringing me comfort and even a few happy moments that I allowed myself to enjoy because without them I couldn't have gone on. Now there was Tommy, and that was far more than I could have hoped for.

Kieran was something different, and I certainly had no right to the kind of thrill I'd felt when he kissed me, the ease of talking to him, the pleasure at seeing his eyes crease with a smile and his hand holding a glass. I touched my lips. There had been times when I could recall Steve's kisses so vividly that I could still feel them, but not today.

Watching the sun setting over the sea, I tried not to hear Kieran moving overhead. So close. I knew he was walking across to his window and looking at the same view.

I turned away, opened the laptop and checked the train times, then sent a message to Emily to say when I'd be there and I'd call her when I was on my way. After that I emailed Tom. I kept the tone light and didn't mention last night, just told him I'd keep in touch while I was in Cumbria.

I was about to switch off when I thought about Lorna. I believed her when she said she loved me. And what right did I have to be angry with her because she'd had an affair? She had forgiven me for something so very much worse – I had killed the man she loved.

But I still didn't trust myself to talk to her. At least an email would be a start.

Dear Lorna,

I am so sorry I behaved the way I did the other day and of course I still want us to be friends. You will always be my dear fairy godmother and I just need a little while to get used to the idea of you and Dad.

Lorna, if I'm going to help Tom, I have to know everything about the time around the accident. About anything at all you remember that could be relevant. I still have the feeling you're keeping things back and if it's because you're trying to protect me, it isn't working.

Above all I must find out why I took those pills and how I got hold of them. But I've realised other things may have been different to the way I imagined them. So please will you rack your brains for anything that might be relevant about me and Steve, about Dad, or about the situation in the firm at that time.

Clare

I hesitated for a second then added, *with love*, before my name and a kiss after it.

As I left the flat next morning, Nic opened her door, still in her dressing gown and slippers.

'Hi Clare, you couldn't spare a drop of milk could you? I've run out again.' When I turned back to my door she must have registered the holdall. 'Oh sorry, you're off somewhere. I won't keep you.'

I had plenty of time before my train, so I brought her a carton from the fridge.

'Thanks, babe,' she said, her shiny eyes crinkling at me. 'Going somewhere nice?'

'To see my cousin.' Her nod and beaming smile somehow made it impossible not to add, 'The Lake District.'

'Ooo, you lucky thing,' she said. 'How long for?'

'Just till Friday.' I turned to open the front door.

'Hang on a sec and I'll get dressed and give you a lift to the station. Molly'll enjoy the ride.'

'No really, I've got plenty of time and I'd like a walk.'

'Well, if you're sure. It's really no trouble. Don't know why I keep paying out for that car. Only use it once or twice a week for shopping.'

She reached into her own hallway and I edged closer to the door, but when she turned back to me she was holding a pad and a pen. 'Here are my phone numbers.' She scribbled something and tore off a scrap of paper. 'I've got your landline one, so give me your mobile number too.' She laughed, waggling her head so her blonde, uncombed curls flopped back and forth. 'You know, in case your flat catches fire or something.'

It would have been rude to refuse and after all she was just trying to help: to be a good neighbour. And I nodded when she said to give her a ring if I wanted a lift from the station when I got back, although I knew I wouldn't do so.

On the train up north, I asked myself what on earth I was doing, churning up the past when I couldn't even get a grip on the present; couldn't deal with ordinary life and still looked at normal people as if they were enemies. But it was too late to turn back, and resting my head on the carriage window, I tried to put everything, and most of all the fear of what would happen when I saw Emily and Matt, out of my mind. As the miles rolled by, and the rain began to sheet down over fields that became greener and greener, I finally slipped into a dreamless doze.

I was woken by my mobile and I fumbled for it still half asleep. 'Hello?'

'Hi, Clare? It's me, Emily.'

My heart thudded; she was ringing, no doubt, to put me off.

'I won't talk for long because you're probably on the train and I hate people who chat on their mobiles. What time do you get in?'

'4.30, but don't worry … '

'Just wanted to tell you to forget all this taxi rubbish. I'll meet you at the station.'

*

Emily, who once could hardly heat beans without burning them, had evidently become a keen cook and I sat in her kitchen at a big pine table as she stirred a risotto on the stove. They'd done a lot of work on the house and it was very different from the little place I remembered her and Matt buying a few months before their wedding. But it still felt very much like Emily: warm, untidy, and with touches of bright colour everywhere.

I'd asked if I could help, but she laughed and told me to relax and sit where she could see me and every so often she turned to beam at me, her brown eyes sparkling. 'It's so good to have you here. Wish you could stay longer.' She ladled stock into the bubbling pan.

'I wouldn't have blamed you if you never wanted to see me again.'

'Don't be daft.' She shot a teary smile at me. 'Let's just start again, shall we? I promise I won't talk about the past. Just relax and enjoy a little holiday.'

I asked, 'When does Matt get home?'

She turned away, her voice muffled as she searched through packets and jars in a cupboard. 'He's in Scotland, not due back till late Thursday, so you won't see much of him. He was so disappointed to miss you.'

I swallowed down my frustration. 'Oh well, never mind, that gives *us* more time to talk.'

As if my words had some kind of negative power, an awkward silence descended. Emily ground pepper into the pan, put dishes to warm, and occasionally hummed to herself, while I looked around the room.

It had been extended since my last visit a couple of months before the wedding, but they'd kept the rough brick walls of the original cottage, and the one opposite the table was covered in framed family photos.

Emily had dark hair and eyes, like me, and in one picture – the two of us throwing dried leaves at each other in her parents' garden – we looked like a couple of little gypsies.

That day was suddenly in my mind more clearly than yesterday. The smells of autumn bonfires in a nearby garden, the chill air against my hot little cheeks, and the joy of knowing I would be staying with Uncle Alan and Auntie Rose for a whole week. Away from Mummy's complaints about my untidiness and noise. Here I could forget, for a while, what a bad girl I was.

The picture below was one of Alice's birthday parties. Mum must have been having a good day because she looked radiant, blonde hair cascading over her shoulders. There were eight candles flickering on the cake and Alice grinned over them, her smile identical to Mum's apart from a lost front tooth. Dad had insisted Emily and I, awkward young teens, should be in the picture too and Emily had managed a stiff smile, whilst I looked down at the cake, hiding my face with a fall of hair.

There were various old wedding photos scattered around. Emily's parents as toned- down hippies: Alan in a blue shirt with ruffles and a white jacket, and Rose trailing flowers from her mass of hennaed hair. A black and white of a couple I didn't recognise – Doris Day and Rock Hudson lookalikes – were all tuxedo and frothy chiffon. Our shared grandparents, Dad and Uncle Alan's mother and father, were there too: my grandfather in tails, top hat in his hand, and his new wife, very French and stylish, in tight-fitting white satin. A single photo of Matt and Emily tucked in amongst the group was the only evidence of their own wedding day.

As we ate we discussed asparagus and Italian cheese, Emily seeming to be as uncomfortable as I felt.

When we'd finished I told her to take it easy while I made some coffee, and as we drank it, I looked up at the paper smiles gleaming through the glass on the wall behind her head.

'I notice there's only one wedding photo of you and Matt.'

She shifted in her chair, rubbing a hand over her bump. 'Well, they all went into the album.'

'And you didn't take one or two down from the wall when you knew I was coming, I suppose?'

'No I didn't, and to be honest I never look at the album either.'
Her brown eyes flashed at me for a moment, before she looked
down at her plate again. 'I'm sorry, Clare, but honestly it doesn't
matter anymore, at least not to me. Matt and I are happy now
and the past is past. So we don't really talk about it.'

'That's just it though, Emily. I need to.'

'But what good can it do, going over painful things that can't
be changed?'

'I have to understand what happened. Tom's asking questions I can't
answer for one thing and well … I just need to know. I thought maybe
the photos might help me to remember something from that day.'

She ran her hand through her hair, and pulled herself upright,
her bulk making her stagger. 'I'm too tired to look for them tonight.
Let me show you your room and if you still want to see the album
I'll find it tomorrow.' It was clear she was upset, but at the door
of my room she seemed to revive.

'Honestly, Clare, I think you should let it go. I was at the wedding
too, remember, and if there was anything I thought you should
know don't you think I'd have told you by now?'

I smiled and squeezed her arm. 'Of course. But I suppose I just
need to remember for myself.'

She turned away. 'Let's talk about it in the morning.'

I told myself at 3 a.m. that I was just going down for a glass of
water, but instead, I wandered through the downstairs rooms,
keeping the lights dim, quietly checking bookshelves, opening
drawers and cupboards. It was wrong to sneak about like this,
but I guessed Emily would try to avoid the subject of the album
in the morning, and I dreaded having to raise it again.

There was no sign of it and when I opened the final cupboard,
the one under the TV, I wasn't surprised to find only DVDs and
a few old videos. But then I saw a DVD box that looked different
to the rest. It was plain white, a little dusty and labelled in curling
gold letters – *Our Wedding*.

I was shaking as I pulled it out. It had clearly not been looked at for a long time, and Emily might even have forgotten it was there.

At least I had to hope so, because it was going back home with me.

Chapter Fifteen

Neither of us mentioned the wedding album next morning and Emily seemed relieved when I chatted about other things. She had a doctor's appointment at 10.30 so she wasn't surprised when I said I'd go for a walk.

She waved me off and when I reached the main road, out of sight of the cottage, I took out my mobile and rang for a taxi.

My last memory of that dreadful day was of pulling up, a little late and very anxious, at the church. The building had haunted me ever since, yet standing in front of it, as the taxi drew away, it seemed no more familiar than something seen in a picture postcard. It was more chapel than church, with a tiny graveyard to the side, on the edge of the little village of Bramstone. In one direction a lattice of fields stretched away, and in the other, the fells rippled down in green waves to the lake at the bottom of the valley. The air was transparent in the way that seems particular to the Lake District.

Matt's parents had owned these fields and the reception was in a marquee beside their farmhouse. They'd sold up a couple of years ago, and the marquee, of course, was long gone, but I thought the church might yield something.

Inside, I breathed in a mixture of polish and dying flowers. A Victorian stained glass window overpowered the small altar. It was a nativity scene: the pale Pre-Raphaelite virgin clutching a roly-poly Jesus, his plump face scowling up at her, no doubt wanting his next feed.

It sparked no memory, nor did the pews, each with its own embroidered kneeler. I sat cradling one of them, the purple fabric emblazoned with the motto: *Let he who is without sin cast the first stone.* Well, I certainly wouldn't be doing any stone throwing, I thought, as a laugh escaped, only to turn into a sob. There was nothing here I remembered, nothing that meant anything. I banged the pew with my fist as I stood.

'All right, love?'

How she'd managed to get right up behind me with her bucket and mop I couldn't understand, but I choked out that I was fine.

David Hillier was the second witness to arrive at the scene of the accident. At the time, he lived in Bramstone and I'd planned to ask Emily to help me locate him, but I realised, unless he'd moved, I should be able to find him myself. After all, Bramstone was just a hamlet and, apart from Matt's family farm and the church, there were only four or five houses. So it shouldn't be too difficult to track down Hillier, if he still lived there.

The road to Bramstone led nowhere else, and much had been made at the trial of how surprising it was that anyone was around in the early hours of a Sunday morning. Hillier was returning from visiting his dying wife in hospital and the other witness was the young biker, Jacob Downes, who'd just been riding around.

I suddenly had a clear memory of Downes at the trial, scratching fiercely at a mop of dark, unkempt hair as he reddened and stumbled out a kind of apology when the judge asked, with startling irrelevance, if he took into account the fact that his noisy engine might spoil the sleep of other people.

At the time, Hillier had been a headmaster, and would have retired so I gave the first cottage a miss when I saw the little trike in the garden. The second, a neat bungalow, fronted by a perfect lawn edged with lavender and petunias, looked more promising.

He came to the door seconds after I rang the bell and I suspected he'd seen me through the panoramic living room window. Inside, the radio was playing something classical. He greeted me with a smile that suggested my face was familiar but he couldn't quite place me. His professionally warm, 'Hello, dear, and what can I do for you?' made me guess he had put me down as an old pupil, or perhaps a parent.

'I'm Clare Glazier ... you remember ... from the trial.' It was clear before I finished speaking that he did. The smile vanished, and his face flushed as he began to close the door on me.

'I'm sorry I've nothing to say to you.'

But I'd anticipated this and held up my hand. 'There's no need to be frightened, Mr Hillier. I'm out of prison and I hoped you might be able to help me. I can't remember that night, and I thought if I talked to some of the people who were there, something might come back to me. I still have a son, you see, and I want to tell him the whole truth.'

He looked doubtful but no longer alarmed and stepped back to let me into the cramped hallway. 'Oh ...Well, I really don't think I can help you, Mrs Glazier, but as you're here ...' He gestured for me to go into the front room. The mantelpiece and the two brimming bookshelves were cluttered with framed photos, most of them of smiling youngsters. In the middle, a studio portrait of an attractive middle-aged woman – the dead wife, I guessed.

The room smelt of pipe smoke and bacon with a hint of something alcoholic. He lowered himself into an upright armchair, wriggling to straighten the crumpled cushions behind him. Then turned the music down, picked up his pipe and gestured to the sofa. It was covered in a tweedy material that pricked the back of my thighs through my thin trousers, so I sat on my hands and leaned towards him.

'I was just hoping you might be able to press some buttons. You know, recall some details. It doesn't matter how silly or irrelevant they seem to you. My therapist said anything can trigger a memory.'

'And you still remember absolutely nothing?' I shook my head. 'The trouble is my own memory isn't what it was,' he said. 'Also, to be honest with you, Mrs Glazier, it was a difficult time for me altogether. There was my wife's death, the funeral and all that. And then I had to contend with the trial.'

'I am sorry to bring it up again, but if there's anything at all …'

He sucked his pipe for a moment, then took it out and stared thoughtfully at the shiny mark left by his lips on the mouthpiece. 'They told me there was no point in staying that night. She was in a coma by then, morphine-induced I suppose, and they assured me she would last another couple of days and I should go home.'

'It must have been after two in the morning and the road was very dark, of course, only the cats' eyes for light. And just a couple of miles from here, that nasty bend … well you know where it happened.' I nodded, trying to see what was in his mind. 'I was very far away in my thoughts, with Gloria in that bleak little room.'

His hand shook as he poked strands of tobacco into the bowl of his pipe. Then he looked down at it muttering, 'Filthy habit, 'and tossed it onto the crowded little table beside him where it slipped down between a pile of books and a bottle of Scotch.

'So, you didn't hear anything?'

'No, but there were the flames. Thought it was some idiot with a bonfire out of control. But then I saw the two of you, and the car against the tree.'

'So Downes, Jacob Downes on the motor bike, got there a good while before you?'

'That I couldn't say, but by the time I arrived the car was already alight and there was no chance of helping the others … although at the time, I didn't realise there were any others.'

I swallowed and forced myself to say it. 'So you didn't hear any … any screams, or anything?'

'Oh no, nothing like that. I'd have gone to help if I'd even thought …'

'You see, I sometimes think I remember screams.' As my breath caught I saw his face contort too, and realised how awful this was of me. I couldn't lay my guilt onto an innocent old man.

He stood and laid a hand briefly on my shoulder. 'Cup of tea I think, eh? Nice and strong.' I walked to the window and stared out as I listened to him potter in the kitchen. The sun had gone in, and a fresh wind was bothering the petals of the petunias. The lavender however stood stiff and unmoving.

'No biscuits I'm afraid. Gloria banned them when I started to put on weight and it's funny, but I never fancy one nowadays. Will you pour?'

I was tempted to tell him to get on with it, but I waited till he was sipping noisily at his tea. 'I know you probably said all this at the trial, but I can only remember snippets. You were saying you saw Jacob Downes right away. Where was his bike?'

'I really can't remember. In fact, I thought at first he was with you. Then I realised he was a local lad, just another passer-by like myself.'

'And he was helping me from the car?'

'Well no, by the time I got to there you were on the ground and definitely unconscious. I'm sorry this isn't much help but, really, I saw very little.'

Something he'd said struck me then. 'You said Jacob Downes was local. Did you know him before the accident?'

He put down his cup and looked at me. 'I'm not sure that's relevant.'

'I was wondering if you might know how I could contact him.'

A sigh. 'Look, Mrs Glazier, I can see how difficult it must be for you – the not knowing – but I doubt very much if Jake can help you any more than I can.'

Jake, not Jacob, I leaned towards him. 'I'm not looking for anything dramatic, Mr Hillier. I accepted long ago that the accident was my fault. It's just … some tiny detail could be the key to unlocking my memory and helping my son.'

Another sigh. 'I can understand that, of course, but from what I know of Jake Downes I doubt he'll be willing, or even able, to help you. It's true he was an ex-pupil from my school but, as headmaster, I didn't know him well. I checked his records after the accident, just out of interest, and some of his teachers talked about him. Unfortunately, he was a very vulnerable young man. If I recall correctly, he lost his father when he was still at school and his mother was ill too, so he was in and out of foster homes. During the trial he seemed terrified of the police and it was clear, from the way they dealt with him, they knew him of old.'

His stirred his tea, the spoon loud against the china. 'I'm telling you this in the hope you'll give up the idea of contacting him.'

'So you won't help me find his address?'

'I'm sorry, no, and I honestly don't think he'd be any help to you.'

I gritted my teeth; it was hopeless. 'Well, did he talk to you during the trial or when you were giving your statements to the police?'

'No, they kept us pretty much apart. Didn't want us comparing stories, I suppose. And he was obviously somewhat uneasy with me, as his ex-head teacher.'

I brought the image of Downes in the witness box to mind again. Thin, scruffy, and not too bright. Yes, that made sense.

I stood, and as he ushered me to the door, I could almost hear his sigh of relief. 'Well thank you for your time, Mr Hillier.' But I knew I couldn't leave it there. 'I can understand why you won't give me Jacob's contact details, but would you consider speaking to him for me?'

I touched his arm as he began to shake his head. 'You could reassure him that all I want is to learn exactly what he saw. I certainly won't be trying to get the police to reopen the case or anything like that. So it would just be a chat with me, by email if that was how he wanted it.'

I pulled a slip of paper from my pocket. 'This is my address, phone numbers, and my email, if you do get in touch with him, or if you think of anything else yourself. '

'I'm sorry, but frankly I want to forget the whole incident. It might seem harsh to you, but I've had a good deal of tragedy in my life, Mrs Glazier, and I can tell you it doesn't do any good to dwell on it.'

I decided to walk back to Emily's, but I'd overestimated the distance and it ended up taking far longer than I expected. I tried her on my mobile, but her phone was engaged, so I hoped she was too busy to worry about me.

The sun had come out again and by the time I reached the cottage I was sweating. There was no reply to my tap on the front door so I walked round to the back, remembering the kitchen had a stable door. As I expected, the top half was open to let in the breeze, and I could hear Emily talking. She was still on the phone, but her voice was so shrill I stopped in my tracks. Better to wait till she finished and avoid embarrassment.

I told myself I stayed where I was because she might hear my footsteps, but in reality I was eavesdropping. I learned in prison that eavesdroppers may not hear anything good, but they can find out many things that will help them avoid trouble. Emily's voice was quieter, but still audible, and still with a note of suppressed anger. 'I told you, tomorrow … OK. I'll see you on Saturday then, instead. Yes, me too … Phone me from the station. Bye. Yes, OK, bye.'

She made an odd little noise and I heard water running, but I stayed leaning against the wall. The caller was obviously Matt, but was the conversation about me? I'd told Emily I had to leave tomorrow, so was Matt staying away to avoid me?

When I thought I'd left it long enough, I crept back to the front door and tapped. Emily's face looked a bit red, but that could have been caused by the heat. 'Oh there you are, I was just about to send out a search party,' she said.

She had made some sandwiches and we sat in the garden. The table was under a tree and there was a view all around of the wide fells, the breeze making it a little chill. Emily yawned.

'Didn't you sleep well?' I asked. Had she heard me wandering around in the night?

'Oh yes, like a log, but I'm always tired these days.'

I decided to risk it. 'So how's Matt?' After Dad died, the firm had been taken over by a big American company, and Matt had been promoted rapidly. I had never been able to see him as a boardroom man, though. Unlike Dad, Matt always seemed like a real scientist, but when I'd seen him last he had actually looked the part of the successful executive.

Emily stroked her stomach and we both contemplated the bump for a moment. 'Thrilled about the baby, but not happy at work. He hates being part of a conglomerate and what he has is basically a desk job. They had to keep some of the people from Parnell Pharmaceuticals on after the merger and, of course, the money's pretty good.'

I brushed some crumbs from my lap. 'But it's not Matt, is it?'

'No, and that's one of the reasons he's going to all these conferences, trying to network with other chemists. What he'd love is a university post, but they're few and far between these days.'

I looked across the fields, the blood beginning to drum in my temples. 'I went back to Bramstone this morning.'

'Oh, Clare, why?'

'I hoped it might trigger something. Called in to see Mr Hillier too.'

She folded her arms, shivering slightly. 'Who?'

'The old chap – the witness.'

'And?'

'He couldn't help.'

She stood, shaking her head, and began picking up our plates. I grabbed the cups and said, 'Leave this, I'll do it.' But she carried on, letting out a small gasp of exasperation as she dropped a knife and tried, and failed, to bend for it.

I picked it up and followed her back to the house.

'Look, I'm tired, I think I'll go up for an hour,' she said.

After she'd gone I went back into the garden. It was very quiet and my mind began to circle endlessly again. I asked myself what I was doing. I'd upset Emily, I'd hurt Lorna, and I was no closer to having Tom back with me.

Alice had always assumed I would come to live with them when I got out, but I'd been determined to be independent. I'd talked for hours to Ruby, building up a fantasy where Tom and I would live happily together. We would get a little cottage and put the past behind us to be a family again. It suddenly seemed ridiculous.

The wind was really blowing now and I realised I was very cold. It was the kind of bone-deep cold you feel when you're ill, and inside, I huddled near the Aga, pulling my mobile out. I wanted only one thing – to speak to Tom.

'Hi Mum. OK?'

Keep it light. 'I'm fine. How's it going?' All I wanted was to listen to his sweet, gruff voice, to know he was there.

'Yeah. But, Mum, have you found out anything? From Emily or Matt?' His voice had the slight squeak I knew betrayed excitement.

I explained that Emily and I had talked and I'd visited one of the witnesses. 'Mr Hillier was really kind, but it was difficult to get much out of him.' Then, because I couldn't bear to disappoint him, 'But it's good to be up here and maybe it will help my memory. The doctors say these things are often gradual. So I'm hoping … What about you? How's the revision going?'

He was obviously reluctant to let the subject go. 'OK. Good. But, Mum …' Alice's voice in the distance now. 'Oh, yeah. Got to go. Music lesson. Will you call me as soon as you get back?'

'Of course. Bye …' The dialling tone cut me off and I sat feeling lonelier, more mixed up, than ever. The Aga, giving off waves of gentle heat, had warmed my hands and feet, but the cold stayed lodged inside and I wrapped my arms round my midriff, rocking myself slowly as if to thaw the block of ice trapped there.

By the time Emily surfaced I had taken a hot shower and put on some make up and knew at least I looked normal. I'd offered to cook, but she suggested we walk to the village pub for dinner. 'It's a shame,' she said, 'but I had a call from Matt. He can't get back tonight after all. So you won't see him.' She was taking a jacket from a hook in the hall and putting it on, not looking at me, as she spoke. I didn't say anything.

In the pub, as we waited for our food, I found myself talking about Ruby and some of the others I'd met in prison. The kind of hopeless lives many of them had.

Suddenly Em was scrabbling in her bag. 'Sorry, sorry …oh damn.' She pulled out a tissue and blew her nose. 'I'm so emotional at the moment, but it's awful to think of what you've been through, all those other women too. I used to wish so much I could help somehow and – oh I don't know.'

'Well you can help me now by trying to remember even the smallest details about that day and the days around it.'

The barmaid called, 'Lamb casserole and fish pie,' as she clunked two plates onto the bar and I was forced to break off and collect them. Back at the table, Emily was pulling another tissue apart. I waited till we'd sorted cutlery and she'd begun to poke at her pie.

'Emily?'

She sighed. 'You don't seem to realise I've been over and over it through the years. If there was anything that could excuse what you did, don't you think I'd want to find it?'

'I'm not looking for an excuse. Just an explanation.'

'Well I don't have one.'

In the silence that followed, we both made a pretence of eating. I knew she wanted me to leave it alone, but I couldn't. 'Did you know about Dad and Lorna? That they had an affair that lasted years?'

It was obviously no surprise. 'Well, I suppose I had an idea from things Mum and Dad said, but I've never given it much thought. And it doesn't matter now, does it?'

'It does, because it makes me think differently about people and about the past. To realise how blind I was.'

Emily threw down her fork, looking with disgust at the potato and fish she had stirred into a mess of grey lumps. 'Matt said you were asking about anyone we knew who might have supplied you with the amphetamines.'

'Yes, because I know I didn't have any with me. Hadn't touched anything like that for years.'

Her brown eyes, when she raised them, were hard. 'Has it never occurred to you how easy it would have been to get hold of them at our wedding? Half the people there worked for a pharmaceutical firm, including your dad, Lorna, and Matt. And Alice is a doctor. So you have plenty of suspects there.'

She struggled into her cardigan, her bulk and her distress making her clumsy. I reached out to help her, but she shrugged me off. 'Are you finished?'

We didn't speak as we walked, and when we got to the house I expected her to go straight up. Instead, she went into the living room and slumped into an armchair.

I sat opposite. 'I'm sorry, Em, I just can't give up now.'

This time her eyes were gentle. 'You know how stressed everyone at the firm was at that time so I'm sure some of them were self-medicating. But that doesn't mean anyone supplied you. If you were really upset you could easily have seen a pack in someone's bag and pinched them.'

That was something I'd never thought of, but it was true and, even if the person had realised, they'd hardly have come forward to the police. 'In that case I still need to find out why I would want them.' My voice wobbled and Emily reached out towards me, but couldn't lean far enough to touch me because of her pregnant stomach.

She dropped her hand with a sigh and her voice wobbled too. 'I thought you'd got over all this, Clare. Have you ever thought it could be a good thing you can't remember the accident? Matt and I had already left on our honeymoon so we were spared some of the aftermath, but think about what Alice and my poor dad had to go through that night and the next morning at the hospital. And Lorna too, for that matter.

I shook my head, but couldn't speak, and she pulled herself up, breathing heavily as she made her way to the door. Then she turned back. 'I think you need to ask yourself if you really want to start probing the wound again.'

Chapter Sixteen

Emily insisted on cooking me a big breakfast next morning. We ate with hardly a word, and when I said I'd be fine getting a taxi to the station, she sighed. 'I am a bit tired … if you don't mind.'

I reached out across the table and touched her hand. 'I'm sorry if I've upset you.'

'It's all right.' She looked at me. 'You *will* come again when the baby's born, won't you? See Mum and Dad as well.'

'If you still want me to.'

'Of course we do. Dad always blamed your father for what happened to you anyway.'

'I was the one driving.'

'He meant earlier, when you went off the rails. Adopting a child is a serious business and turning up with you the way Uncle Robert apparently did, as if you were a pet or something, Dad said he guessed it wouldn't turn out well, even at the time.'

'I can see that – poor Mum.'

'And, according to Dad, she'd already had one or two breakdowns.'

'But I thought it was post-natal depression.'

'From odd things Dad said I think it was a longer term and more serious condition and it just got worse after Alice was born.'

It made sense: Mum's attitude to me, mostly cold, but with occasional furious tirades, and even more occasional bursts of affection. Her feelings for Alice were too intense as well. I remembered her crying for a whole weekend once when Alice went to stay with a friend. And then there were the periods in the private hospital, often preceded by days in bed with the curtains closed and silence throughout the house.

There was a hoot from outside: my taxi.

At the door I put down my bag and kissed Emily. 'I can't give this up however much I would like to. I need to help Tom to understand, but I'm so sorry if it brings back bad memories.'

'I know,' she said, with her old sweet smile, her hand rubbing her bump. 'I've been thinking about it overnight and you can't refuse him that. I'll try to think of anything that might help.'

'And what about Matt? Could you ask him to tell me all he can remember about the scandal? He must have known Dr Penrose, and Lorna says Dad used to talk to him too.'

'Of course I will. If it's so important to you.'

When I turned to say goodbye. Emily clutched me to her for long seconds, and it was clear, from her quivers, that she was fighting the tears. There was a pain in my throat too.

I'd made sure I had plenty of time to spare before my train, and asked the taxi driver to head for Bramstone and stop just short of it. Then I got out and crossed the road to look back at the crash site.

Like many accident black spots, this was a winding country road surrounded by trees and fields. The first time I recalled coming here was when the police tried to get me to admit I'd caused the accident deliberately.

The woman detective was soft-voiced. 'I know this is going to be difficult for you, Clare, but if you can remember anything that will help us it will make things easier for everyone and especially you and little Tommy.'

It was raining that day, a lacy curtain that shrank everything down to a few shrouded yards; a drizzle that crept into every gap in my clothes and made my scalp itch. My head still pounded and I had difficulty focusing my eyes. Every few minutes, I had to remind myself that this horror was my new reality. My baby, Toby, was dead and nothing could bring him back – Steve and Dad, too.

The policewoman said again and again, 'Look around, Clare. Try to put yourself back in the car. What kind of a car was it, my love?'

I dragged out an answer, wanting only to get away. 'A Mercedes – Dad's.'

'That's right and you were driving.' When I nodded, her voice became warm. 'That's great, Clare, you're doing really well. You were upset weren't you? Maybe you'd had an argument with Steve. Good-looking lad like that, you had to keep your eye on him, didn't you? Was he playing around?'

I wiped at my face. Her words meant nothing. I just wanted to get out of the drizzle that tickled my scalp so much it almost hurt. I didn't want to see the swerve of skid marks on the road and the scarred tree trunk with the grass burnt black beneath it.

'Something, made you unhappy didn't it, Clare. Was it your dad? It can't have been easy being adopted. Did he say something to upset you?' Her voice drilled on. 'You wanted to keep cheerful – not to spoil the party. So you took something to help. Was that it?'

What she was saying began to make sense and I think I shook my head, scratching and pulling at my wet curls, my feet slipping on the crumble of soil, as I tried to pull away from her grip. 'No, no, I wouldn't have.'

'And Steve was supposed to take Toby off early, wasn't he? Why did you stop him?'

I shook my head to help me return to this new day of brilliant sun. Those weren't the memories I wanted; it was the night of the accident I was desperate to recall. I looked at the curving road. The overhanging trees and lack of street lights would make it very difficult to negotiate on a dark night. Hillier had been heading home to Bramstone and he'd probably stopped on the grass verge, more or less where the taxi was parked now.

Jacob Downes' evidence was more dramatic. He said he was about five minutes behind me, heard the crash, and arrived as the car burst into flames, to find me staggering about, just before I collapsed. He'd been riding aimlessly round the area and had actually gone right into Bramstone. Seen the Mercedes pull out of the farm track, and then ridden up to the church before turning to follow the same route I'd taken: his only option. At one point he told the prosecution he thought perhaps I was *weaving a bit*, but got flustered when my defence pressed him on this and admitted he couldn't be sure.

'Perhaps it was clear there'd been a party at the farm and you made the assumption that anyone driving away might be intoxicated. Is that possible?' I remember Downes nodded and muttered, yes he might have, pushing back a lock of greasy hair, and I also remember wondering if he knew what *assumption* meant, or even *intoxicated*.

The mini cab driver hooted, warning me I would be late for my train, and I took a few quick photos of the place with my phone, knowing they were unlikely to help. Then I climbed in beside him and he began to turn the car. As he did so a van passed us, the sun flashing on its wing mirror.

And something stirred again.

The flash became a different flash, something blinding that made me flinch back as I felt a jolt and the steering wheel twisting in my hands, the car swerving into a skid. *No!*

And I was back in the taxi my hands pressed to my lips and the driver asking me if I was all right.

It's wasn't until I was on the train again that I was able to think. Couldn't remember the taxi ride and everything at the station was a blur. What remained was the sense of dread I felt as I came close to remembering it all. The psychiatrist had warned me about this – my mind was protecting me and it might be dangerous to try too hard for recall before I was ready. But ready or not I had to risk it – for Tom.

As the train raced onwards I asked myself what, after all these years, had made the difference. Talking to people and going back to the scene had to have had an impact, but maybe it was as simple as the fact that I finally wanted to remember.

The accident happened in the dead of night, so there was certainly no sun around. There was often a light in my dreams and I'd thought it was a memory of the car bursting into flames. But I was sure now it something else. Headlights – the flash of headlights from an oncoming vehicle. On that dark road, a sudden light could have startled me enough to make me lose control.

Neither of the witnesses had mentioned seeing another vehicle and it wouldn't make me any less guilty, but it could only help to know more about the exact moment of the crash.

Mr Hillier had been coming towards us, but he had arrived minutes after the accident: after Downes. And Downes had been behind us, so this other vehicle would have passed him. Then why hadn't he mentioned it to the police? Maybe he had, but they were so sure of my guilt they told him to say nothing about it. He had certainly seemed very anxious giving his evidence, as if scared of saying the wrong thing.

Thinking about that, it crossed my mind that maybe there was just one headlight – the one on Downes' motorbike. What if he had been coming towards us, like Hillier, not following as he'd said? Maybe even doing something dangerous? It would have been easy enough to move the bike before the police arrived.

Then something Hillier said came back to me. '*I was very far away in my thoughts…* ' Had I been fooled, had the police been fooled, by the impression of integrity he presented? I saw a different scenario and one that now seemed very possible. Could Hillier, distracted by grief, have been driving back with his headlights full on, to blind me and make me crash. If Downes knew him as his old headmaster, it would be easy enough, surely, to persuade him to twist the facts just a little. At the time they didn't know I was high, so Hillier could have feared being charged with dangerous driving himself. A vision of the whisky bottle on the table close to his hand came to mind.

I could almost see and hear it. The headmaster, used to giving orders, with his hand on Downes' shoulder. 'Maybe we should keep it simple, Jake. You say you got here first and I doubt there'll be too many questions after that.'

Now I'd thought of it I wondered why I'd never considered it before or realised how important that burst of light was. Whatever else I saw in those brief moments of clarity, the brilliant flash was always there.

It didn't explain the drugs in my system, or lessen my guilt, but it did mean I must talk to Hillier again. And to Downes.

The underground between Euston and Charing Cross was frighteningly crowded on a Friday evening. I'd got used to keeping out of people's way in prison, but here it was impossible. The heat, the smell and the noise, the pressure of bodies against mine as I clung to a bar in the Tube, made me want to jump off every time the doors slid open. But I needed to get home, so I closed my eyes and clenched my teeth.

On the Hastings train, I called Tom's mobile and then Alice's home phone, but got the answer system on both. I left messages that I was still travelling, but I was looking forward to Sunday and would call them tomorrow.

When my phone bleeped with a text, I hoped it would be Tom, but it was Nic asking when I would be back and reminding me of her offer of a lift. I was tempted to call her, hoping her chirpy voice would cheer me, but talking to her might mean I'd miss Tom, so I texted back not to worry. I wouldn't be in till after nine and Molly would be in bed.

The walk to the station on a bright morning had been pleasant, so I didn't even consider taking a taxi on the way back. But in the dark it was very different and when I reached the steep road to the flat I was almost stumbling. There was no pavement here and

I kept close to the hedges, but everywhere was quiet and when I was in sight of the house I could see a welcome gleam from Nic's flat. All I could think of was falling into bed.

A roar and a blaze of light – and for a second I was transfixed, reaching for that memory again.

Then I realised what was happening and threw myself away from the car speeding down the hill.

As I slammed against the metal gate it gave way and I lay shaking on the path, floored by pain and shock. Alice had warned me about the road that first day, and I'd always been careful before.

Eventually, I dragged myself to my feet, my legs shaking as I scrabbled for my key, my curses more like grunting sobs than words.

'My God, Clare, are you all right? Here I'll get your bag.' Kieran was behind me, his hand on my elbow. 'I saw that, chased after the bastard to try and get his number, but he was doing a ton.' He opened the door and without his saving hand I would have fallen through. I muttered something about being all right and tried to shut my own door on him, but somehow he was inside too making me sit on the sofa.

Then he was holding a steaming mug in front of me and sitting beside me – too close. I closed my eyes to shut him out and sipped the drink, letting the warmth calm me, and ignoring the urge to rub my aching hip. 'Thanks. I'm fine now.'

'You don't look it. Are you sure you don't want me to call a doctor? Or I could drive you to Casualty.'

'No, no. I'll just have a bath and get to bed.'

'Did you get a look at the car, or the driver?'

'No, it was all so fast.'

'I couldn't describe them either, but we should call the police anyway.'

'No.' My voice was a seagull shriek, and Kieran put his hands to his ears, with a wince and a smile.

'OK, OK, it was only a suggestion. Don't suppose there's much point anyway, as neither of us saw anything useful.' He headed for the bathroom. 'Right, you relax, while I run you a bath.'

Despite my throbbing side, the coffee and the soft cushions soothed me and I began to feel I could have slept. But I was too aware of Kieran, and when he came back to tell me the bath was ready I jumped up, anxious to lock myself away from him.

The world lurched and he caught my arm and steered me back onto the sofa. 'Sit still for a minute more. Get your breath, then I'll help you. Don't worry, I'm not going to offer to undress you, but I think I should sit out here until you're finished. Don't want you drowning.'

I swallowed the rest of my drink and stood very carefully. 'Just moved too quickly. Honestly, I'm OK.' He followed me to the bathroom door, but I closed it firmly against him, calling from inside to say he should go home, I was absolutely fine. He shouted back something about checking on me soon, and I heard the door slam – there was no way I would let him in again.

As I sat in the warm water I began to cry, huge sobs with no thought behind them and, despite the heat of the water, I was shivering when I got out. I pulled on a sweatshirt, pyjama bottoms, and socks and sat on the sofa too weak to do anything else.

When I heard Kieran's tap on the door I ignored it, but he called through, 'Clare, are you all right? I'm coming in.' Then the door opened and he was in the little hallway.

I went to the living room door. He was smiling and brushing a curl of dark hair from his forehead. 'You didn't drown I see.'

'How did you get in?' I was aware that my voice was shrill, but he didn't seem to notice.

'I still had your spare key.' He waved it in front of his face. 'Couldn't take a chance you'd collapse on me, could I?'

I could barely get the words out. 'How come you've got my key?'

'I told you, I helped out when the place was for let. Showed a few people round. Forgot I had it.'

'Well, I'll keep it now, thank you.'

He handed it to me with one word, 'Fine,' and left, closing the door quietly behind him.

Chapter Seventeen

I'm making love with Steve, his body pounding into mine as I clutch at him. Then a burst of light stabs the darkness and I realise the man isn't Steve, but Kieran. Through the dazzle I see we're in a prison yard, our naked bodies squirming under the brilliance of a spotlight. And then he's gone and I'm alone, shivering under the harsh beam, as voices mock and catcall.

I woke to bright daylight, hot and tangled in the sheets, my bruises throbbing. The dream hung over me as I showered and dressed for work, and I could see just where it had come from. Last night I had wanted nothing more than to call Kieran back, to apologise for being so ungrateful. And, if I was honest, to have him hold me; to help me forget everything for a few hours.

But I had promised myself I would steer clear of men. I had thought Steve loved me, but, in Holloway, remembering the insinuations at the trial, I often wondered if I'd been fooling myself all along.

Stories of happy marriages were non-existent in prison and nearly every woman there had been through too many dreadful relationships, too many painful break ups. That didn't stop them hoping the next time would be different, and affairs were starting up, and breaking up, all the time inside too.

It wasn't just the real lesbians who fell in love either, many women became prison bent, as they called it, reaching out instinctively for love and companionship. These affairs nearly always ended badly: one of them would be released and go back to the man who hadn't bothered to visit her, or a new girl would arrive on the block to cause a split.

Ruby and I became the closest of friends, but maybe because we only ever hugged we were able to support each other through the bad times. She always said she was done with romantic relationships. 'All the troubles I've had have been caused by the bastard men I've got myself involved with. And I'm not gonna make the same mistakes again, even with a girl. It's gonna be just the kids, me, and my mum when I get out.'

At first, I couldn't even imagine getting out and it seemed wrong, after what I'd done, to think of a life in the real world. But, along with Alice and Lorna, Ruby helped me see that I was being selfish and that Tom still needed me. 'He might give you a hard time, and I guess you deserve that,' she said, 'but you gotta be there for him.'

She was right and I had to be there for Tom, with no distractions. So perhaps it was just as well Kieran might want to avoid me in future.

I could hear his usual jazz playing upstairs, so I felt safe to leave the flat, but as I reached the door I froze. A creak on the stairs told me someone was coming down. I waited, my breath caught in my mouth, as the soft footsteps paused in the hall. I imagined him contemplating my door, but then another door – it must have been Nic's – opened and closed quietly again.

At work, Stella was shocked by my bruised face, and despite my protests, she told me to go home early.

When I got in, the flat felt grubby and neglected, with my holdall spilling clothes in the middle of the living room. It smelled even mustier today and suddenly seemed far too big, with too many windows, too many doors, and I was tempted to go for a walk rather than face what I knew I must do.

Gritting my teeth, I dragged the DVD from the bag, slotted the thing into the machine, then walked over to unlock and push up one of the windows, the movement sending condensation dripping down onto the sill. A draught of cooler air touched my face and shook me into action. *Just do it, will you.* I pressed *PLAY,* my finger moving at once to hover over the *STOP* button.

Whoever held the camera was no expert, zooming in and out at inappropriate moments, giving sudden drunken close-ups of doors and chair legs. Here were Emily and Aunt Rose in dressing gowns, laughing with her bridesmaid and waving the camera away as they fiddled with headdresses and shoes. A stomach-churning view of the stairs, the banister, swaying in and out of shot, and Uncle Alan, in the living room adjusting his buttonhole and tugging at his silk waistcoat. Another drunken lurch upwards showed Emily descending the stairs, in her froth of white, the clapping and whistles off-camera making her laugh and press her bouquet to her face.

Then inside the church, just recognisable as the one I'd been in the other day, but full of people and resembling a wedding scene from Thomas Hardy, with pews garlanded with flowers and trailing ribbon. The camera, more steady now, panned over the congregation, and I moved to kneel in front of the TV, peering hard, my heart loud in my ears.

The off-key organ wheezed into *The Wedding March*, and there was my lost self, turning to smile at Emily. She, Clare, was mouthing something and I lip-read the word 'Lovely'. Next to her, Steve, oh so handsome, turning and smiling too. That other Clare – young, uncrushed, undamaged – looked almost beautiful in a violet silk dress, a chiffon stole over her shoulders.

And I was biting my hand and stifling the groan that wanted to burst from under my ribcage as I watched the laughing crowd in the churchyard ignoring the harassed photographer.

A little girl, in a pink dress and angel wings, romped round the gravestones, chased by a boy – my boy – my Toby. He was laughing straight into the camera now, as that other, long-gone, Clare gestured for him to join the family group. With the little girl in tow, he bounced back behind another gravestone, peeping out to shake his head, as the video camera zoomed in. It swayed for a moment over the headstone, the words *In Loving Memory* standing out black against the white marble, then moved to focus on Toby. I pressed the pause button and leant forward on my knees to stroke his laughing face, smoothing his hair with my finger. He'd had it cut specially for the wedding and I remembered for the first time since that morning how tender the strip of pale skin, newly exposed at the back of his neck, had looked in contrast to his tan further down.

I pressed the button to play again, but when Toby stepped from behind the gravestone, I paused it once more. My fingers curled on the screen as if they could hold him, as if, somehow, even now, I could pull him from behind the glass.

How long I stayed like that I don't know, but there was only one thing I could do for Toby and that was to help his brother. I had to face this for Tommy's sake.

The reception was in a marquee in the grounds of Matt's parents' farm, and during the best man's speech the camera scanned the guests again. There was plenty of laughter, although the jokes were pretty lame, but I remembered what Emily had said about people being under stress and watched carefully.

Dad was smiling, but I knew how well he could conceal his emotions. Lorna was nowhere near him, on a table with some people I didn't know, and was looking down at her plate when the camera stopped on them. She must have been aware of it because she looked up, touched her hair, and there was her usual serene expression, but was I imagining it or had there been real misery on her face as she stared at the table? I would have to look back again later, for now I was desperate to get to the end.

Matt was shaking the best man's hand and standing to give his own speech. He was good, not many jokes, but he soon had everyone chuckling with genuine amusement. A glimpse of myself and Steve, both laughing, and another of Dad.

I pressed pause again – there was something in Dad's expression as he watched Matt. Again I told myself it could be nothing, my own suspicions conjuring up something that wasn't there. But I knew Dad and this time he wasn't bothering to hide how he felt. And I was sure that look was one of dislike.

I played the moment back and forth. Matt was saying the usual silly bridegroom things. It wasn't his words that had upset Dad, it was Matt himself.

I watched on. There were glimpses of that other me: the one I hated for what she was about to do, dancing with Steve, dragging a red-faced Toby up for a few uncoordinated turns to the music. And all the time I was smiling, a real smile. I looked happy. So if something had upset me, I was hiding it well.

Now I was sitting with Alice, both of us waving the camera away and looking a bit the worse for wear, although I only had a coffee cup in front of me.

A flash of the trial, here, as I recalled my sister in the witness box, insisting I'd seemed fine and she was sure I'd had nothing alcoholic to drink. The prosecution barrister asked her if most people were drinking all evening. 'Well it was a wedding,' she said, looking at the judge with those big blue eyes. He smiled at her and nodded, I remembered, and it almost made me smile.

'And you'd been drinking yourself?' the barrister pressed on.

'Yes, but just champagne and I was getting a lift back to the hotel.' She had looked so young and vulnerable all alone up there, but she spoke clearly and when he tried to get her to admit she was too drunk to tell what state I was in, she said firmly that she was quite capable. He rephrased and tried again until the judge told him to move on.

When my barrister asked if she thought Steve and I were happy together, she nodded and said, 'Yes, very happy,' turning to the jury as she said it. As she left the witness box she gave me a tiny nod and a tremulous smile.

Here were the older ones, watching the dancing: Lorna, Dad, Uncle Alan, and Aunt Rose. Dad still looked grim. Perhaps he was just tired, but that seemed unlikely, he always loved parties and was a real night owl. This was something I had to look into. Surely other people must have noticed his mood.

The camera seemed to have missed Emily and Matt's departure because the evening was obviously coming to a close. Then a series of camera lurches towards the exit, as people began leaving. Alice went with a young couple who wanted to get away early because of their baby. She couldn't be late either. She had to work at Newcastle General next day. In the end she spent that day and those following in a different hospital, by my bed.

Then, on screen, I saw Lorna, car keys in hand, waving to someone as she waited for the people she was driving back to the hotel.

Another twist of pain as I watched myself covering Toby with a coat while he slept on a pile of cushions. In the background, Steve's slurred voice, saying something silly about yummy mummies, as the camera zoomed in on my backside. A woman speaking then, faint and muffled, obviously asking a question. We both turned to her and my husband's reply was clear enough.

And there it was, the oh-so-simple explanation to one of the questions I'd agonised over all these years. 'Don't worry, Sylvia, you get off. Toby's fast asleep, and it'd be a shame to disturb him. I'd like another drink anyway. Then I'll prise Robert away and Clare can drive us all.'

Oh no, Steve, don't say that. I had a crazy impulse to rewind the thing. To hope that this time he'd change his mind, and take himself and my baby away in the safe car with Aunt Rose's friend Sylvia, who would – this time – deliver them whole and well to the hotel.

So that was why the police had given up trying to make me say I persuaded Steve to stay – the evidence was clear: he made the decision.

The recording rolled onwards to take in the empty marquee and the debris of the day. Aunt Rose, shoeless, wandered from table to table, dropping bits of rubbish into a bin bag and waving the camera away, telling Alan to turn it off now.

But here we were again: Dad, his voice too loud as usual. 'Bye, Alan. Goodnight, Rose.' He looked drunk, which again was unusual for him. He could down a whole bottle of Scotch with no apparent effect.

Steve followed, carrying Toby. Then me, chiffon stole trailing on the floor.

At the exit, Steve stumbled and a woman rushed forward to steady him. One of Toby's legs hung loose, and she tucked it back into Steve's arms, patting his shoulder as she did so. I recognised her too from the trial. She was a friend of Matt's mum, drafted in to help with the clearing up. She confirmed we were the last to leave. Said she had noticed nothing odd about my behaviour, although she looked doubtful when asked if I seemed drunk or drugged and just said she wouldn't know about that.

But now, watching myself, I did know. I was no longer in the frame, but I was certainly nearby. So why had I made no move to help Steve: to protect my son? The answer was in the sound recording – I had laughed – as Steve nearly dropped my child and another woman rushed to save him – I had laughed. A silly, reckless laugh: the kind of laugh I remembered from prison. The one that told us a visitor had managed to smuggle in some dope.

I sat on the floor, hugging my knees and rocking. My mind filled with those images of Toby, playing around the graves, then red-faced and embarrassed as I made him dance with me. And finally, that thin, vulnerable leg, dangling, helplessly, while I laughed my frenetic, junkie's laugh.

I told myself I could at least be sure I never intended to hurt Steve and Toby. It was Steve who wanted to wait and by that time I was obviously too out of it to know I shouldn't be driving.

There were things I needed to look at again, to think about, but still no clue as to when I had taken the stuff, where or who I'd got it from and most of all what had made me want it. And no stir of memory. Nothing I could tell Tom.

I was brought back to myself by a tap on the door. 'Clare, are you in? It's Kieran.' I clutched my knees tighter, hardly daring to breathe until I heard his footsteps on the stairs, then moving about over my head.

Finally I got to my feet, splashed my face with cold water, and took the DVD from the machine, putting it back into its case and telling myself that was enough for today.

When I dialled Alice's number, Tom answered and my heart gave a small skip. 'So what happened?' he said as soon as he heard my voice.

'I found out Mr Hillier knew Jacob Downes, the biker, and I've asked him to contact Jacob for me.' I knew I must let him help me. 'So, Tom, have you got any ideas about what I should ask if I do get to speak to him?'

He was breathing fast. 'Yes, I've been thinking about that. I know it was a quiet road, but we should ask both of them if they're sure they didn't pass any other cars.'

Clever boy. 'Yes, that's just the kind of thing I mean. Maybe you could write out a list of possible questions for me. We've got a whole day together tomorrow so we can talk about it properly then.'

'What about your memory? Did you remember anything?'

'I really feel as if something may be stirring, but it's all very vague and I think I need to let it become a bit clearer before I talk about it. Is that all right with you?'

'Yeah, that's OK. Alice says minds are delicate and we have to give you time.'

'Thanks, Tom. And I'm glad you've been speaking to Alice about all this. We mustn't shut her out.'

'OK.'

When I talked to Alice she asked about Emily.

'She's great. Matt wasn't there so it was just the two of us.'

'And you're OK? Glad you went up there?'

'Oh, yes.' I knew she'd notice the bump on my forehead when she came over so I told her about the accident.

'Oh, Clare, I warned you about that road.'

'I know, but I was tired and thinking of other things.'

'Bet I can guess what things they were. So are you any further forward?'

'Maybe.'

'Have you remembered something?'

'Not really, but I've seen the wedding DVD and Dad didn't look happy at all. Did you notice on the day?'

She was quiet for a moment, obviously thinking. 'I can't say I did, but he was under terrible strain just then, you know that.'

'And what about the end of the evening?'

'Well, it all kind of fizzled out after Emily and Matt left so I can't remember anything much about it.'

'What time did they go?'

'Now you've got me. I think they just disappeared. I know they were flying out first thing next morning so I suppose they left fairly early. Do you know, I can't even remember Emily throwing her bouquet.'

'It isn't on the DVD either so it looks like she didn't do it,' I said. 'But that's odd because I remember talking about it at the hen night, don't you?'

'Yes I do, now you mention it. She promised to throw it to me. I suppose she forgot in all the excitement.'

I wanted to talk about my sense of a real memory coming to life and my theories on the headlights, but I needed time to process all that. I told her I'd seen Hillier and I hoped he'd lead me to Jacob Downes, and left it at that.

'Please be careful,' she said. 'I remember that biker from the trial and I didn't like the look of him at all.'

Chapter Eighteen

When the knock came again, I answered the door.

Kieran was dressed in dark trousers that looked to be part of a business suit, his white shirt was open at the collar, and he'd rolled the sleeves back. He was smiling, head to one side. 'Am I forgiven?'

'Sorry?'

'What an arse you must think I am. There you were, in shock, and first of all I frighten you by letting myself in, and then throw a wobbler when you, quite rightly, tell me to piss off.'

I tried to laugh. 'I didn't tell you to piss off, just … well as you say, I'd had a shock. I was rude. You were only trying to help.'

'OK, let's call it evens shall we? But only if you take me up on my offer of a meal. I've had a bloody awful day in London and I've already started cooking, so if you say no that really will be rude.'

He turned and walked towards the stairs, looking back at me with a lopsided smile. 'And you're quite safe, Nic's already up there. So, see you in five minutes.'

After I'd closed the door on him I leaned my head against it. In the living room the DVD waited, heavy with its burden of pain. If I stayed here I knew I would watch it again and again. Hoping this time it would be different.

*

Kieran's flat smelled of garlic and onions. Nic was sitting on the sofa, a large glass of wine on the table in front of her and Molly asleep in her arms. 'Are you all right?' she said, her face crumpled with concern. 'Kieran told me what happened.'

'I'm fine. Just my own stupid fault.'

'That road is terrible. I tell you getting the buggy up and down there you take your life in your hands.' She stood up, Molly lolling in her arms. 'Here, have a seat. I was just going to put her down on Kieran's bed.'

I was grateful he stayed in the kitchen chopping and frying, while she was gone. Billie Holliday was singing something about heartache in a low voice and, instead of sitting, I wandered round the room – an exact replica of mine, but more cluttered and comfortable. A book shelf sagged in one corner and an untidy desk with a wide screen computer and a large printer stood in another.

Most obvious of all were the photographs on the walls. They all featured people: some close ups of individual faces or figures, but also group studies. Most of the pictures were black and white and the faces were interesting rather than attractive. On one wall, there was a small group of old people, and some of what looked like down and outs sitting around fires on waste ground, or standing in shop doorways. Then a larger collection, evidently taken in hospital wards or hospices.

I was looking at them as he came in with cutlery and a bowl of bread. 'Those are from the book I'm trying to interest a publisher in – no luck so far.'

'They're very good.'

'Thank you, I think so.' He pointed to a small dark man in a dressing gown sitting on a hospital bed. 'That's my dad, just a couple of days before he died. I took that set of pictures in the hospice – wonderful place.' His finger stroked the frame, then he sighed and turned back to the kitchen.

The food was good and Nic chatted non-stop while she demolished at least a bottle of wine, so it was easy just to sit and smile as I resisted the temptation to have more than a couple of glasses myself. Once or twice Kieran caught my eye and I knew I was blushing, and when we'd finished I collected the dishes, saying I would wash up. It hadn't been too bad, but all the same I was glad to be alone in the kitchen.

Molly started to grizzle from the bedroom and I heard Nic say, 'Well that's it. Better get her to her own bed before she wakes up properly.' She poked her head into the kitchen, hanging on the door with one leg raised. 'Bye, Clare, take care.' Then, laughing, she almost overbalanced, 'Whoops, did I drink that much?' Kieran raised his eyebrows at me as he carried Molly through the door.

The sink was still full, there was no way I could leave, but I very much wanted to, not only to avoid being alone with Kieran but because Nicola's drunken stumble had reminded me of the DVD.

Kieran was back within minutes. 'I see you're house-trained,' he said, taking a tea towel to start drying. I tried to relax and to clear my mind of the image of that other Clare – to drag out some casual remark – but it was impossible and the silence grew heavier as the minutes passed. At last, I was able to drain the sink and dry my hands.

Kieran took my waist and turned me to face him. My skin flared at his touch. 'Clare,' he said, 'I need to tell you something.'

I met his eyes and his expression stopped my breath for a moment. Then I forced a laugh. 'What?'

He took my hand. 'Come and sit down.' I let him lead me to the sofa and, as I took in what he was saying, I slumped back. 'I know who you are,' he said. 'I didn't at first. Just thought you looked familiar. But it niggled at me and I couldn't let it go. Must have remembered your face from the papers … '

As I stood, he caught my elbow. 'No, Clare, don't go. I'm sorry, that was clumsy. I just wanted you to know it doesn't matter.'

I pulled free and turned away, folding my arms across my chest. 'If it doesn't matter, why did you say anything?'

'Because I want to be honest with you. And I'm hoping you can be honest with me.'

I walked over to the window, gripping the sill until my fingers hurt. The darkening sky was streaked with orange and purple. I couldn't keep the bitterness out of my voice. What a fool I'd been to think I could try to fit in with normal people again. 'So you know I'm a criminal and an ex-junkie? Then how can you want anything to do with me?'

His voice was soft. 'Because that's not you. Maybe if I hadn't got to know you first I would have … '

'Would have what?'

'Well, made assumptions about the kind of person you might be, I suppose, but I've seen what you're like and … '

I cut him off. 'Have you told Nicola?'

'Of course not. Oh, Clare.' He was behind me now and I turned to face him. His voice was thick. 'It's come out all wrong. I'm not going to tell anyone, and I won't mention it again if that's what you want. But I thought maybe you'd be glad I know, and that it doesn't make any difference to me.'

I knew I should stop this now. Go down to that dreary flat and, tomorrow, find somewhere else to live. Instead, I stared at his white shirt, at the place under his shoulder where I longed to rest my head.

He was still talking. 'I realise this isn't the best time for you to start seeing someone, but I like you very much. We don't need to rush into anything, but … '

I was suddenly too tired to hold out any longer and, when I leaned into his arms, his shoulder was as comforting as I knew it would be.

Kieran held me, saying nothing. But I could feel his heart beating faster and my own drumming urgently, too. Before it was too late, I pushed myself away and went to sit on the sofa. Kieran held my hand in both of his and I found myself telling him everything. It felt wonderful, talking to someone who had no connection with any of it and who, for some reason I knew, I could trust not to judge me.

'But I need to think about Tom and only Tom. I can't let myself get too close to anyone else.'

He laid his warm hand on my knee and I was just able to stop myself leaning into his arms again. 'I understand that, Clare.'

'I should go down.'

He came to the door with me and kissed me very gently. 'It's not my place to tell you how to deal with your son, but I was a thirteen-year-old boy once and I think you can trust him to understand. Whatever the truth turns out to be.'

My bruises, and the thought of what had happened with Kieran, kept me from sleeping well, but I couldn't be unhappy because I was going to spend the whole next day with Tom. I got up before seven and made some coffee and toast to eat as I watched the TV news.

I was still aching, so I ran a bath and soaked in it for a long while. The warm water was soothing and I let my mind play with fantasies of my future with Tom. The little house we would live in, how I would let him decorate his own bedroom and have his friends over. But when I started to visualise the garden, big enough for him to kick a ball about, but with space for me to grow some vegetables, I stopped. *Oh Steve!* We always joked that if any of his clients ever saw our own garden they'd be horrified because he never had time to tend it.

And I saw him handing me a glass of wine as we sat, amid the scrubby grass, in two old deckchairs I'd found in the shed when we first moved there. The twins were babies, asleep in their pram next to us and Steve was looking at me, head to one side, his grey eyes crinkling at the corners.

'What?' I said.

'Just that you're gorgeous and so are our sons.' Then he leaned over and kissed me, his hands twined into my hair.

I could almost feel his fingers on my scalp as I lay back in the bath and he seemed closer than he had for so many years. The tears were hot on my cheeks and I pressed my hand to where my heart must be – where the pain throbbed white-hot. One enormous sob burst from me with such force it sounded more like the cry of a wounded animal. It frightened me and I moved my fingers to my mouth, holding it shut so it wouldn't make that noise again.

And, slowly, slowly, the pain began to ease. Steve was gone, but I knew he would want Tom to be with me. For us to make a new life together.

I was in my dressing gown, a towel wrapped round my hair, when I heard the tap on my door. It was too early for Tom and Alice, and no one had buzzed the main door, so it could only be Kieran or Nic.

I wiped the steam from the mirror. My face was blotchy from the hot bath, and for a moment I hesitated. But I couldn't worry about that. I didn't want Kieran to be here when Alice and Tom arrived.

When I opened the door, the ground shifted beneath me.

Two uniforms filled the space: a young fresh-faced policeman and a bulky WPC, a spit for one of the worst screws on my last block in prison. I swayed and clutched the dressing gown around me, very conscious of my naked legs and feet. A million thoughts, all of them horrible, fought with each other in my head. They'd come to arrest me, to take me back to prison. Or worse, it was something to do with Tom. *Oh God Tom was hurt.*

'Mrs Glazier?'

I managed to nod, dislodging the towel on my head, so it flapped over one eye.

'We're here about your accident.'

'What?' I pushed the towel back, goggling at him helplessly, until I saw the woman's eyes on my legs, taking in the bruises. 'Oh you mean the other night? It was nothing, my fault. I didn't look.' I knew I was babbling, but I couldn't stop. 'I didn't report it.'

The young man looked at me, and I squirmed again, aware of my naked body under the thin covering. He flipped open a notepad. 'We've had a report, apparently from you.'

'No, no it wasn't me. I'm sorry. There's been a mistake.'

The woman spoke, now, more kindly. 'They do speed down that road and if you were hit, we really should look into it. Don't forget, there's kiddies live round here.'

'Yes, but it was my fault and I don't want to take it any further. I'm sorry.'

The man closed the pad with a click, and moved his hand to the radio on his shoulder. 'Well, if you're sure, Mrs Glazier …'

They glanced at each other, as if considering saying more, but then the woman shrugged and they turned away. I closed the door, shaking and weak, waiting for what seemed an age until I finally heard the front door open and close and watched them stride off down the path.

I dressed quickly, half-fearing they would come back, my bruises throbbing with renewed viciousness. Then knocked on Nic's door.

'Hi there, babe,' she said. 'Come in and have a cuppa.'

I made an effort to keep my voice even. 'Sorry, I can't stop, I'm expecting visitors. But I've just had the police here about my accident. You didn't call them, did you?'

'Not me, babe, wouldn't go sticking my nose in like that. I let them in, that's all. Went to the front door to collect Kieran's paper before the boy shoved it through the letter box. Molly's asleep and it makes such a racket it always wakes her up. The cops were coming up the path so I held the main door open for them. When they said they wanted to speak to you I guessed it was about the accident. Thought *you'd* called them. Have you asked Kieran if it was him?'

It was the last thing I wanted to do, but she held out a plastic bag with the *Observer* inside. 'You can give this to him while you're up there.'

I couldn't think of a way to refuse and she watched as I started up the stairs. 'Thanks, Nic, sorry to have bothered you,' I said, but she stayed where she was, smiling and leaning on the side of her door.

I was almost relieved when there was no answer from Kieran and I left the paper outside his flat. When I came down Nic was gone, but I heard my own phone ringing. I ran inside and grabbed the handset without looking at the caller id. 'Alice?'

'No sweetheart, it's me, Lorna.'

I took a breath. 'Hello.'

'I've been thinking hard about your email, doing some heart-searching, and I've decided there's something I have to tell you.'

'What?'

'I can't talk about it on the phone. My knee's very bad, so could you come and see me? I'm having the op this week – what about visiting me in hospital?'

'All right, I'll do that of course. But surely you can tell me whatever it is now. Is it about the arthritis drug situation?'

'No, but … '

'Lorna, please.'

'Well there *was* more to that than I said, although I don't think it could possibly have any bearing on what happened to you.'

I sat on the sofa, softening my voice. 'I'd like to know anyway because it's what Tom seems to have focused on.'

There was silence for a moment, then she said, 'I'm sorry to say this about Dr Penrose, when he's dead and can't defend himself, but he was incompetent and always making mistakes. Your father sacked him and that's why he was so determined to get his revenge. They could never be sure about it, but the mistakes with the data were probably his errors.'

'So there were mistakes.'

'Your father thought so, yes. But that didn't mean the pills were dangerous.'

I let that go. 'What about Mr Gardner, the families' rep? What do you know about him?'

'Well, he and your dad reached some kind of agreement and he went away very happily, if I can put it like that.'

'Dad bribed him you mean.'

'I honestly don't know, but there was a lot of bad feeling from some of the other families. Mr Gardner had apparently persuaded them to settle and later they began to think they could have got much more.'

'So Tom's theory does have legs. There were plenty of people who were angry with Dad. And I don't blame them.'

'They were mainly upset with Mr Gardner, not your father. And Robert was only following his lawyer's advice and doing what was best for the company.'

'And for himself.'

Her voice was cool. 'For his family too, Clare. As he always did. And you weren't there so you can't understand the kind of stress he was under. There was an enormous amount of bad feeling in the firm. And it was just about the time when the Americans were trying to take us over. People were in fear for their jobs. Rightly so as it turned out.'

'You said Dad was close to Matt, but were there problems between them at that time?'

'If there were I didn't know about them. To be honest, I was wrapped up in my own worries. Robert and I were no longer that close and, in any case, he had never confided in me about work issues that didn't concern my job.'

We were silent for a while and her voice was gruff when she spoke again. 'But that's not what I need to tell you. It's something much more important.'

A thump inside. 'What is it?'

'Clare, I really can't, not on the phone. Please come and see me. I'm having the op on Tuesday, so any day from Wednesday onwards.'

'Give me the address, then, and I'll come on Thursday.'

I put down the phone knowing it would be agony to wait because I was sure she was going to answer one of my most urgent questions: who I got the amphetamines from.

*

169

Alice was laughing as she and Tom came into the flat. 'I hope you're prepared. He says you're going to let him choose whatever he wants to do and he's already wearing his swimming trunks.'

He was in a white T-shirt and long blue cotton shorts and looked taller today, dumping his rucksack on the sofa as he made his way into the kitchen and threw open the fridge. 'Oh good, you got some cokes.'

I swallowed and bit my lip. He was beginning to treat the flat as his home.

Alice pulled me back into the hall. 'You sure you're OK? You don't look all that well to me. I could hang around for a bit if you like.' When I told her I was fine, she said, 'Have you got a swimsuit?'

'No, but it's only five minutes to the shops. We can go there first.'

She smiled. 'Just as well I thought of it then.' She opened her large handbag and pulled out a plastic carrier. 'Got you this at the supermarket yesterday, just a cheap thing, but it'll do for today.'

For some reason I wanted to cry. 'Oh, thank you.'

She waved her hand in front of her face, her eyes glistening. 'Shut up,' she said. 'I just grabbed it when I was shopping.'

I put my arms round her and for a moment we stood like that. She smelled lovely: of clean hair and warm skin with just a hint of floral perfume. And I whispered the words I should have said so many times before. 'Thank you, Alice, for everything.'

She stroked my hair then pulled away. 'Well, if you want to make me happy, go and have a lovely day with your son. You both deserve it.'

I couldn't meet her eyes, shaken by my own rush of emotions. It seemed as if something really was thawing inside and I didn't know whether to be glad or frightened. I managed to ask what she was planning for her own day. 'Lunch with Gareth.' She laughed and gave my arm a little push. 'And before you say it, we're still not serious.'

When she'd gone, I went to the bedroom and slipped on the swimsuit, covering up again before I could get anxious about the bruises on my legs.

Tom was on the sofa and when I sat beside him he gulped down the rest of his drink and began poking in the side pocket of his rucksack. 'I've got some questions you could ask Jacob Downes and Mr Hillier.'

'That's great, but what say we look at them on the beach? The weather's set to cloud over later on and we don't want to waste the sunshine.' When he looked sideways at me, his mouth turned down, eyebrows pulled together, I added, 'Besides, there's something I want to tell you first. Something I just heard about from Lorna. We can talk as we walk down.'

As we stepped through the main door, Tom stopped to retie his laces, and Nic opened her kitchen window. Her eyes moved from him to me, then to the towel under my arm. 'Off to the beach, Clare?'

I smiled, she'd obviously been on the lookout since Alice and Tom arrived. 'While the sun lasts. This is my son, Tom, by the way.'

If she was surprised she hid it well. 'Hello there, Tom, I'm Nicola, Nic.'

Tom gave her a little wave and outside the gate he turned to me, his eyes sharp with interest. 'What did Lorna tell you, then?'

I explained that Lorna thought it was possible that Dr Penrose himself had been responsible for any mistakes in the report. 'Your granddad had to sack him, so that was probably why he wanted to cause trouble.'

'But didn't Granddad tell anyone about the mistakes?'

A vision of my dad smiling as we sat in the garden of Beldon House one weekend, watching the twins playing with the miniature cricket bats he'd bought them. He wasn't one to show emotion, but I remembered him rubbing my shoulder and saying, 'They're great lads, Clare.' He really loved them and they had adored him.

'I don't know, but whatever he did I'm sure he had good reasons. And he paid the bereaved families compensation, even though nothing was proved.'

He turned to face me, bouncing along backwards so fast I was frightened he'd collide with a lamppost. I shook my head, 'Please, Tom, be careful.'

He twisted back round, panting as he spoke. 'But people were still angry with him, I've read about that.'

A deep breath. *Careful, careful.* 'Some of them thought they didn't get enough I suppose.'

He turned towards me again, stopping dead. 'You don't think he cheated them, do you?'

This was awful. 'No, I don't, at least not intentionally. And remember he had the business to think about too. All those people who worked for the firm. It must have been really difficult to know what to do.'

He started moving again. 'Yeah, but if they thought he cheated that would make them really angry with him.'

Chapter Nineteen

The beach wasn't too crowded and when we spread towels on the shingle, Tom looked towards the calm, blue sea then back at me, his face bright. I said, 'Come on let's have a dip first, plenty of time to look at your notes after that.'

He was wearing his swimming trunks under his clothes and he wrapped a towel round as he pulled off his shorts, and sat down with it still covering him. I felt suddenly embarrassed too. 'Don't wait for me. You've got swim shoes on, but it'll take me ages to hobble down there with all those stones.'

He grinned and leapt up and I watched as he raced down the beach and splashed into the water. Sparkles leapt around him, gilding his shining brown skin, and a lump came into my throat: he was going to be handsome like his father. I pressed my fingers to my lips at the thought of Steve, who would always be young, who was younger now than I was. And of my little Toby who would never grow tall and strong like his twin.

I shook my head and started to pull off my clothes as an elderly couple came to sit nearby. I hid my bag under a towel, wondering if I dare leave it behind and sensing that the woman was watching me. Maybe I wouldn't swim after all.

The woman's voice made me jump. 'It's all right, dear, we'll keep an eye on your things.' For a moment that voice came into my head – *don't trust anyone* – but when I looked at her she was smiling such a kind smile that I was able to smile back and thank her. Then I staggered down towards Tom, forcing myself to ignore the impulse that told me to turn back.

After the first cold shock, the sea felt warm and I lifted my feet off the sharp shingle and swam over to Tom. It was wonderful to stretch through the water and we were soon matching stroke for stroke: my aches and pains seeming to disappear. But I was out of condition and it wasn't long before I was treading water and waving to Tom that I'd had enough.

When he came out, he was shivering and hopping from foot to foot as he held a towel around him and dripped icy water. 'I'm starving,' he said.

'Fish and chips then?'

He towelled his hair and more cold drops flew at me. 'Yes, please.'

'Shall we have them here or go to a café?'

'Café, please. Then we can talk about the questions for those witnesses.'

We found a little place across the road from the beach and sat upstairs overlooking the crazy golf course and the boating pool where pedallos, in the shape of swans, sailed around. As we sat waiting for our plates of cod and chips, Tom pulled out his notes and handed them across to me, taking a huge gulp from his glass of cold milk as he did so. 'Mark helped me with them,' he said, rubbing his mouth with the back of his hand.

It was a set of bullet points, neatly printed:

- As you approached the accident site did you see or hear any other vehicle (even if it was some distance away)?
- Did you notice anything at all that you didn't tell the police?
- Did the police ask you to miss out any of your evidence?
- Was there anything unusual about the way the other witness acted?

- Can you remember anything else at all that might trigger Mrs Glazier's memory?

I moved the paper to one side as the waitress brought our food. Tom cut a huge piece from his fish and forked it up with a pile of chips.

'These are very good points,' I said. 'But the one asking about the other witness might be a bit awkward.'

He spoke with his mouth full, but this wasn't the time to say anything about that. 'I know, but we'll only ask when we get them on their own.'

'OK, it should be all right, unless we have to pass the questions to Jacob via Mr Hillier.'

He ate on steadily, his face flushing and I waited. Had I upset him again, I was so clumsy with him still. But then he looked up. 'Yeah, we need to try to talk to Downes himself. Mark and me have searched for him on Facebook, Twitter, and everywhere else we can think of, but we haven't found him yet.'

He put down his knife and fork and rubbed his palms on his T-shirt before pulling his bag onto his lap and fumbling in the side pocket. His face was very red. 'I've written this for Mr Hillier.'

Dear Mr Hillier,

My name is Tom Glazier and it was my dad and brother (and my grandfather) who were killed in the accident. Now there's only me and my mum (Clare Glazier) and we both want to know more about the accident so we can move on. Please, Mr Hillier, will you try to think of anything that might help Mrs Glazier get her memory back and please will you also speak to Jacob Downes for us and ask him if he'll talk to her too.

I would be very grateful for your help with this.

Yours sincerely,
Tom Glazier

It seemed as if hours had gone by when I felt Tom's hand tap mine. 'Mum?'

His face was still red and he looked away as I raised my eyes to him. 'Oh, Tom, this is wonderful.'

He picked up his fork and began poking at his chips. 'Do you think it's all right then?'

'Of course. I would never have thought of anything like this.'

His smile was huge and he pushed another forkful of fish and chips into his mouth chewing as if he was still starving. 'Good, we can send it right away then.'

I needed to think about it and I was glad he seemed satisfied with my silence. He pushed his plate away. 'What shall we do now?'

'Whatever you like. The aquarium, Smugglers' Caves, amusement arcade.'

'The arcade, and then maybe the funfair, if that's OK. I brought some money.'

A clench from deep inside, 'No, I want to treat you today.'

At the amusements I gave him a handful of coins and he dived straight into the bubbling turmoil of electric noises and flickering lights. I called, 'Meet you at the door,' as I lost sight of him. I knew there was no reason to be anxious, but the tinny music battering at my ears and the crowding bodies made me flinch into myself and I began to feel sick.

I pushed my way to the door and sat outside on the step, breathing deeply.

'You can't sit there, madam.'

I was on my feet, wrenching my back, before he'd finished speaking, so familiar was that tone from my time inside. It isn't the pettiness of prison rules as much as the fact that, for some reason, you never know precisely what they are; never know how to avoid breaking them.

So I found myself looking at him with the kind of childish rebelliousness you relearn inside: the only way to assert some kind of individuality. I said nothing, of course, just stared at him until he slouched away, looking back at me to show he'd got my number. Oh yes, I could see him as a prison warder.

On the beach I'd imagined I was nearly back to thinking like a normal person, *what a fool*. I was damaged in so many ways that I wondered if I could ever really heal.

'Mum? You OK?'

'I'm fine. A bit hot that's all.'

'I won £4 on the horse race game.'

'Great, well let's go and see what you can spend it on.'

We walked to the little funfair, stopping en-route to spend Tom's winnings on comics and a bag of sweets. At the fair he insisted we go on the Big Apple – surely the tiniest big dipper in the world. As we bounced along I laughed and clutched at my stomach and Tom patted my back. 'It's all right, Mum.' My eyes misted as I gripped his arm, wanting to squeeze it so hard we would never be separated again.

He was content to go on the next few rides alone and bought a candyfloss as we walked away.

At the door to the flat I heard the phone ringing, but the answerphone cut in before I could get the key in the lock. The voice was very clear.

'Hello, Clare, it's Kieran. I'm not sure how we left it last night, but I just wanted you to know I'm thinking of you. I've had to come to Lancaster to be with my mum. She's been taken ill. I should be back soon and maybe we can talk then.'

Tom looked at me. 'Kieran? Is that the man who brought me to your shop?'

I headed straight to the kitchen to avoid his gaze. 'Yes, it's my neighbour.'

'He's nice,' he said. Then, 'Can I turn on your laptop?'

I brought my coffee out and stood behind him as he whizzed around showing me that Jacob Downes was not on any of the normal social media sites.

He'd put his list of questions and the personal letter to Mr Hillier on the little table. I said, 'We don't want to push too hard yet, so I think I should write him a letter too and send it with yours. Keep the questions until they agree to talk to me.'

'OK.' I could see he was distracted, looking at the bookcase next to the desk. 'What's this?' He held up the DVD of Emily's wedding.

Damn, I hadn't thought to hide it. For a moment I considered lying to him, saying it belonged to a friend, but I couldn't. 'It's Emily and Matt's.'

'Can I watch it?'

He was looking at me very hard and I felt my fingers curl as I resisted the urge to snatch the thing away. *Be careful.* 'Come and sit down, will you?'

I moved to the sofa, praying he would follow me. He did, sitting in one corner, his fingers drumming lightly on the DVD case. He asked, 'Have you seen it?'

'Yes. I didn't want to look at it, but I had to, in case it might jog my memory.'

'And did it help?' He still wasn't looking at me and his voice was tight.

'Not really, but you never know, it might take a while. Might have started something moving.'

'Did you see yourself on it?' He was making circles with his index finger on the DVD case, his eyes focused on the imaginary patterns.

My heart gave a huge thump. I could see where he was going with this and I'd promised to be honest with him. 'Yes I did and at the end of the evening, just before we left, I do think there was something wrong with me.'

'Did you look drugged?'

I laid my hand over his so that his finger stopped circling, but he wouldn't look at me. His jaw and neck were flushed pink.

'It did look like that,' I said. 'But there was nothing on the film to help me work out when it happened.'

He glanced quickly at me then away again. 'If you let me see the DVD I might spot something you haven't.'

I bit my lip, *what to say*? 'Yes you might, but I really don't think it would be good for you, Tom. Can you leave it for a bit and we'll talk again later on?'

He was silent and I held my breath, expecting another outburst, but then, still without looking at me, he handed me the DVD. 'All right.'

It was best to leave it now. I put the DVD back on the shelf and went towards the kitchen. 'You're probably not hungry after that big lunch. I don't suppose you could force down a sausage sandwich and a piece of chocolate cake could you?'

He didn't answer, but at least he followed me into the kitchen and when I handed him the cake box he found plates and a knife in the cupboard. After that, I gave him a series of little jobs to do, chatting all the time as if nothing had happened. Eventually, his answers became more than monosyllables.

Then, as we sat at the kitchen table, him tucking into a sandwich and me drinking tea, he asked, 'When are you going to get that put-you-up so I can stay the night?'

'Soon. Let's talk to Alice about arranging the first sleepover, shall we? And I'll make sure I've got everything sorted by then.'

'OK.' And his smile made my heart sing.

After Tom and Alice had gone I wrote to Mr Hillier:

I'm enclosing a note from my son, too. He was keen for you to hear from him personally.

Then I begged him to try to arrange for me to talk to Jacob Downes.

All I want is anything that might help me regain my memory. Whatever you tell me, or he tells me, I'll keep to myself. I definitely won't talk to the police again. I've served

my time and I don't want anyone else to suffer. But please,
please, help me if you can.

I went straight out to post it and came back to watch the DVD
again. I couldn't believe it would be a good idea to let Tom see it
and I certainly couldn't do that without talking to Alice about it
first. For now I had to hope he'd forget it.

There didn't seem to be much more to learn about Steve, or
myself, and looking at Toby was so painful that I concentrated on
the others. After what Emily and Lorna had said about the stress
people were under I could see that the whole event was not the
totally happy occasion I'd always imagined.

Alice seemed very tired and Lorna depressed. Matt and Emily
looked suitably dazed at the centre of all the attention, but I was
sure now that there was something wrong about the way Dad
looked at Matt. Lorna had said they were close, but if their relationship had soured I needed to find out why.

When I took the DVD from the player I hesitated. Although I
didn't really think Tom would forget about it, at least there was
no reason to leave it where he might spot it again. So I put it in
the bedroom drawer with his folder, the photo albums, and the
baby shoes.

When the phone shrilled, I jumped, but let it run on to the
answer system. '*Still not there, baby girl. Well never mind ...*'

I answered before she could ring off. 'Ruby, oh God, it's lovely
to hear your voice. How's it going?'

She told me what I already knew: she was just hanging on in
there. 'If I keep my nose clean, and I'm going to, I'll get through
all right. But what about you? It's not all sunshine, I can tell. So
what's up?'

Very quickly, conscious of the inevitable queue waiting behind
her to use the phone, I told her as much as I could. A couple of
times she sighed and I knew she was thinking what a mess I'd
made of it all. 'I thought you promised to get on with your life,'

she said, when I stuttered to a halt. 'I should really tell ya just to leave it alone, but it sounds as if it's too late for that now.' A pause where I could hear her breathing. 'And you did say you'd do anything to get Tom back. So if this is what he needs I guess you got to finish what you started.'

I was desperate to find out what Lorna wanted to tell me, but she had asked me to come in the afternoon, so I decided to use the morning to try to see Matt. Lorna's hospital was in central London, but Parnell Pharmaceuticals' offices, and their lab complex, were in the south east suburbs, in Orpington. It had been an easy commute for Dad from Wadhurst and was on the train line from Hastings, too. I could get off the train there en-route to see Lorna. The chances were Matt wouldn't be in the office today, but it was worth a try, and I didn't want to call ahead to warn him.

The walk from the station was difficult. It was a lovely day, but it reminded me so much of coming here over the years and especially of the summer I spent working with Lorna. When I met and fell in love with Steve.

The office was one of the better '60s designs: a long low building with lots of glass. As the architect had no doubt intended, it resembled an expensive private clinic. The discreet Parnell Pharmaceuticals' signs I remembered had been replaced by bigger and more numerous ones reading, Global Meds: the U.S. conglomerate that had been Dad's rival for years. He had fought the takeover, but first the scandal and then his death meant it became inevitable.

As I reached the gates I felt a pang, not because of the signs, but because Steve's lovely landscaping, which had once stretched out in front of the building, had been replaced by a second, large car park.

Inside, things were more plush than I remembered, with a dark blue carpet and matching chairs dotted around small glass tables. The glossy reception desk was larger too, more like something from a top hotel. The girl behind it was unfamiliar and showed no sign of recognising me. When I asked to see Matt Bradshaw she raised her eyebrows. 'Do you have an appointment?'

'Not exactly, but please let him know Clare Glazier is here. I can wait, if he's busy.'

With eyebrows still raised she picked up the phone. 'Please take a seat.' I wandered towards the door that used to lead to the executives' offices, feeling her eyes on my back, but she called out, 'He'll be with you in a moment.'

It was only a matter of seconds before the door opened and Matt came out, looking every inch the corporate man in his striped shirt, and blue tie. His smile was the same, though, and he seemed genuinely pleased to see me, grabbing me into the familiar bear hug. 'Clare, this is a surprise, but you couldn't have timed it better. I've just had a meeting cancelled and I need an excuse to avoid the paperwork.'

He led me through the door and along the corridor. His office was opposite the one Dad used to have, with new furniture, but otherwise just like Dad's. 'Come in, come in.' He pointed to a black leather sofa and opened a door to call through, 'Sandy, can you bring us a couple of coffees, please.' He grinned back at me. 'And make one of them very strong.'

He sat on the armchair opposite, his long legs stretched out. 'I was really sorry to miss you in Cumbria, but I'm guessing this isn't just a social visit.'

'Did Emily tell you what I said?'

'That you want to find out everything you can about the situation here at the time of the accident? Yes, she did.' His secretary came through with the coffee and he paused, smiling and thanking her, before turning to me again.

'She called it probing the wound,' I said. 'And it must seem like that to you but, I'm sorry, Matt, I have to do it.'

He sighed and picked up his coffee cup. 'All that stuff about total honesty and facing facts has always seemed overrated to me, and I can still remember the way people were after the accident. It was awful, Clare, do you really need to keep reminding them?'

As I went to speak, he held up his hand. 'Oh I know it was dreadful for you and I can't begin to imagine how it's affected Tom. But Emily was devastated too and so were her parents. And Emily thinks Alice has only begun to recover properly in the last couple of years. At the beginning we worried she wouldn't get through it.'

'And I suppose you think I'm too wrapped up in myself to care about the rest of you?'

He gave me a gentle smile. 'It would be understandable if you were.' He seemed to be waiting for me to speak, but when I didn't he shook his head. 'OK, you win, I know you're trying to do what's right for Tom. So ask away and I'll answer if I can.'

I took a long drink of my coffee, put down the cup, and forced myself to meet his eyes. 'First I should tell you, I've seen the DVD of your wedding. I borrowed it when I was at your house.'

'Emily didn't mention it.'

'That's because I took it without telling her.'

Another headshake and the hint of a smile, but this time it was grim rather than gentle. 'I see. Well, neither of us has ever looked at it. The police had it for a while and when they finally gave it back to us we couldn't bring ourselves to watch. So did it help?'

I didn't blame him for being angry. 'It confirmed that I was high when I left the reception, but seemed perfectly happy most of the day, which was only what I expected. There are other things, though, little things that might be important, and I need to look at them again.'

He carried on drinking his coffee, his eyes fixed on my face. I spoke carefully, making sure I said it the way I'd planned, making it sound more definite than it was. 'Something I did notice was the tension between you and Dad. What happened?'

He stood and walked over to sit on the front of his desk, hands in his pockets. After a couple of minutes he raised his shoulders and let them fall again on a gusty breath. 'It was a bad time here – you know that already. I'd always got on well with Robert and he was very pleased about Emily and me. But I saw what was happening with Dr Penrose, not to mention those poor devils affected by Briomab, and their families. I wasn't supposed to do it, but I checked Penrose's results and I was sure he was right. The final report had been altered.'

'So did you tell Dad?'

'Tried to, but he wouldn't listen.' He paced back to me. 'And I was a fucking coward, Clare, and did nothing. Let poor old Penrose go it alone and get shafted.' He sat opposite again, leaning forward with his hands clasped on his knees. 'Then I found out about the huge payment to Gardner, the families' rep, and I went to see your dad again. Same story, he told me I'd got it all wrong. Said it was all a pack of lies that Global was spreading to discredit the firm.'

'What did you do?'

'Nothing, chickened out yet again.' He leaned back, scrubbing at his face so that red blotches showed through the tan. 'But that was when Global offered me a job. I think Robert found out and assumed I'd been having talks with them all along. He thought I was going to get out, then shoot my mouth off.'

'Were you?'

'Honestly? I didn't know what to do. And then, of course, there was the accident.'

'So you're saying Dad was corrupt?'

'I'm sure he didn't think of it like that. He was fighting for the firm. I've been in the business world long enough to understand that sometimes you do have to be ruthless. But I was still just an idealistic young chemist in those days. I went into this work to help people, not to make money.'

I sat for a moment, until Matt moved beside me on the sofa. 'And, you know, I still don't really understand commerce, or like what it does to people. Despite all this,' he waved a hand to take in the spacious office, 'like I told you, I'm trying to get out.'

But he had certainly done well as a result of the takeover. 'Global didn't keep on too many Parnell staff, did they?'

'And there were plenty of the old guard who called me a traitor, but after what I'd seen, what I suspected, I felt no loyalty to Parnell. So I make no apologies for that.'

Lorna's hospital was a private place and her room looked out onto grass and trees. She was propped up in bed with one leg heavily bandaged. As the nurse showed me in, she held out her hands to me, her smile hesitant, 'Hello, Clare, my love. Sorry, I can't get up.'

I stayed at a distance. 'How are you?'

Her hands fell back into her lap. 'Pretty well, considering. They say I'm making good progress.'

I moved to look out of the window. I had been tempted to press Matt again about who might have had amphetamines at the wedding, but after his reaction last time it seemed pointless. And in any case that must be what Lorna wanted to tell me.

I turned to her and she cleared her throat. 'Please, Clare, I need to know if we're still friends.'

I sat on the chair next to the bed and looked into her dark eyes. This was still my dear, dear Lorna and who was I to judge her? I smiled, 'Of course we are.' My voice had trembled and when I touched her hand she gripped mine and closed her eyes. I did the same and we sat for a while, the squeaks from a trolley passing in the corridor outside the only sounds.

I cleared my throat. My stomach was churning because what she had to tell me must be something big. I had to make it easy for her to be completely honest. 'Lorna, I think I know what you're going to say. It's about how I might have got the drugs, isn't it? But please don't worry, I won't get angry and I won't start accusing anyone. I just need to know. Emily said she thought there were people there who might be self-medicating and I could easily have pinched the stuff. If that's the case then they wouldn't be to blame.'

She glanced away from me, then back with a shake of her head. 'You'll have to ask her about that.'

'So she never said anything to you?'

Lorna shifted and winced, her hand coming up to smooth her hair in that familiar gesture. 'She did tell me something similar after the trial. She had an idea who might have had amphetamines at the reception. I think she tried to raise it with you when she visited the prison, but you wouldn't listen.'

I couldn't remember it, but then I'd been very angry with Emily in those early days because she seemed to be trying to persuade me to accept my guilt and I was still convinced there must be some other explanation.

Lorna took a deep breath. 'But that isn't why I asked you to come.' She pointed to a notepad and pen on the little table beside the bed. 'I was going to write to you, but how to explain something like this in a letter?'

I was scared now. 'What is it then? Something to do with Dad?'

She folded her hands under her chin as if in prayer. 'You know about Robert and me already. We were in love for so many years, but it petered out, and when your mother died it was long over. But we were still close and he knew how much I loved you and Alice, so we often talked about you.' She twisted her fingers together. 'Oh dear, this is so difficult and I'm still not sure I should be telling you.'

'Lorna, please, what is it?'

She took a shuddering breath. 'There's no way to make this easy, so I'll just say it.'

I looked into her eyes and the Earth stopped turning.

'Clare, my love,' she said. 'You were, you are, your father's real daughter.'

The world rocked, and I think I let out some kind of cry. The silence that followed her words was denser than any silence I'd known. It was as if I had been struck deaf and all I could do was stare at her.

The only thing that made sense at this moment was her smile – such a tender smile.

'So you? You're … '

She shook her head. 'Oh no, my darling, I wish so much I could say I was your mother, but, I'm not. I didn't even know about it till he told me the last time we spoke properly.'

I fumbled for my bag, pulling out a bottle of water and swilling the warm liquid down my bone dry throat. Then I began to pace the little room, knocking my thigh on the end of the high bed. It hurt one of my old bruises and I was glad of the pain. 'So my mother *was* Romanian?'

There was the ghost of a laugh in her voice. 'I doubt it, but I don't think she was from this country. He said he met her at a conference in Italy and they used to get together abroad whenever they could. She died, I'm afraid, and Robert felt he should take you on. The Romanian story was for your mum, for Elizabeth's benefit.'

'And to hide it from everyone else.'

'Yes, I suppose so. But, Clare, he loved you. And he told me he loved this woman – your mother – too.'

'Why didn't he tell me then, when Mum died?'

'I don't know. I suppose it was difficult after so long, but he was going to tell you some time over the wedding weekend. I have no idea why he decided to do it just then either. Maybe it was that heart scare he had.'

'And you've never thought to say anything to me or Alice during the past five years?'

'Of course, I've thought about it, but I couldn't because, you see, I've always wondered if he *did* tell you, and that was what sent you over the edge that night.'

A cold stillness came over me as her words penetrated and I saw what this meant. It was the answer to the question that had tortured me all these years. The thing that had been so shocking, so world shattering, that it could have turned me back into the angry teenager I had once been.

Lorna's voice cut through my frozen brain. 'You said you needed to know everything.'

All I could do was whisper, 'Yes, I did.'

187

'Maybe I should have spoken up before, but it wasn't my secret to tell and I had no idea what damage it might do.'

I could hear her words, but there was a buzzing in my head, like a bad radio signal. 'And I had the impression he was going to tell Alice first,' she said. 'Afterwards, after the trial, I talked to her, trying to give her a chance to say if she did know, but it seemed obvious she didn't, so I guessed he'd changed his mind and I felt I had to respect that.'

We sat in silence for a while then Lorna reached for my hand and squeezed it. 'Did I do the right thing in telling you?'

'Yes,' I could only whisper the word because it hurt so much. 'It could explain everything.'

'But remember, we don't know if he did tell you.'

I wanted to scream at her, but I wasn't sure whether it was to beg her to take it back – to unsay it – or to ask her why, oh why, she hadn't said something sooner.

'Clare my love, I won't stop thinking about that night and the days leading up to it. If I can remember anything at all that might give you something more positive, I'll let you know. I promise.'

It was a pointless promise. I guessed we both knew that. She'd supplied the missing piece, the reason I'd been searching for, the shattering news that could have sent me in search of chemical comfort. And nothing could change that.

I leaned over to kiss her as I said goodbye and she clutched at my hands and held them, looking deep into my eyes so I couldn't turn away. 'Goodbye, my darling. I hope I've done the right thing.' I could only nod.

When I turned at the door she was leaning back in bed, still watching me, and I wanted nothing more than to run into her arms: to have her say everything would be all right, the way she always used to.

I was hardly aware of travelling back to Hastings, but somehow I got there. When I came out of the station I couldn't bear to go back to the flat, but I needed somewhere to sit and think.

I remembered the little café perched on the cliff edge of the West Hill. The climb would take more energy than I had today but this hill, like its eastern twin, had an old funicular lift. I walked to the tiny station and bought my ticket.

Thankfully, I was on my own in the cabin as it clanked up the steep slope, the wooden bench hard on my bruises. But it was only minutes to the top and, as I'd hoped, it was almost deserted up here today. The café, though, was open and I took my tea and a bowl of soup out onto the small terrace that felt to be almost hanging over the cliff edge.

The sea was bright blue, as still as a piece of wrinkled silk thrown out along the shoreline. I sipped my soup, putting off the moment when I would have to face my thoughts. A gull landed heavily on the table next to mine, huge wings flapping for a moment as it fought to regain its balance, its eyes pinpoints of jet following the movement of my spoon. I groaned and pushed the soup away and the gull hopped onto my table, staring, with what looked like disgust, into my half-empty bowl.

What Lorna had told me was true, I knew that, although I'd never for a moment suspected it before. Yet, knowing it was true didn't help me to take it in, or to understand.

Why had my father – my real father – deceived me for all those years? I could hardly believe Mum had been fooled, and even if he thought she was, what had stopped him telling me when she died?

It was obvious too that his affair with Lorna was one of many. He was an adulterer and a liar and, if Lorna was right, it was only the awareness of his own mortality that had prompted him to consider coming clean.

I had so many questions and now there would never be any answers. My real mother was not the Romanian peasant I'd imagined all these years and I felt further away from knowing about her than ever. What a bastard he was. And this was my real flesh and blood. Right now I hated him.

I stood, almost upending the plastic table so that the gull was thrown, squawking, into the air. I wanted to scream and kick and hit out at something, someone – anyone. The expression on my face and my clenched hands must have betrayed my thoughts, because a young couple coming out onto the terrace exchanged wary glances and carried their tray to the farthest corner.

Walking on the grass a moment later, my fists still clenching and unclenching, I asked myself if the kind of helpless fury I felt would have been enough to make me do something desperate. What was it the detective had said? *You were upset. Did you take something to keep you cheerful?* My answer was still the same one I had given her then, *no, no I wouldn't have.* But how could I be sure?

It was as I travelled down on the funicular that it happened again. A sudden flicker of sunlight through the window of the little carriage was all it took.

And I was that Clare again.

Not fighting with the steering wheel this time, but standing, staring into the dark. To one side I could feel a terrible heat that stung my skin. And I could hear the crackle of something, too, something I couldn't turn to see. What I did see, were the two dim shapes ahead. And I could feel my throat straining to force out some kind of sound; to scream at them for help.

My head banged hard on the wooden frame of the funicular window. We'd come to a stop halfway down the slope, with the other carriage, the twin of the one I sat in, right next to us on its way up. A little girl, kneeling on her seat, her face pressed to the glass, waved at me and somehow I managed to wave back.

As we moved off again I forced myself not to think. I had to get home first.

Back at the flat, I sat facing the window, but aware of nothing outside. Two figures: that's what I'd seen. Two people watching me as I stood, feeling, and hearing those flames. None of it was clear. There was a haze all around me and inside me too. Whether it was smoke, or the shock, or the drugs roiling through my veins I didn't know. But I was still certain I had seen two figures and I'd tried to shriek to them for help before the dark overwhelmed me.

Hillier said he arrived when I was already collapsed on the ground. So the two people couldn't be him and Jacob Downes. Unless he was lying; unless they were both lying.

But what was the point of struggling to remember? Whatever Hillier and Downes could tell me, Lorna had told me the one thing that mattered; the reason I'd taken those pills.

I poured myself a tumbler of the vodka I'd bought on the way home and began to drink.

It was ten in the morning when I opened my eyes from a deep, dreamless sleep and lay in peace for a few moments before my head started to thump and I remembered. *You are your father's real daughter. If he told you that night, it could have pushed you over the edge.*

Yesterday I was convinced she was right, but now I couldn't believe it. Surely even that wouldn't have sent me back to drugs? But I'd promised Tom the truth and I would have tell him. What would he think; what would it do to him? And to Alice, too.

When I'd had some coffee and a couple of aspirins, I called her mobile, asking her to ring me urgently. Ten minutes later, she was on the phone. 'Are you all right?'

'Yes, but I need to see you as soon as possible.'

A pause. 'Is something wrong?'

'No, not really. Nothing for you to worry about anyway.'

'Well, I'm only working this morning. So do you want to meet for lunch somewhere?'

'I'd rather come to you, if you don't mind. I'll get the train and bring some food.'

'OK. You've got your key so let yourself in and I'll see you about half one.'

As I put down the phone I marvelled at how normal I'd been able to sound.

When I arrived at Beldon House, I made sandwiches and cut the cake I had brought. Then I took a big plaid blanket from the sofa in the living room and laid it under one of the old trees in the garden. Alice's key sounded in the door as I was putting ice cubes into a jug.

I didn't wait for her and was already sitting under the tree with the picnic spread out in front of me when she came into the garden, pulling off her jacket and smiling. 'What's wrong with the table?' she asked.

It was hard to keep back the tears so I looked down, gesturing to the blanket. 'This is how we used to have picnics. Don't you remember?'

She sat beside me kicking off her shoes. 'You've done egg and cress sandwiches, and that's not lemon barley water, is it?'

My voice wobbled. 'Of course.'

'Oh, Clare.' She pulled me to her. She was very warm and smelled faintly of antiseptic. This was my sister, my real flesh and blood, and somewhere deep inside I had always known it.

She reached for a sandwich. 'Mmm, haven't had egg and cress for so long.'

I hadn't expected to be able to eat, but now I was hungry. We ate and drank in silence for a while, but when she took a long drink and leaned back against the tree, I knew I had to speak.

'I went to see Lorna yesterday and she told me something. Something unbelievable.' My tone must have startled Alice because she raised herself on her knees, as if ready to jump up, and bumped her drink down on the grass beside her so quickly that it tipped over.

I told her then, as plainly as Lorna had told me. She looked away for a long moment. 'Alice?'

She spoke without turning. 'I'm all right. Tell me the rest. Everything she said.'

There wasn't much, and when I'd finished her face was pale. 'I don't know what to say. That changes everything, doesn't it?'

We went back inside, neither of us speaking, and I made coffee while Alice loaded the dishwasher. By the time we were sitting across from each other at the kitchen table she looked herself again. 'Can you believe it?' she said. 'That he kept up the lie for so long, I mean. He was … well I don't know what to call him.'

'A lying, adulterous bastard?' I said. 'That's the best I've come up with.'

A tiny laugh. 'Yes that'll do.'

We both sipped our coffee and I tried to catch her eye, but she was staring out into the garden. 'I wonder if Mum guessed?' she said.

'That's something we can never know. Like so much else.'

'It was awful when you went away.' She was still gazing out, the sunlight making her squint. 'I was, what, ten, and you were the centre of my world, my big sister. At first I kept asking Mum where you were, when you were coming back, and she just said to ask Dad. Of course, he was never here, so it was hopeless. Then the odd times you did come home you were so different. I remember you smelled bad, and your hair looked awful, and you just stayed in your room.'

I swallowed. She'd never said any of this before.

'I used to save up things to tell you, but you never wanted to speak to me.'

Although so much of that time was a blur for me, her words brought back a sudden memory. Little Alice, holding a plant pot and standing outside my bedroom door as I opened it. 'Look, Clare, do you like my sunflower, I'm going to grow the tallest one in my class.' That was what she said, or something like it, but I just pushed her out of the way, needing to get to the bathroom.

'I'm sorry,' I said, years too late.

She hardly seemed to hear. 'Dad was away more and more, and Mum's good days happened less and less often. If she wasn't

193

depressed, she was angry. Anything seemed to set her off and I remember her saying, more than once, that I was behaving just like you.'

'So maybe she did guess we were really sisters. Poor Mum.' I reached over and touched her arm. 'And poor you.'

'She was never as hard on me as she used to be on you, but I had to be so careful not to upset her and I was scared every time I came home from school.' Her fears had been justified, because, one day, she did find our mother unconscious and she died that night.

The silence stretched and finally Alice sighed and picked up our mugs. As she put them in the dishwasher she seemed to shake herself, and when she spoke her voice was lighter. 'But that's all in the past. This is nothing to be miserable about. We're real sisters after all and that's wonderful. I just wish we'd known it all those years ago.'

She came to sit next me, her hand gripping mine and we were quiet for a while. Then she said, 'But I suppose it answers the question about what happened that night. I mean if he was as stupid as to drop a bombshell like that, without preparing you, it must have been an enormous shock.'

'I know.' I moved to stand half out of the French windows, leaning on the door jamb. 'And I've got to find a way to tell Tom.'

She twisted towards me. 'I was going to talk to you about him anyway. I've been worried about the way he's going overboard with this accident stuff, so I spoke to my psychiatrist friend. To be honest, I think she feels we've made a mess of it so far.'

'I have, you mean.'

'No, both of us. Like you said at the start, I should have worked harder to make him see there was no point in thinking about what happened in the past. Should have talked to him more about the future. And I certainly shouldn't have let him watch that bloody miscarriage of justice TV programme. Though how I could have stopped him from seeing it at Mark's I don't know.'

She stood and went to the fridge. 'The lemon barley water was lovely, Clare, but I think this calls for something a bit stronger.'

She poured us both a glass of white wine and we took them out to the table on the patio.

After the half bottle of vodka I'd drunk the night before the wine didn't tempt me, but Alice took a long drink then ran her fingers through her hair and shook her head. 'I thought we were doing so well.'

My head thumped again and the sunshine seemed to bore into my skull. It wasn't her fault and here she was taking the blame. 'I'm the one who should have dealt with it and it's up to me to try to help Tom accept this. I just wish I knew how.'

'Well, Emma, my friend, said we should go gently with him. Be as honest as we can, but don't burden him with too much all at once. Above all, we need to show a united front to help him come to terms with it.'

It made sense and we agreed I'd stay and see Tom in the evening and take the first steps towards telling him the truth.

'It's not going to be easy.'

'He'll understand, Clare. I'm sure he will. He's begun to know you again – the real you – and he loves you so much.'

'Does he?'

'Oh yes.'

For a moment, we looked at each other, and Alice took my hand again. 'It's going to be all right. We'll get through this together, you, me, and Tom,' she whispered. Then she leaned over and kissed my cheek. 'And thanks for the picnic, big sister. It was perfect.'

Chapter Twenty

We were in the kitchen when Tom burst through the front door, his face shining and pink. He was wearing his P.E. kit and trainers. His rucksack bounced on his back, the zip gaping wide, and he brought with him the unmistakable odour of steamy school changing rooms. The door slammed behind him as he beamed at me. 'Hey, Mum, didn't know you were coming.'

He shrugged off his rucksack, narrowly missing the copper vase on the hall table, and throwing open the fridge to pour a glass of orange juice. Alice raised her eyebrows at me.

'Before you do anything else, upstairs and in the shower,' she said.

He turned to her. 'All right, cool it will you, let me talk to my mum first.'

My breath caught in my throat and I looked from his face – so certain I was on his side – to Alice. She flushed and I said, 'Please do as Alice says, Tom.'

He stared at me for a long minute, his grey eyes sparking anger, his mouth set but betrayed by a tiny wobble from his chin. I had no idea what I'd do if he defied me. Then he turned away and slouched towards the stairs.

'Okaaay, be like that. I just had something important to tell you, that's all.'

When he'd gone, Alice gave a huge sigh and shook her head, looking at me with clouded eyes.

'Is he often like this?' I said.

'Not often, but more and more lately.'

'I'm sorry.'

'Well, he's a teenager, so a bit of rebellion is only to be expected. You'll have to be prepared for that when he comes to live with you again.'

My heart gave a small skip at her use of the word *when*, but that wasn't the issue now. 'What can I do to help?'

'Just what you did then – back me up. My divorced friends tell me it's the kind of thing they get all the time – playing one parent off against the other.'

Tom took a long time with his shower. Alice had some paperwork to do, andI got things ready for a spaghetti bolognaise. The glass of wine I hadn't fancied earlier seemed very attractive now and I was onto my second, and back at the kitchen table pretending to read the paper, by the time Tom appeared in jeans, bare feet, and a T-shirt, his damp hair sticking up in spikes. I tried to keep my face neutral.

He shuffled from foot to foot. 'Sorry.'

'You should say that to Alice, not me.'

'OK.' I heard him speaking quietly in her little office and her answering, 'All right, that's fine then. Go and tell your mum what was so important.'

I tried to look interested, although I could hardly focus on anything for the voice in my head telling me to get it over with and explain what Lorna had said.

'You know you were writing to Mr Hillier?' he said.

'Yes and I've done that. He should have got it by now.'

He pulled up a chair and sat down, leaning across the table at me and passing me a scrap of paper. 'Well, he's in the Cumbria area phone book and I've found his number. So there's no need to wait for him to write back. We can ring him.'

That was the last thing I wanted to think about. 'But he'll only just have got the letters.'

'I know, that's why I think we should put some pressure on him. And, Mum, I've been thinking about that DVD and I really want to see it.' I tried to speak, but he rushed on. 'I promise I won't get upset, but I might spot something you've missed.' He looked at me, his eyes sparkling. 'Is that OK?'

I tried to speak slowly, to calm us both. 'There's something I need to tell you before we even think about doing anything else.'

He sat up, completely alert again. 'What?'

I didn't tell him about Dad and Lorna, there was no need, just what he had told her about my parentage. Tom listened calmly enough, nodding when I said Granddad must have had an affair with my birth mother and had invented the story about Romania to cover it up. 'So Granddad was my real father and your real grandfather,' I said.

Alice had obviously been listening in because she came behind Tom and put her hand on his shoulder, rubbing it as she smiled at me. 'And that also means your mum and I are actually sisters and you, my lad, are my genuine nephew.'

He twisted to look at her. 'So you're really my aunt? Hey that's cool.' He jumped up.

'Where are you going?' I said.

'To get my phone, tell Mark.'

He bounded upstairs and Alice laughed. 'Well, that went all right. And to think we were so worried.'

I got up and started to fry the onions and garlic I'd chopped earlier. 'He hasn't realised what it could mean, though. I still have to find a way to explain how it changes everything.'

'But not yet. Leave it to sink in for a few days.'

I added the mince and spoke above the splutter of frying. 'He might work it out for himself, of course, and that would probably be for the best.'

'Yes, and it's got to be easier if he's had time to think it through when you do explain it fully to him.'

'What have you got to explain to me, Mum?' Tom's voice booming out made me jump. His arms were crossed and his look fierce. Alice glanced at me, but didn't speak.

There was nothing for it. A tiny noise from Alice suggested she might want me to hold back, but I had promised to tell him the truth. I took a deep breath and leaned against the worktop. 'It's great we're a real family, and I'm so happy about that but, according to Lorna, my dad was planning to tell me the news around the time of the wedding.' Seeing him about to say something I spoke quickly. 'If he told me such incredible news during the reception, then I might have been really upset and that could explain why I took those pills, which is the one thing I've never understood. '

He moved restlessly. 'But why would you be upset?'

The pan behind me spluttered fiercely and I moved to stir the meat and turn down the gas. 'Because he'd kept it a secret for so long. You see, it would have meant so much to me, when I was younger, and to Alice as well. And he could have told me years before.'

'So ...?'

Alice took a can of tomatoes from the cupboard. 'Come on, Tom, leave it now. There's plenty of time to talk it all through.'

'Mum?' His arms were crossed again, his face set.

I moved towards him. 'Do you remember what I said that day in the woods when we talked about all this? I told you drug addicts can go back to their old ways after years and years, if something bad happens.' I was aware of Alice behind me, tipping the tomatoes into the pan and grinding in salt and pepper.

I knew she thought I should leave it, but I couldn't stop. I wanted so much to see that bitter look gone from Tom's eyes. 'It would have been a huge shock to learn that everything I'd thought about myself, and where I came from, was a lie. And it was just the kind of thing the police thought must have happened.'

His face became harder, hands clenching at his sides. 'So I suppose that means you're giving up. Not even gonna try and remember anything else? Well fine.' He headed for the stairs, turning back at the bottom to call to Alice, 'And I'm not hungry.'

I watched him go, longing to run after him, to force him to understand, but he was gone, and when I looked back at Alice she shook her head. 'Best leave him for a bit.'

When the food was ready we called him, but he didn't answer. Alice told me again to let him be, but I went up and knocked on his door. 'Tom, will you come down? I have to go as soon as we've eaten.'

There was no answer.

Stella took one look at me next morning and gestured to the little back room. 'Look,' she said, closing the door, 'whatever's happening in your life is none of my business and I knew when I took you on that you might find things difficult, but it's obvious you're not coping.'

I explained I was having problems with Tom and promised to pull myself together at work, although I knew my weary tone was unlikely to reassure her.

She rubbed my forearm. 'I know what kids can be like – you wouldn't believe the trouble I had with Harriet when she was that age. But, Clare, this business is my livelihood, and my daughter's, and I can't afford to carry passengers. You started so well, but we can't go on like this. Please try to focus a bit more while you're here.'

I managed to bite back my tears and gave her a nod and some kind of smile, and we left it at that. She was out most of the day and it was quiet, so I got through it somehow.

Back at the house, on the hall table there was a handwritten letter addressed to *Mrs C. Glazier*, and when I turned it over I saw it was from Mr Hillier. I ripped it open as I walked inside.

I was still taking the single sheet of paper from the envelope when I looked up and noticed the room: the books on the floor, the upturned chairs, the scattered cushions.

For a moment I was confused. How could this have happened? A piece of furniture or a heavy book falling and causing some kind of chain reaction? A seagull trapped in the room? Finally my brain jolted to life again. I'd been burgled.

The flat was silent and I went round every room, checking that all the windows were closed and locked. Nothing else seemed to have been touched and eventually I began tidying the living room. I wasn't going to call the police, so fingerprints and other evidence didn't matter. And it looked as if they hadn't taken anything, just made a mess. For some reason this upset me even more.

There was a scrunched up ball of paper in the middle of the sofa and when I flattened it out I saw it was Tom's list of questions for Mr Hillier and Jacob Downes, thrown from where I'd left them by the laptop. I felt a surge of anger that anyone should tamper with his stuff and took the paper to the bedroom, putting it into his folder in the drawer.

It was then I realised something *was* missing – Emily's wedding video.

The phone rang and, while I was looking for the handset amidst the mess, Alice's voice cut in sounding tight and high. 'Clare, are you there?' When I answered she said, 'Oh thank God – it's Tom. After last night I told him to come straight home from school, but he's not here. I've rung his friends and apparently he left school after registration and none of them has seen him since. He's not come to you, has he?'

'No, he hasn't. Have you called the police?'

'Not yet, it's too soon.'

'He's only thirteen.'

'I know, but he's done this a couple of times before and that's what they've told me. I shouldn't worry, Clare. I'm sure he'll be back when he gets hungry. Just stay where you are in case he comes there and I'll try to think of anyone else I can ring.'

I wanted to ask why she hadn't told me about his disappearances, but this wasn't the time. We agreed we would both stay where we were in case he came to either place. 'I'll call you if he's not back by dark,' she said.

She had more patience than I did, and when I heard jazz from upstairs I knocked on Kieran's door. He was obviously just out of the shower, wearing only a towel around his waist, his hair wet and standing up in jagged points, but I was too anxious to be embarrassed. My face must have told it all because he asked, 'What's wrong?'

When I tried to turn away, apologising for my bad timing, he was having none of it. 'Stop that now,' he said. 'What's happened?'

I told him and he sent me back down, promising to do a careful drive around. Alice rang and said Mark's dad was doing the same in their area, with Mark advising him where to look.

I could do nothing except peer from the windows of each room in turn and pace the floor, my whole body clenched. After a few minutes of this I could stand it no longer and knocked on Nic's door.

'What's up? You look awful,' she said.

I explained about Tom. 'He lives with my sister and he's disappeared.'

'I'm sure he'll be all right, darling. I mean we've all been teenagers, haven't we?' I thought of my teenage years and how lucky I was to survive them,, and almost laughed. It would have been a miserable kind of laugh, however, because by now I was really panicked.

It was all my fault. Of course Tom was vulnerable. When he talked about Toby it was clear he was carrying a huge burden of guilt. And I had done nothing to help him.

I called Alice and she said she had rung the police, but doubted it would be a priority for them. When Kieran came back he said he'd take a walk through the town and check all the arcades, the funfair, and the cafés. He told me to ring his mobile with any news, otherwise, he would keep looking.

It was near midnight when I heard him in the hall, but my surge of hope was short-lived. He was alone, looking exhausted. 'I'm sorry,' he said, following me inside.

The phone rang.

'He's here,' was all Alice said, and I sank onto the sofa, a throb deep in my chest. I managed to ask if he was all right and she told me he was, her voice sounding as drained as I felt, and we agreed to leave anything else till morning.

It wasn't until Kieran said, 'I'll get it,' that I registered the tap on the door. As I heard him talking quietly to Nic, I felt a huge weight descend on me. I just wanted it all to stop.

Then Kieran's warm hand was on my neck and I stood and moved into his arms. After a while I looked up and kissed him. His hands cupped my face, and his lips were gentle, but I pressed hard against his mouth. My hands moved down his body, the solidity, the pressure of him against me, making me frenzied, desperate to wrap myself around him, to have him with me, in me, right now.

He pulled back and looked into my eyes, but I didn't want to look at him, just to have him filling that aching emptiness. I pulled him towards the bedroom.

Chapter Twenty-One

'Clare, are you sure?' Kieran asked.

I didn't answer, didn't want to talk, and when I kissed him again, he began to pull at my trousers and thrust me back onto the bed. I kicked my legs free and, just like that, the desperate need disappeared and I looked down from a great distance at my naked legs, made ridiculous by the sock hanging from one foot. He was still fully clothed, his face concentrated, very dignified in contrast to me with my sweatshirt rucked up to reveal a pallid stomach.

I pulled myself up to sit on the edge of the bed, unable even to look at him.

He knelt in front of me. 'What's wrong?'

'It's not you ... I'm sorry.'

He looked down at my feet and, with a smile, pulled off my sock and kissed my foot very gently. I shivered and he pulled the duvet around me. As he turned to go, I caught his hand.

'Please, Kieran, stay.'

He lay beside me, outside the covers, and I rested my head on his chest. His heartbeat was strong and steady and I focused on listening to it, thinking of nothing.

After a while he started to talk. And it was the kind of talking you might do after you've made love. A rambling account of his life, his breakdown, and his hopes for his photography. I said nothing, but he seemed to understand that I was happy just to listen. Eventually he told me how worried he was about his mum. 'She was diagnosed just a few weeks after Dad died – cancer too. So she thought that was it. But they caught it in time and she's been fine. Until now, when it's come back with a vengeance.'

'I'm so sorry. And I've been bothering you with all my problems.'

His answer was to kiss me and, as I pressed closer, he pulled back the covers. He looked steadily at me as I took off the rest of my clothes. But when I felt his warm skin against mine and looked up into his green gaze it was suddenly Steve's grey eyes I saw. I turned away, feeling the tears slide from under my closed lids as I muttered, 'Sorry, I'm sorry,' again.

Kieran touched my shoulder and I turned back to look at him. He stroked my wet cheek. 'You're thinking about your husband,' he said. I could only nod and close my eyes as they filled up once more. Kieran kissed my cheek and the corner of my mouth where I could taste the salt of my tears. 'He would want you to be happy.'

I shook my head. *I killed him, I killed Steve. I don't deserve happiness.* But when Kieran kissed me this time I felt myself respond.

Our lovemaking was quiet and gentle, as if our bodies already knew each other.

Afterwards, suddenly shy, I turned away again but he held me close: the length of his body pressed against mine, his face buried in my hair. The bedroom curtains were open and the sky looked faintly milky with a suggestion of dawn; only this moment existed: my body in a state of peace, my skin humming from his touch.

I spoke to him, then, about what Lorna had told me and how it might explain why I'd taken those pills; about Tom's reaction to the news and even what I had told no one else: the details of those flashes of memory.

After a while he lifted my hair to kiss the back of my neck, and sat up. 'I don't want to move; want to stay just like this,' he said, 'but I'm starving.'

As soon as he was gone, the calmness I'd been feeling disappeared, and my brain began twisting and turning again until I felt it would burst. Had I betrayed Steve? And had I used Kieran to stop myself from thinking? To stop thinking about the fact that I knew why I might have been tempted back to drugs? About why my dad had kept his secret all those years? And, above all, to avoid facing the knowledge of how troubled Tom was and how angry with me he must be?

Because I knew it must have been Tom who'd taken the DVD and torn the place apart.

I pulled on my dressing gown and found Kieran coming out of the kitchen with a tray.

'I was bringing it back to bed,' he said.

But I walked over to the window. 'Can we stay out here for a bit?' I stood staring into the night. The hint of dawn had disappeared and a single light shone in the black absence of the sea: a boat moving slowly through the nothingness, night fishing.

He was behind me and, as I felt the warmth coming from him, I had a sudden memory of Alice on that first day here. Had it really been only weeks since then? I leant into his body, welcoming his closeness.

We stayed there as we ate the toast he'd made. Then I faced him again and he opened my dressing gown and began to kiss my yellowing bruises, one by one. But his lips on my skin seemed to light something inside and I didn't want gentleness from him now. I grabbed his hand and pulled him back to the bedroom. We made love again, so fiercely this time that, at the end, we lay apart as if afraid to touch.

He slept for a while, but I was wide awake and as it became light I knew I must make sure I was fit to cope with work today. In the kitchen, as I made some tea, I saw Mr Hillier's letter on the table. It hardly seemed possible that I'd only opened it last evening. I wiped away a smear of butter and took the letter back to bed.

Mr Hillier wrote:

> *Your visit made quite an impact on me, as did your letter.*
> *I was particularly moved by the note from your son, of course.*
> *It must be some considerable consolation for you to have such*
> *a loyal young man by your side and I do hope the two of you*
> *can begin to make a new life for yourselves. Believe me, Mrs*
> *Glazier, I have always felt a lot of sympathy for you. As a*
> *parent myself I know the terrible loss you have suffered was a*
> *far greater punishment than anything the law could inflict.*
>
> *In fact I have managed to speak to Jacob Downes, by*
> *phone, on your behalf. Unfortunately he refuses to have any*
> *contact with you, which doesn't surprise me. However I did*
> *persuade him to talk a little about that night. Mostly this*
> *was a repetition of what he told the court, but he said some-*
> *thing several times that I'd never heard before and I think it*
> *might comfort you. His words, as precisely as I can recall*
> *them, were, 'She tried to help them, really tried and so did I.*
> *So we didn't do anything wrong.'*
>
> *Of course you were unconscious by the time I saw you,*
> *but if what he says is correct, it seems clear that you were*
> *desperate to save your family, despite your own injuries. He*
> *probably still feels guilty that he couldn't do more. That was*
> *certainly the impression he gave me.*

It was kind of him, but it didn't help much. I'd never doubted I would have tried to get to them if I'd been able. He'd added his phone number and email address so at least it looked like he'd be prepared to talk to me again.

Kieran stirred and reached out for me and part of me longed to fall back into his arms again. Instead, I passed him the letter.

'Not much use is it?' he said, when he'd read it. He lay back on the pillows and picked up the photo frame from the bedside table, studying the three faces. 'This is Toby then. He looks a lovely lad too.'

He didn't mention Steve, but I was very conscious of my husband's face smiling out of the frame and suddenly I needed only to be alone. Bone-weary, I crawled from bed, knocking over my full mug. I left the tea to soak into the carpet and dragged myself to the bathroom, asking myself what the hell I was doing adding Kieran to the rest of my worries.

The phone rang. 'Hi, Clare – Stella.' I stared at the clock; it was only just after 7.30. 'I'm ringing to say, take today off.' Before I could tell her I was fine, she went on. 'I happened to call Alice last night, and she told me about Tom. I've just spoken to her again and I gather he didn't get back till all hours, so I can imagine you didn't sleep much and you already looked done in yesterday.'

When I tried to protest again, she was firm. 'I'm not arguing with you. You'll be of no use to me anxious and exhausted. Have a day to sort yourself out. Harriet can do your shift.'

It sounded like an ultimatum, but I was too tired to care. There was nothing I wanted more now than to sleep, but that would have meant going back to bed. And to Kieran.

Thank God, he came out already dressed. I pretended to be searching for something in the fridge, but he put his arms around my waist, his lips close to my ear, and I felt the thrill of his touch shiver through me again. 'It's no good, the cupboard is bare,' he said. 'But I've got bacon and eggs upstairs. Back in a minute.'

He must have left the door ajar because I heard, 'Morning, Clare. Everything all right?' and Nic stood in my hall, Molly in her arms. 'Kieran said your boy got back all right.'

I tightened the belt of my dressing gown, feeling the heat rise in my face. 'Yes. Thanks so much for looking out for him.'

She raised her eyebrows as Kieran ran downstairs. 'Morning Kieran. Sorry I can't stay for breakfast, some of us have to work.' Was I imagining it or did she look upset? I told myself I must have been because as she went out the front door she gave a little laugh and shouted back, 'Don't do anything I wouldn't do, will you?'

'Well, so much for keeping it to ourselves,' he said, as he put a pan on the stove.

Alice phoned when I was trying to eat a little of the breakfast Kieran had cooked, very conscious of his warm hand on my bare knee. I took the phone over to the window.

She said she was keeping Tom home from school. Following advice from Emma, the psychiatrist, she had said nothing much when he got back last night and he had gone straight to his room. 'I've left him to sleep. Martha, our daily, will keep an eye on him and ring me if there are any problems and I can be home early this afternoon. I'll talk to him then and let you know.'

I told her about Stella. 'I've got the whole day free, so I'll come over and try to speak to him myself, shall I?'

'Best leave it, Clare. I've been through this kind of thing with him before.'

A surge of real anger went through me. *This was my responsibility.* I took a breath. *Be calm.* 'But this is different. It's all to do with what I told him the other day and if I avoid him now it'll be like telling him I don't care if he's upset.'

Her voice was very calm too. 'I just want to make sure he's ready to hear what you have to say.'

'I think I can manage.' I wanted to tell her that Tom was my son and I knew how to talk to him, but of course that wasn't true. I willed her not to argue because I was afraid of what I might blurt out if she did.

'OK, Clare, fine. Just be careful will you?'

'Of course I will.' I made an effort to make my voice warmer. 'And when you get home you can relax while I cook us all some dinner.'

She gave a small laugh. 'That's the best offer I've had today. See you later.'

I went straight to the bathroom to shower and dress, putting Tom's crumpled list of questions in my bag, along with Hillier's letter.

Kieran had washed up and was standing by the window in the living room. He turned and smiled. 'How are things with Tom?'

'Alice is keeping him home from school today. I'm going over to see if he'll talk to me.'

He stretched and yawned. 'I could do with some fresh air. I'll drive you.' My doubts must have showed on my face because he laughed. 'It's all right, I'll make myself scarce.'

It seemed easier to go along with him and in the car I pretended to doze, wondering what the hell kind of mess my life was in. The trouble was, my anxiety about being in a car, especially on a country road like this, made it impossible to sustain the pretence for long. And I was soon sitting upright, one hand on my door, my foot pressing at an imaginary brake, as I looked out at the trees, the light slanting through their branches.

Gradually, our speed increased on the long straight road and I gripped the edge of my seat. As the trees flashed by, Kieran glanced over at me. I swallowed, trying to get a look at the speedometer, certain we must be going too fast. Then I saw a lorry approaching on the other side of the road and clutched at Kieran's arm.

The car swerved and there was a blast from the lorry's horn. It passed within inches of us as we slowed and bumped onto the grass verge. When we were stationary Kieran turned to me, his face twisted.

'What the fuck are you doing?'

My breath was coming in harsh gasps that hurt my chest, and it seemed an age before I could speak. 'I'm sorry, but you were going so fast.'

'It's a clear road and dead straight.' He turned off the engine and, in the silence that followed, my breath began to steady itself, but I needed to get out into the fresh air. I bent over, certain I was about to be sick, but as I stood on the grass, with the quiet countryside all around me, my heart slowed and the churning in my stomach calmed.

Then Kieran was behind me, solid and warm, holding me close and whispering that he was sorry too. 'I should have thought. You're bound to be scared of speed. I just enjoy putting my foot down but I promise, never again.' He turned me towards him for a long kiss, until a hoot and a shout from a passing car had us pulling apart. Laughing, Kieran gave the driver the finger. 'Come on, before we get arrested.'

After that, he drove sedately, smiling over at me every so often. Finally, he put his hand on my knee. 'I realise this is difficult for you, and that's fine. I just want you to know I can wait and I'd love to help in any way I can. Or I can keep out of it if that's how you want it.'

I had no idea how to respond with anything more than a, 'Thank you,' but he seemed happy enough with that.

'You know earlier, when you got upset about my speeding?' he said. 'I wondered, for a minute, if you'd had one of those memory flashes.'

'No, nothing like that. I was just scared.' As I watched his neat brown hands on the wheel, my skin quivered to a different memory: the memory of his touch. Then I forced myself to think, not about him, but about what I needed to do for my son.

'I know Tom's never going to be happy until I can tell him I've remembered everything, but what if I never do?'

He didn't answer for a moment, concentrating on the road as another car overtook us. 'Well, I suppose you could always tell him you *have* remembered.'

'No, I promised I wouldn't lie to him.'

'Even if it's for his own good?'

I had nothing to say to that and, as we reached another stretch of straight road and his speed increased, I couldn't stop my hand clutching at my seatbelt. He glanced over, said, 'Sorry,' and slowed down.

'You see, I'm pretty sure the light I keep seeing in my dreams is a real memory, and it has to be another vehicle on that corner. So why won't my mind let me remember it properly?'

'Well, you were under the influence, so maybe you were so out of it that the light was all you ever registered.'

211

It was very possible, but … 'Oh, I don't know. I just wish I could speak to Jacob Downes myself. I'm sure he must know something. Either it was his headlight, or he saw another car. And why do I seem to see another figure with him?'

He said nothing for a while, then, 'Well, when Mr Hillier arrived you could have been half conscious. Just enough to be aware of his presence and of the two voices.'

That made as much sense as anything else.

As we pulled into the drive of Beldon House, Kieran whistled, 'Nice place, bit different to the two up two down I grew up in.'

'But you were happy there, weren't you?'

'Yeah, we were. It was great until Dad got ill.'

I thanked him, feeling awkward again, but when he leaned over and gave me a light kiss it felt completely natural. 'Good luck. See you later,' was all he said.

When I'd introduced myself to Martha, she said she'd banged on Tom's door to tell him she was here, but had heard nothing. I went up and knocked, 'Tom, it's Mum. I'm coming in to talk to you.' He was out of bed, but still in his pyjamas, sitting on the window seat that overlooked the driveway. He must have seen me arrive.

He shuffled his feet and looked down, speaking in a stran-gled voice. 'I'm sorry about last night, Mum. Alice said you were worried. She shouldn't have told you.'

'She had to. I'm your mum and I need to know these things. Besides, she thought you might have come over to me.' He was scraping at the carpet with his foot and I forced myself to go on. 'Where were you all that time?'

'Just round here, walking. Went to the park for a while; kicked a ball about for a bit too.'

'A very long bit.'

'Yeah, but that's all.' He looked up at me, 'Honest, Mum.'

'Have you apologised to Alice?'

'Not yet.'

'But you will as soon as she gets home?' He nodded. 'We were so worried about you, both of us, and Alice says you've done it before. Why, Tom?'

'Dunno.'

'So what now?'

''Spect I'll be grounded for the week.'

'And you know you deserve that, don't you?' He shrugged, but it seemed best to leave it there. 'Look, I know all this is very difficult for you and I'm sure I'm doing everything wrong, but I am trying. Will you promise to talk to me or to Alice when something upsets you in future?'

He looked out towards the road. 'OK.'

'OK, what?'

He turned back with a hint of a smile. 'OK, I promise.'

My knees felt suddenly weak and I sat on the warm, crumpled bed. How on earth could I ask him about the break-in without setting him off again? The heat didn't help. 'Can you let in some air?'

He wrestled with the old sash window for a few minutes. 'It's stuck, sorry.'

'Tom, you *didn't* come to my place yesterday, did you?'

'Nah, I told you I was just round here.'

Careful. 'Only I haven't been able to find that DVD and I wondered if you might have borrowed it.'

His eyes met mine and I saw only suspicion of me there, no sign of guilt. 'You've lost it?'

'Yes and I can't understand, because I thought I knew exactly where I put it.'

He stood up, his whole body tensed, hands clenched at his sides in the way I was beginning to recognise too well. 'And you think I took it? Well I didn't. I wanted to see it, but I wouldn't take something like that without asking.' His chin came out and his voice wobbled and broke on the words. 'All right?'

'Of course it is.' I believed him. 'I just have to ask anyone who's been in my flat recently, that's all.' I took Mr Hillier's

213

letter from my bag and held it out to him. 'This came for us, from Mr Hillier.'

I didn't move from the bed. If he wanted to read it he would have to stop standing there, glaring, and come towards me. It took a minute, but he did so even managing a short, 'Thanks,' as he took the paper.

He read it, flushing when he reached what must be the comments about himself.

'And he's put in his phone number so I'm guessing it would be all right to phone him,' I said.

When he looked up his eyes were bright. 'Can we call him now?'

I needed to think about that one. 'Why don't you get washed and dressed first and I'll see you downstairs?'

Martha was in the hall. 'Your sister phoned,' she said, her arms crossed, voice thick with disapproval. 'I told her you were here and she said, if you're staying, I could go.' She looked as if she thought I was planning to kidnap Tom after ransacking the place.

I made myself some coffee and pulled Tom's list of questions from my bag. Perhaps he was right and I should call Mr Hillier right away.

When he came down he poured himself some cereal and sat opposite me. 'Oh, good, you've got the questions.'

'Mr Hillier probably won't be in at this time of day, but I'll give him a try.'

As I clicked the number, and listened to the ringing from the other end, Tom watched, spooning cornflakes so fast into his mouth that streams of milk poured back in the bowl.

Hillier was obviously surprised by my call. 'Oh, Mrs Glazier. You did get my note, didn't you?'

'Yes, and I'm ringing to thank you. I'm very grateful, but there was something else I wanted to ask you.'

His, 'Yes,' was guarded.

I told him I was now sure I had seen headlights, coming towards me. 'So are you certain you didn't see another car?'

'As certain as I can be after all this time.'

'And the police didn't suggest you simplify your evidence.'

'Certainly not.'

'You said I was on the ground when you arrived, but was I actually unconscious?'

'Mrs Glazier, I'm not a doctor and it was years ago, so I can't be sure about that either.'

I told him I needed to talk to Downes about it.

'I don't think that's a good idea. Speaking to him the other day it was clear he's in a state of great anxiety.'

'Well then, I know it's a lot to ask, but maybe you could talk to him again. Tell him I saw headlights and all I want is to hear about it from him. Was he coming towards me rather than following, or did he see another car? I mean, if he's worrying about something it might help to get it off his chest with someone he trusts. And I really have no intention of talking to the police, whatever I learn.'

I heard a sigh down the line and I could imagine him standing in his little hall, holding the old-fashioned phone, and wondering how to get this bothersome female off his back. 'All right, my dear, I suppose, having stirred up the hornet's nest, I should try to help calm it down.'

He said he would ask Downes to call round. 'Better to do something like that face to face. Have a proper chat. And I gather he's living a rather aimless existence, so I may be able to help him to sort out his life a bit.'

I could hear a spark of enthusiasm: the old shepherd wanting to help the sheep that had gone astray. He promised he'd be in contact.

Chapter Twenty-Two

As I put the phone down, Alice came in the front door. She placed her bag on the hall floor with great care, reaching out to steady herself on the little table by the stairs. Her face was paler than the creamy wall behind her and she let out a huge sigh and stood for a moment as if too tired to take another step. This was what I'd done to her.

Then she became aware of us in the kitchen and shook her head so that the shine of blonde hair spun around her face and she seemed her pretty self again.

'Hello, Clare.' She stood in the kitchen doorway, hands on her hips, looking from me to Tom. 'You're up, I see.'

He glanced at me and I gave him a tiny nod. 'I'm sorry, Alice, I shouldn't have done that yesterday.'

'Tom's promised he'll talk to us first if he has a problem in future.' I said. 'And he expects to be grounded for the rest of the week, don't you?'

He was looking with great concentration at the table where his index finger rubbed and rubbed at a tiny mark, but he nodded. 'Yeah, I deserve it.'

'Well,' Alice said, 'since you don't seem as tired as us oldies, why don't you make the most of today and get some of that homework out of the way so you can have more free time at the weekend.'

He headed upstairs with another glance at me, obviously wondering if I was going to tell Alice about the call to Mr Hillier. I made some coffee and we took it into the sitting room. One of Alice's colleagues would be covering her patients for evening surgery so she could relax for the rest of the day.

'Thanks for dealing with this, Clare,' she said. 'You were right. It was best that you talked to him. And I'm so tired I would have made a mess of it.' She leaned back in the armchair and closed her eyes.

'I'll cook something for us all a bit later,' I said. 'Why don't you go up and have a sleep.'

She stood and rested her hand on my shoulder. It felt very heavy. 'Thanks, Clare, I think I will.'

Nic was in the hall, sorting through the papers and junk mail on the hall table, as I came in and for once she seemed too occupied with what she was doing to want a conversation, just gave a small smile and said, 'All right?' as she went back into her flat.

I'd cooked for Tom and Alice, but we'd all been too tired, or preoccupied, to say much and I'd told myself that was the reason I hadn't told Alice about the phone call to Mr Hillier.

The flat felt chilly and even after I'd pulled on a jumper I was cold, so I switched on the central heating for the first time, then sat staring at the TV as an old film played out. After a while, I rested my head back on the cushions, beginning to doze.

When I jerked awake I knew I'd been dreaming of storms and dark seas. But there was fire too: dark fire that burned on the surface of the sea and was untouched by the rain that poured down on it. The flat was very hot, a clammy heat complete with an ominous burning smell.

I ran into the kitchen and switched the heating off. Then checked all the rooms. In the outer hallway all was still and quiet and there was no smell.

Back inside it was less noticeable. In the bedroom, the tousled bed reminded me all too vividly of last night, and even though I was dog-tired I changed the sheets, the pillow cases, and the duvet cover before I could think of sleeping.

The phone rang twice in the night, but cut off quickly. I'd left the handset in the living room and didn't bother to get up to look at it. I was asleep again almost at once.

When I dressed in the morning, and was drinking my first cup of coffee in the kitchen, I picked up the handset to see if there was any record of the numbers from the night. It shrilled in my hand. A mobile number: and not one the phone recognised. I pressed to answer, but didn't speak.

A male voice, 'Hello, hello?'

A cautious, 'Hello?'

'Clare, is that Clare?'

'Yes.' I held my breath.

'It's Matt.'

I breathed again. 'Oh, Matt, I didn't recognise your voice.'

I could hear his smile. 'I'm not surprised; I've been up all night. Emily's had the baby. It's a bit early, but they're both fine. Both lovely.'

'Oh that's wonderful. What is it?'

'A girl. We're calling her Lily, and Emily wanted you to be the first to know, after our mums and dads.' Those wretched tears sprang to my eyes again and no words would come. 'Are you still there, Clare?'

'Yes, I'm sorry. I'm so happy for you both.'

'Thanks, it's wonderful. Exhausting, but wonderful and, can you believe it, they're letting Em out later today if everything seems fine.'

'She'll be glad to be home.'

'She made me promise to tell you to ring her tomorrow. Think she wants to persuade you to come up again as soon as possible.'

Before he rang off, I asked if he'd called in the night. 'Oh dear, I think I did ring your number once before I realised how late it was.'

'Only once?'

'Yes, sorry if I woke you. I was in such a state I didn't know what I was doing.'

'Nice skirt,' said Stella, her brown eyes taking in everything about my appearance as I clanged through the shop door. 'How are things?'

'Fine thanks. That day off was just what I needed. I'll be OK now.' I was surprised that I sounded almost confident, even to my own ears. To emphasise the point, I busied myself with the watering can, refilling the flower buckets and vases, and humming just loudly enough for her to hear.

It seemed to reassure her and she left me to it. At 10.30 she came out of the back room and told me to have a break and bring her down a coffee when I'd finished. Upstairs, I checked my mobile. There was a text from Kieran.

Hope it went OK with Tom. See you tonight? XXX.

I didn't reply.

Back in the shop, I told myself the only thing I needed to do for now was to focus on keeping my job, but when Stella went out to visit a wedding venue my thoughts began swirling again. I couldn't think about Kieran, had to concentrate on the break-in. I hadn't told anyone about it and I didn't intend to. When Tom swore it wasn't him I had believed him absolutely, but if not him, who else? Had I just persuaded myself my son wouldn't lie to me? I knew I should ask Alice what she thought because, painful though it was for me to admit, she knew Tom – this strange teenaged Tom – better than I did. But, no, there was no need. I did believe him. And if I did, that meant there was someone else who was able to get into my flat, someone who wanted to stop me watching that DVD again.

The other thoughts I couldn't stop were about what Lorna had told me, but this time it wasn't my dad I was thinking of, but my real mother. Although Lorna had said she was dead I wondered if that was true. Presumably Lorna only had Dad's word for it and I now knew what a liar he was. With my adoptive mum's history of mental illness it was feasible the doctors might have told them to avoid a pregnancy and he persuaded my birth mother to give me up. I could just about imagine him doing that. Which meant she might be still out there, somewhere. One day, one day when I'd sorted out the mess my life was in, I would have to find out for sure.

At the flat, I could hear the TV through Nic's door, but there was no sign of Kieran. I took the phone into the bedroom and dialled Emily's number as I lay on the bed. Matt answered, speaking very quietly. 'Sorry, Clare, I know I said to ring and Emily is desperate to speak to you, but would you leave it for a couple of days? Neither of us has had much shut-eye the last two nights. The sprog's finally gone off and Em's sleeping too, but after being on top of the world yesterday she's a bit down today.'

'Of course. And don't worry about it, Matt, it's natural. She'll be herself again soon.'

He sighed. 'I know.'

'Just try and get some sleep yourself. Give Em my love and tell her I'll speak to her later in the week.'

There was a sound as if he was sitting down, no doubt exhausted. 'Before you go,' he paused, 'when you do talk to her you won't mention this business with the amphetamines, will you?'

I half sat up, leaning on one elbow. 'What?'

'Only Lorna called a day or so ago and said you'd been asking what Em knew about how you got hold of them and that you were going to raise it with her.'

'Of course I won't, not at a time like this.'

'I mean, just because Alice had them in her bag, doesn't mean you got them from her.'

I sat up properly and swung my legs over the side of the bed, going dizzy from the sudden movement. I couldn't catch my breath couldn't speak. *Alice, he'd said Alice.*

Matt's voice again from far, far away. 'Oh, God, have I put my foot in it? I'm so tired, Clare, I'm not thinking straight.'

I needed to make some sense of this. 'No, no, it's fine, but Lorna didn't say anything about Alice to me.'

'Well just forget I did then.'

'I can't do that, Matt. Please tell me.'

'All I know, is that Emily seems to think Alice was using something like that at the time. It wouldn't be surprising either when you think what it's like for junior hospital doctors.'

I managed to choke out, 'OK, thanks, Matt.' He sounded doubtful, but we said our goodbyes and I threw the phone onto the floor and lay back on the bed, my hands over my face. I couldn't think; could do nothing except listen to her name echoing in my head: *Alice, Alice, Alice.*

Keeping my eyes closed, I pressed my hands over my ears, and as if the words were sounds from outside rather than in my head, they died away. I lay with my ears blocked, grateful for the silence.

And then, behind my lids, I saw Alice and me sitting together at the wedding reception. For a breathless moment I thought it was a memory. But then I recalled the DVD. It was what I'd seen there.

I sat up, feeling dizzy again, and looked around the bedroom, almost expecting it to have changed. This, it seemed, was the truth I'd been searching for. The two questions I'd started with were: what could have sent me back to drugs and how did I get hold of them? Lorna had answered the first question: the shock of learning my real parentage had made me want to blank things out for a while. And now Emily and Matt had given me the probable answer to the second. Emily had said any number of people at the wedding would have had access to drugs and mentioned Alice as well as the people from Dad's company. It had hardly registered then, but now I realised she was giving me a hint. But why had she never said anything before? And why, oh why, did none of it feel right?

When Kieran tapped on the door I didn't hesitate. I couldn't face the next few hours alone with my thoughts. He could obviously see something was wrong. 'Clare?' He moved us gently inside bending to look into my face. 'What's happened?'

We stood together looking out of the window. The sunset was misty today, the faint streaks of colour like a spill of fizzy orangeade above the flat sea. 'I've just heard something that could explain how I got hold of those pills. Seems someone close to me had been self-medicating and I could easily have stolen them.'

The coloured lights along the promenade flickered on: purple, red, blue, and green. Kieran put his arms around me and I leaned back against him. 'So that could answer all my questions.' I could feel his chest moving in and out very steadily as he thought, perhaps worried he might say the wrong thing.

Finally he said, 'You don't sound convinced.'

I pulled away from him and headed for the sofa. Kieran perched on the window sill, looking steadily at me. I said, 'It just doesn't feel right. None of it feels right. And stupidly I imagined if I got to the truth my memory would come back.'

He shook his head. 'But I don't think you have got the whole truth yet. I mean, what about that light? Maybe you still need to find out if there was another vehicle involved in the accident.' He stood and smiled. 'You'll think more clearly when you've eaten. I'm too tired to go out, but if you give me ten minutes to clear up I can find us something to eat.'

As I walked upstairs a few minutes later, an ache, like a stitch after running, clutched at my side. I felt as if I was in some kind of dream and for the first time I noticed the tiny multi-coloured dots speckling the blue stair carpet. Kieran was right. Two people were at the crash site in that flash of memory. So either David Hillier or Jake Downes was lying, or both of them were. And, as for Alice, I needed to know if she really had the speed in her bag and if she realised I might have taken it.

Kieran's door was ajar and he was talking softly on the phone. When I tapped he gestured for me to come in. But when he threw down the handset I realised something was wrong. He looked so different from the way he had only minutes before.

'Are you all right?'

He ran his fingers through his thick, dark hair. 'It's my mum. She's been rushed to hospital. Apparently she's adamant I'm not to come up yet, but …'

There was nothing to say after that and we sat at the table together, playing with the food, watching, as the lights in the town turned on and the stars emerged over the black sea to fill the darkness with a tinselly glitter.

He kissed me then, on my eyelids and my cheekbones, and pulled me to my feet. 'Stay here tonight, please. I don't want to be alone and you shouldn't be either.'

In his bed, I held him and he lay, breathing steadily for a while, until we began to kiss and then to move urgently together. But even as our bodies joined I knew his thoughts, like mine, were far away.

Chapter Twenty-Three

Ringing jolted me from fiery dreams. It was still dark and I lay for a moment, confused about where I was. Then the ringing stopped, the light dazzled me, and for a split second I felt a memory stir again – so close, so very close.

'Shit.' Kieran dropped the phone and the bed shook as he leant over the side to reach it.

And the memory slipped away.

I closed my eyes, hating my hopeless brain.

Kieran's voice was angry with sleep. 'What? Right I'm leaving now. I'll be with you in a few hours.' He threw down the phone, letting it bounce off the bed onto the floor again, and began pulling on trousers and a sweatshirt.

'Kieran? Is it your mum?'

'Yes.' Under the early morning growl his voice had a bitter note. 'They're doing an emergency operation.'

'Shall I get you something to drink?'

'No. I've got to go.' He pulled his arm away and finished dressing. I lay back, not knowing what to say or do but, when he sat on the bed to tie his laces, he took an enormous breath, reaching behind to touch my hand. 'I'd never forgive myself if I wasn't there.'

'What can I do?'

'Nothing, except think hopeful thoughts.' He brushed his face briefly against mine, his breath tickling my hair, and a moment later the door closed quietly behind him.

I lay there, wide awake, wishing I could have done something to help him. After a while I got up. It wasn't even 6 a.m. but it didn't feel right to be alone in Kieran's bed. I switched on the living room light and I stood for a long while studying the photographs on the walls.

The picture of Kieran's father – so frail and looking into the camera with sunken eyes that saw death approaching – kept me fascinated. I thought of my own dad, with his huge laugh, his expensive clothes, his enjoyment of all the good things in life. And his ability to smile at his wife and children while he lied to them. And yet I still loved him and hated myself for what I'd done to him.

I closed the door very quietly, crept downstairs, and let myself into my own flat, hardly daring to breathe – the last thing I wanted was to see Nic because I still wasn't sure how she felt about me and Kieran.

Outside the windows the morning was grey and inside it felt bleak, but after I'd showered and dressed I took care with my make-up: I needed to look under control when Stella saw me. The flat was so chilly I shivered and had to scrabble around for a warm jumper. As I did so, the phone rang: Emily and Matt's home number. And it was Em who spoke.

'Hi, Clare, is it too early? Only I've been up most of the night with Lily and she's finally asleep.'

'No, it's fine and I'm so glad you called. Are you OK now?'

'Yeah, tired but very happy, just a bit weepy yesterday. Matt said he'd told you not to ring for a day or two so I thought I should call you.'

'Well, I want to know all about Lily and the gruesome details of the birth, of course, but I have to go to work. Can we talk again later?'

225

'OK, this evening if I'm still awake then. But, Clare, I gather Matt put his big fat foot in it and told you about Alice. I'm so sorry. You haven't mentioned it to her have you?'

'No, but is it true?'

'Yes, sort of, but it wasn't at the wedding. It was on my hen night. You know we all got changed at my place, well, her bag was on the floor and I kicked it over. It fell open and I had to shove everything back inside and saw the pills then.'

'Did you say anything?'

'Oh no, I mean she was the doctor so I guessed she knew what she was doing. And I wasn't surprised because I knew she was working all hours at the hospital and didn't seem to be coping well. You must have noticed?'

I hadn't and once again I realised how blind I'd been to everything outside the bubble of my own little family. Emily was still talking. 'But I know she wasn't the only one who was on something. The situation at the firm was a nightmare just then.'

I wondered, but didn't ask, if that applied to Matt too. 'Don't worry,' I said. 'If I pinched the stuff from Alice, or from anyone else, I'm still to blame. I just wish you'd told me before.'

I heard her sigh. 'I did try to say something all those years ago. That's when you turned against me. And afterwards, when you got out, I just wanted us to be friends again, like before.' Something in her voice told me she was crying. 'I'm a coward, I know, but I've always thought we should try to put it behind us.'

I looked at the clock; I couldn't be late to work. 'I know and it's OK.'

I was about to say goodbye when a rush of words came from Emily. 'You know, I've only been a mother for five minutes, but I've realised something of how you must feel. How important it is for you to find the truth for Tom. I looked at Lily this morning and I knew if I was in your position I wouldn't rest until I'd answered all her questions.'

'Thanks, Em, that helps.'

'But I want to help properly. Don't forget we're close to where it happened and Matt grew up in Bramstone. He knows people from around there.'

I'd forgotten about Nic, and in the end we were both closing our doors at the same time. It was impossible not to hold the front door open, and then the gate, to let her manoeuvre the buggy through, and inevitable that we should walk together. There was a sea mist hovering over the town. The road was shiny with moisture, so we had to concentrate to avoid slipping on the steep slope.

'Did I hear Kieran rush off in the middle of the night?' she said when the road flattened out.

'I expect so. His mum was taken ill.'

She smiled at me, expecting something more. Her eyes were as bright as always even in the dull light and I felt a rush of affection for her. It might be good to talk to her about some of it, about Kieran and me, at least. I was going to suggest we share a meal tonight when Molly threw her blue rabbit onto the road. I retrieved it but, as I tried to pass it to Molly, Nic grabbed it and shoved it into the bag on the back of the pushchair, shaking her head and giving a heavy sigh. Molly had managed to slip off her shoe and before I could reach her she'd thrown that too, giving a little giggle.

I went after the shoe as Nic kicked the brake of the pushchair. Her, 'Molly for goodness sake,' came through gritted teeth and when she crouched to put the shoe back onto Molly's waving foot her voice was sharp. 'You'd better go, Clare. Don't want you to be late for work as well.'

I left her struggling and headed away. And as I walked I thought better of talking to her about Kieran. After all, I still didn't know how she felt about us getting together.

On the way home I got a text from Ruby. She must have borrowed an illicit mobile:

Hey you, guess what. I'm out soon. Wish me luck!

I texted back:

Great news, call me.

But somehow I knew she wouldn't. She'd told me there was no way we could still be friends on the outside and I knew this was her way of saying goodbye. I kept looking at her text for a long while, wishing I could call and speak to her. I doubted I would have survived inside without her and she said I had helped her get through it too.

But Ruby told me over and over that when we got out it was time to move on. 'I want to forget about this place and everything in it,' she always said, and after a while I could see she was right. By the time I came to leave I was determined to build a life outside for myself and for Tom, and in order to do that I had to make a fresh start.

The phone rang. 'Mum?' Tom's voice was anxious. 'Are you all right, you sound funny?'

'I'm fine, just a bit breathless because I'm walking home from work and it's uphill.'

We talked for a bit as I headed back to the flat, soothed by his voice and his stories of school. 'And, Mum, I'm in a cricket match next week after school. Can you come?'

I let myself into the flat. 'I'd love that. Just hold on while I take off my jacket.' It was difficult to keep my tone light, I was so happy he wanted me there. 'I haven't forgotten the put-you-up, by the way. I found a good one on the internet, so I'll get on with ordering it. Want to make sure it's here by the time you break up for the summer.'

'And Alice was talking to Emily about the new baby and they said you might be able to take me up there for a visit.'

I was just absorbing this when he asked, 'Have you heard from Mr Hillier?'

I'd hoped we could avoid that today, but at least I had one positive thing to tell him. 'Not yet, but Matt may be able to do a bit of digging around up there while he's on paternity leave.'

When I rang off I tried Kieran's phone. No answer, so I sent him a text to tell him I was thinking of him and wishing his mum well.

Then I fired up the laptop to order the put-you-up bed. And there was an email from David Hillier.

Dear Mrs Glazier,

I did manage to see Jake Downes for you and eventually got him talking. First of all, your memory was correct: there was another car there before Jake arrived. He claims to have no idea if it contributed to your accident, however the driver was apparently anxious not to get involved and begged Jake to say he was the first on the scene. It was only after he'd given his evidence that he understood that lying under oath was a crime.

As I told you, he's been in trouble with the law quite frequently and is terrified of the police. So he panicked when he realised how much he had told me and refused to say any more. He is still adamant that he won't talk to you and seems convinced you are out to get him.

However I made him promise to come and see me very soon and, if he does so, I will try to get whatever additional information I can. Although he was considerably shaken by our conversation I'm hoping it's done him good and that what he said may help you and your son.

With very best wishes,
David Hillier

*

I sat back in my chair, almost unable to breathe, my brain reeling. So that flicker of memory was right and a flash of headlights must have been partly to blame for me losing control. The other driver didn't want to be involved, which in the early hours of the morning, meant it was quite likely he had been drinking. The car must have been coming towards me, so it had to be heading for Bramstone because the road went no further. That meant the driver was probably someone from the village. If that was the case, Mr Hillier would know him, so would he tell me even if Jake had identified the person? I needed to talk to Jake myself.

I replied to the email.

> Please tell Jake I don't hold any kind of grudge against him for what he did. He must have been in an impossible situation. If he will agree to speak to me I will make sure he doesn't suffer for it.

I had made some strong coffee, and just swallowed a mouthful, when Emily rang. We talked for a while about Lily and the birth. Emily sounded tired, but with the kind of delirious happiness I remembered from the early days after the twins were born.

'Matt was wonderful, but because she came early he was still in London and we thought for a while he wouldn't get here in time. Just as well the actual labour took so long.'

Then she said, 'I've been thinking about Alice and I'm really not sure you should mention the pills to her. I mean I saw them at the hen night not the reception. And even if she did have them, would she have noticed if any were missing in those horrible days after the accident?' She carried on before I could speak. 'And think about it, Clare, if she did realise and has lived with the thought all these years, do you really want to make her face it now?'

A surge of emotion that said, *yes I do.* But, 'I don't know. I just feel everything needs to come into the open if I'm ever to get my memory back.'

'I can see that,' she said, 'but my brain isn't working well at the moment so why don't you talk it through with Lorna?'

I said I would, then told her about Mr Hillier's letter, the other car, and my own memory of someone else being there with Downes right after the crash. 'Trouble is the other person must surely have come from Bramstone, so was likely to be one of Mr Hillier's neighbours.'

'That's a tricky one. I wonder if he's guessed who it might be.'

'I'm betting whoever they were they must have bribed Downes at any rate. Can't see him lying for anyone out of the goodness of his heart.'

Emily said, 'Look, talk to Matt. He's local and he might even be able to find out where this Downes guy is living.'

We said our goodbyes and, while I waited for Matt to come to the phone, I had another thought. Perhaps the car driver wasn't from Bramstone, but was a guest from the reception coming back for something they'd left behind. Unlikely, I knew, but it was a possibility.

Matt said, 'Right, Em's filled me in and I think I should ask around to see if I can locate this Downes fella and have a word with him myself. Unless he's moved right away, which sounds unlikely, I shouldn't have too much trouble finding him. And I'll get the truth out of him, never fear.'

'Be careful, we don't want to scare him off.'

He chuckled. 'You forget, I've spent the past few years getting down and dirty with the corporate boys. Learned a few tricks about how to get a result.'

I'd decided to discuss the whole thing with Lorna before I talked to Alice so when Alice rang next evening I said nothing about it. She had been to see Lorna in hospital. 'They say she's making a perfect recovery, responding well to the physical therapy, and should be out in less than a week.'

'You don't sound convinced. What's wrong?'

'It's probably nothing, but she seems very low. It's not unusual to be depressed after an op like that, of course, but I had the feeling something else was bothering her.'

When we'd said goodbye I knew I needed to think and I'd do that more clearly out of the flat.

Although it was beginning to get dark it was very warm and the narrow Old Town streets were still crowded. As I wandered along I thought of those first days when I had cringed away from other people. This evening I found the chatter and laughter comforting.

Eventually I stopped at a little place that called itself a café/bar. All the outside tables were full, but there was space inside and I ordered a glass of wine and a toasted sandwich and found a seat in a corner.

I'd brought a notepad and pen and as I ate and drank, I scribbled down my thoughts, smiling as I remembered Tom's flow chart. My jottings were a lot messier than his professional looking production, but I could feel my mind clearing as I wrote.

If Dad told me he was my real father during the reception I would certainly have been upset and if I'd then spotted the amphetamines in Alice's bag it was conceivable I took some, just to keep from breaking down. (This, of course, was what the police suggested all those years ago, although they had the reason for my upset wrong.) Steve and Toby were going to leave early so I wouldn't have worried too much about the drugs impairing my driving. Might even have thought it would be good to drive a little recklessly and give Dad a fright as I told him what I thought of him. By the time Steve changed his mind and decided he and Toby would come with us I knew, from the evidence of the DVD, that I was too far gone to realise I was unsafe.

In any case, we might have got back to the hotel all right if it hadn't been for the oncoming car with its brilliant headlights. The other driver was probably as unfit to be behind a wheel as I was and bribed Jacob Downes to pretend he was first on the scene.

I sat back and took a long drink of wine. My scribbled notes made sense, but they sparked no memories and generated yet more questions. Surely, if the pills were Alice's she must have realised they were gone at some point and, if so, wouldn't she have told me? I underlined her name, running the pen back and forth till I'd made something that looked like a thick eyebrow.

The other questions were: who drove the car with the headlights and where were they going? I underlined the words: *who drove the car* working over it with my pen until it matched the line beneath Alice's name. Two dark brows, straight and stern.

'Everything all right?'

The words came from far away. I was deep underwater. I dragged my eyes from the page and managed a nod for the waitress. Those two stern brows stared at me from the page.

who drove the car … Alice.

It was too awful and yet, and yet … For a mad moment it almost made sense. If Alice got back to the hotel and only then saw some pills were missing she must have realised it was me. Knowing I planned to drive back, she would want to stop me. She'd been drinking for hours herself by then, so it might have seemed perfectly sensible to take her own car. If she'd got to the reception in time she could have warned me. I could imagine her taking me aside and telling me that no one need know anything about it: we could keep the whole sordid incident between the two of us.

But she was too late, we'd already left, and she met us at that dangerous bend with her headlights blazing.

I came back to myself, aware of a man watching me from a nearby table. I must have been staring into space with God knows what expression. Horror, probably, because I was horrified with myself for thinking like this. The idea that Alice might have known I'd stolen the pills from her and kept it from me was one thing, but that she was partly to blame for the accident – how could I think so for even a moment? I tore the page from the notebook, ripped it into tiny pieces, and scattered them along the road as I walked home.

Chapter Twenty-Four

Lorna was in the same room when I got to the hospital next day, but sitting in a chair by the window, her bandaged leg propped in front of her. At the sight of her smile I knelt by her side, leaning over the arm of the chair to lay my head on her chest. We stayed like that for long minutes and I felt her hand, warm, on the back of my head, then moving to stroke my cheek, and when I looked up we shared a smile.

An orderly brought us coffee, which tasted like warm water, but it was lovely just to sit quietly together. After I'd swallowed a few gulps to moisten my throat enough to speak I asked how she was. 'I'm fine, nearly ready to get out of here, thank goodness.'

I went to speak, but she raised her hand. 'Before you ask, I won't need any help. They say I can mostly manage on my own and I've a neighbour I can call if need be.' She smiled again, but I could see what Alice meant: there was a new darkness in her eyes.

A brown bird sat on the branch of a tree outside the window, so still it might have been a toy.

Lorna touched my hand. 'What is it? Tell me, please.'

'First I need to ask if you know anything more about Dad and Matt. I've seen the wedding video. It seems obvious Dad is angry with Matt and Matt has admitted as much.'

She sighed. 'All right, yes, there were big problems between them for a while. Your father knew people were already talking to Global about the possible takeover. Rats and sinking ships he used to say. But Matt upset him much more than the others because they'd been so close and, of course, he was going to be part of the family.'

'That's all?'

'As far as I know, but Matt did work with Dr Penrose and if he thought Penrose was unfairly treated I can't imagine him staying quiet about it, can you? They may have argued about that.'

It made sense and I couldn't imagine either of them avoiding a confrontation, even at a wedding. Lorna's dark eyes were fixed on me. 'But that isn't what's really worrying you, is it?'

'Emily told me about Alice having amphetamines on her at the hen night. Do you think I should ask if she had them with her at the wedding too? And if so, do I ask if she realised I could have taken some?'

Lorna's hand moved to smooth her hair, still as beautiful as ever. 'All I can say is, if I was in your place I wouldn't. What good can it do at this stage?'

'It would stop me imagining even worse.'

The plastic chair squealed as I pushed it back, needing to move, to get away and stop thinking these awful thoughts.

'Clare, don't go,' she said. 'Let's talk it through. You can trust me.' Her eyes gleamed in a shaft of sunlight.

I drew the chair close to her again. 'You know I keep seeing that flash of light? Well, I think it might have been headlights coming towards us on the bend. Mr Hillier has spoken to the biker who was the first witness at the scene and he let slip there was someone else there before him.'

'The biker?'

'You know, the scruffy young guy from the trial. And I've had a memory flash of two people standing in the road before I collapsed.'

There was a tinge of red on Lorna's cheek bones and she leaned forward. 'I don't understand. What does this have to do with Alice?'

I closed my eyes, unable to look at her. 'I keep thinking maybe she left the reception, then saw some pills were missing and realised I'd been acting as if I was high. Do you think she might have driven back to try and stop me?'

Lorna was silent: I couldn't even hear her breathing. When I opened my eyes she had leaned away from me, arms crossed over her chest. Her voice sounded tight. 'This is Alice you're talking about. Do you really believe she's capable of doing that and keeping quiet about it afterwards?'

'She'd been drinking, might even have been on something herself. I doubt she was thinking straight. She would have meant to help us.' My throat was so dry I coughed over the words and my eyes began to water. Lorna waited while I gulped dregs of cold coffee. 'And afterwards she would have been in shock,' I said.

'But all these years?'

'I know, I know, but you see why I have to talk to her. I can't get these thoughts out of my head unless I do.'

'I can help with that.' Her voice was gentle. 'Because I was at the hotel that night, too. I drove to and from the reception and I hadn't had a drink and the friends I'd given a lift to insisted on buying me one when we got back.'

She screwed up her eyes, trying to picture the scene. 'Maggie, Peter, and I were sitting in the bar when Alice came in. We had a bottle of wine and we asked her to join us. Then … let me see … '

She held up her hand to stop me speaking. 'Yes. We were all sitting at a little round table by the window. I was very tired. Really wanted to go to bed, but Peter insisted on getting another bottle.' When she stopped, lost in her thoughts, I waited as long as I could.

'Lorna?'

'We saw the headlights of a car and someone said, "That'll be Sylvia, with Steve and Toby," or something like that. But when Sylvia came in she was on her own.'

I couldn't stop myself. 'So Alice knew they were with me?'

'That's not the point, Clare. What I'm saying is that she was at the hotel hours before the accident.'

'But she could have gone out again.'

Neither of us spoke for a long time. The coffee must have been freezing, but Lorna drained her cup. It clinked into the saucer. 'You're surely not going to say anything like this to Alice herself?'

Having spoken it aloud I saw how mad it must sound and how terrible it would be to accuse my sister. I leaned back in my chair. 'No, but thank you for listening. It was important to say it: to stop it festering away. Now I have to focus on getting more out of Jacob Downes and shaking up my memory.'

'Has much more come back?'

'Apart from the two figures, nothing definite, but I'm sure I'm close. The moments when I feel I'm nearly there seem to be connected to situations like that night. There's usually movement and a sudden flash of light. It's the same kind of thing I've always seen, but much clearer.'

'And you really want to remember? Whatever you discover?'

'I have to tell Tom the truth.'

Her eyes shone and her hand came to her mouth. 'Sorry.'

Tears threatened me too and I closed my eyes to blink them away. Lorna took my hands.

And something happened.

No flash this time; no sense of being that other Clare. Just darkness. And in that darkness, an image. A black gate. It towered there, studded with bolts, barred and padlocked. And a feeling of dread so fierce I couldn't breathe. My eyes flew open.

'Clare?'

I forced myself to breathe again.

'Did you have another memory?' Lorna asked.

'Not exactly. I thought I saw a big gate, just a big, black gate, that's all, but I felt so awful.'

We sat for a while saying nothing until a nurse popped his head around the door to tell Lorna her doctor was coming. As I bent to kiss her goodbye, Lorna held my wrist and said, 'I'm so worried about you, Clare. Will you do me a favour and leave it for now? Take some time to think it through. I'll think too. I'm due out tomorrow, so come and see me at home as soon as you can.'

As I kissed her cheek, Lorna rubbed the back of my head again and whispered, 'I love you, my darling.'

And I left her there, looking out at the little bird, sitting so still on his branch.

When I was on the train, Kieran phoned and I asked after his mother.

'The operation went as well as it could, but it's obviously only delaying the inevitable.' He sounded very low. 'And what about you? Something else has happened, hasn't it?'

'Nothing, I'm fine.'

'So no news from Mr Hillier or Jake?'

I could tell him this. 'Oh yes, apparently Jake let slip that there was another car on the scene.'

'That's good – fits your memories at least.'

'And my cousin's husband lives locally so he's going to try to talk to Downes himself. Until I hear from him, or from Mr Hillier again, there's nothing more I can do.'

There was a silence. I couldn't find anything to say, but I didn't want him to go. Then he said. 'I'd better get back to Mum, but I'll ring again tomorrow if that's all right.'

'Of course it is.'

Chapter Twenty-Five

The phone didn't ring during the next couple of nights, but I almost wished it would. I was hardly sleeping anyway and at least I'd be sure I hadn't imagined it all. I told myself I wasn't paranoid. Unsettling things had happened and I wasn't going mad because I was beginning to think some of Tom's theories weren't too far-fetched. Anyone and everyone could have something to hide and I needed to be open to all possibilities if I was to face up to my memories. But when I closed my eyes all I could see was that image: the black gate, tall and overwhelming. And I knew it was a warning; a warning from my own mind.

Lorna rang twice and left messages, but there was no answer when I tried to call her back. She sounded very subdued each time, just saying she was home and hoped I'd visit as soon as I could. On my next day off work I went up to London to see her.

She had told me she still kept her key hidden under a special stone in one of her window boxes. 'I'm capable of staggering to the door, but it'll be quicker if you let yourself in.'

It felt so much like coming here all those years ago that I stopped for a moment, almost expecting a flash of lost memory, but there was nothing.

A pair of shoes stood on the mat and the door to the courtyard at the end of the narrow hallway was open, giving a glimpse of dappled greenery on the old walls. Although it was cool today, the courtyard, sheltered by the walls, had a Mediterranean look with its stone bench, pots of herbs and red geraniums. I had a sudden memory of Lorna sitting on that bench, cushions piled behind her, looking up with a smile from the book she was reading.

Today the garden was empty, the kitchen and bathroom too. I checked the living room, saying, 'Hello, it's Clare,' before opening the door in case she was dozing in a chair. She wasn't there either so she must be lying down.

I tapped on the bedroom door then eased it open. A shimmer of light filtered through the curtains, a tiny clock ticked on the bedside table. There was an overturned glass next to the clock and the photograph of Dad and Lorna, in its silver frame, lay on the floor.

And Lorna was on the bed, hair and makeup perfect, eyes closed, head to one side.

Obviously dead.

She was fully dressed, but barefoot; one bandaged leg stretched in front of her, the other hanging over the side of the bed. The glass and the photograph were the only things out of place. The room was absolutely still. And from where I stood, gripping the door handle till my fingers hurt, I could feel and smell death.

It had already turned Lorna into something else, something heavy, something solid. I reached out to stop myself from falling, but my hand touched the lumpen thing on the bed and I stumbled down onto one knee.

The carpet was damp and as my hand knocked into the photograph frame Dad's smile wavered, his face distorted by the sheen of water that had dripped from the overturned glass.

I hauled myself to my feet and into the hall, bending over to gasp for breath. After an eternity, I forced myself to look into the bedroom again, pulled out my mobile and sent for an ambulance, all the time staring at the bed, needing to see the thing there, to make myself believe what I was saying.

Then I called Alice, propping myself against the wall to still my shaking legs. 'I'm at Lorna's and, Alice, I'm sorry, she's dead.'

'Oh … ' Silence, then a clunk and a breath, and her voice, quieter, but calm. 'Are you sure?'

'Of course I am.'

'What can you see? I mean what does she look like? Do you think she's had an accident?'

'No, she's just lying there on her bed. It must be something to do with the operation.'

'Yes, that's probably it. Thrombosis … heart. You'd better call an ambulance. Or do you want me to do it?'

'I've done that already.' I felt a twist of irritation; wanting to snap at her that I'd seen death in prison and in far more sordid circumstances than this. But of course this was different. This was Lorna, and my stomach churned, my head spinning again, till I had to hold onto the hall table.

'OK. Look, you must be in shock. I'll drive up and get you. It'll be a while before you can leave anyway. You could try looking for the name of her own doctor and they'll want to know the hospital where she had the op.'

The idea of going through Lorna's things appalled me, but I knew she'd be horrified if the ambulance crew found the place in what she would call a mess. So I picked up Dad's photo, wiped it on the duvet, and replaced it and the water glass on the dressing table in the corner. Then I spotted the slip of paper.

The fountain pen she'd used sat beside it. The paper was folded in half and I hesitated for only a moment. As I read, my eyes focused and unfocused on a few phrases. *Clare, sorry, no other way.* I took a breath and forced myself to slow down, glancing from the mute body on the bed to her words in my hand.

Clare.
   I'm so sorry I have to do this, but I can see no other way. I can't keep a secret like this to myself any longer. Guilt is a

corrosive emotion, I know that very well, and in the end the only solution is to face up to what you've done. I loved your father very much and I think this is what he would want me to do. But please believe me when I say that I also love you.

I hope you can accept that this is for the best.

With fondest love,
Lorna

For what seemed hours after that, I stood in the kitchen staring out at the grey courtyard, my fantasy of Italian warmth seeming as ridiculous now as the single magpie strutting and preening on the stone bench.

It wasn't until the third long ring that I registered the doorbell. I folded the letter and put it in my pocket then let the ambulance crew in, pointing to the bedroom, and standing back to let them brush by me. I hovered in the hallway watching as the man looked at Lorna, then knelt beside her, glancing back at his colleague with an expression that said there was no rush.

The woman turned and led me into the living room. 'You need to sit down, love,' she said. When I'd done so she asked about my relationship to *the lady* and what I knew about her health.

I told her about the operation and the name of the hospital. 'So I imagine she was on some kind of medication.' My voice came from far, far away, but the woman just rubbed my hand and told me to sit quietly for a while. I listened to their voices carrying softly from the bedroom, while Lorna's note crackled in my pocket.

Alice insisted on taking me to Beldon House and I couldn't find the words to object. At least she didn't try to talk much on the way, just said she'd arranged for Tom to stay over with Mark for the night.

She lit a fire and in front of it, in a big armchair, I tried to sip some soup. She sat opposite, and when I placed the bowl on the side table she leaned forward. 'I can see you don't want to talk and I don't blame you. It can all wait till morning. Just go up and get some sleep.'

I felt as if I was coming to myself after a long delirium. 'She left a note.'

Alice leaned closer, blue eyes flickering with sparks of red from the fire. 'What?'

I passed her the paper and she slumped back so heavily the armchair creaked. 'Oh, my God.'

'So it *is* what I think – a suicide note?'

'Certainly looks like it. Where was it?'

'On her dressing table.'

'Clare, you should have left it there.'

'I wasn't thinking straight for one thing and for another, it would have meant involving the police.'

'You're not thinking of destroying it, are you?'

I took the note from her, hating Lorna for being so enigmatic. 'No, but I don't understand it. Why she would want to kill herself?'

Alice held out a mug and I found myself taking it and drinking the coffee I didn't want and trying to focus on what she was saying. 'I've seen a few suicides and the motives are never that clear-cut. One thing we know about Lorna, much as we loved her, is that she was secretive.'

'She talks about guilt and facing up to what you've done.' I wasn't sure if I was speaking the words or if they were just thoughts. 'I've been asking about the accident.'

I smoothed the paper on the arm of my chair. Alice didn't speak and I thought of the scenario I'd mapped out – the one that blamed her. Now it took on another complexion altogether and I saw a new puzzle take shape, one where the pieces fitted just as well for Lorna as for Alice.

She was looking at me with gentle eyes.

'There are things I haven't told you,' I said. 'Things I've remembered. I know I saw two people immediately after the accident.'

'So you were awake when Mr Hillier got there?' Her voice was very quiet.

'No. I think it might have been Lorna.' I told her the theory I'd been putting together: the one that implicated her, but worked just as well for Lorna.

When I'd finished Alice gave an enormous sigh. 'Do you know, there was a moment in the hospital with you ... ' Another trembling breath. 'I heard about the drugs in your system and had a horrible thought that you might have taken them from me on Em's hen night. I had some with me then because work was impossible and I was so tired all the time. But I stopped using them before the wedding because they made me feel worse. I knew I didn't have any with me that day, but I still checked when I got home to see if any were missing.'

'And were there?'

'No.' How ridiculously easy it was in the end.

She went to the fire. One of the logs was spitting sparks and she moved it about with the poker. 'We know Lorna was unhappy and had access to drugs. So I suppose it makes sense. She wasn't drinking at the wedding, but I remember her having quite a lot back at the hotel. I wonder if she went to bed, saw some capsules were missing, and panicked. She wouldn't have been thinking straight.'

'But to keep it secret all this time?'

'How could she tell anyone? God, Clare, she must have been in an agony of guilt at first, but she knew it wouldn't really help you. You were still culpable.'

'But when I started going back over it all, and told her some memory was returning, she knew it would come out eventually. Poor Lorna.'

I put my mug on the floor and we shared a long glance. Then she knelt in front of me, pulled me into a hug, and I dropped a kiss onto her soft hair.

*

Alice gave me a sleeping pill and I didn't wake from my drugged oblivion till after midday: my head and my limbs so heavy I felt like staying in bed forever.

I longed to be able to cry, but the tears wouldn't come. After another hour I dragged myself downstairs. The house was empty. In the kitchen a note told me Alice would be home about six. She had called Emily and also Stella, who said not to rush back to work too soon.

I couldn't summon up an interest in anything to eat or drink. Instead, I crawled onto the big armchair in the living room, and the next thing I knew Tom was looking at me as he cradled a mug.

'Hi Mum, it's half-past four. I've made you some coffee.'

I forced a smile. 'Hello, you,' and raised the mug. 'This is just what I need. Alice gave me a sleeping pill and it's really knocked me out.'

He perched on a footstool, his gaze steady, but his cheeks colouring up. 'Alice said Lorna died, and you found her. That must have been awful. I'm ever so sorry. She was nice.'

'Yes she was.'

He stood, big hands dangling at his side, made a move towards me, thought better of it, coloured even more, and then remembered something. 'Alice says you're not to do anything. She'll cook when she gets in.' His eyes flickered to my dressing gown, then to the stairs. 'Mark's here for tea. I told him to stay in my room.'

I pulled my belt tight. 'Oh right. I'll get dressed.'

I felt so leaden with tiredness that by the time I managed to wash and pull on some clothes, Alice was calling that food was ready. Mark looked at me curiously, but was soon intent on eating. Tom carried my food over, telling me to be careful it was hot, then passed me the bread and jumped up to get me a glass of water. I grabbed a piece of kitchen towel and scrubbed at my face, as Tom and Mark shared a glance.

I refused Alice's offer of another sleeping pill, but slept well all the same. When I woke I felt clear-headed and I was up and dressed before anyone else. Alice came down as I was drinking my second cup of coffee.

She smiled. 'You look a lot better.'

'I'm fine. I'll go home on the train this morning.'

She tried to persuade me to stay, but I was determined, knowing I couldn't even begin to process this until I was back to some semblance of normal life.

Chapter Twenty-Six

As we pulled up at Wadhurst Station, Alice put her hand on my knee. 'You know you could still come and stay with us for a bit. Forget about the job and take some time to be with Tom and me. It would do us all good.'

I raised my eyebrows at her. 'Thought we'd been over this ground months ago?'

She pushed a strand of hair behind her ear, looking in the rear view mirror as a taxi drew up behind us. 'But things have changed. We never expected it to be this difficult.'

'I did.'

She made a small noise and her hand fluttered towards me, but then returned to the steering wheel. I went on, hoping she would believe me. 'OK, I didn't think Lorna would die, but it's been better with Tom than I dared hope and I still need to be independent. You must see that.'

She crossed her arms, but gave me a sweet smile. 'I do, of course I do. It's just … I can't help worrying about you.'

I kissed her cheek and jumped out of the car, leaning back in to say. 'I'm the big sis, not you, worrying's my job.' My train was due, so I flapped my hand at her to drive away. 'Go to work, doctor, there're sick people queuing up for your attention.'

On the train I tried not to think, but it was impossible. I wasn't sure how much of the misery I felt was grief for Lorna and how much was anger. It didn't matter anymore that she might have been lying to me all these years and knew precisely what had happened on that night, or even that the accident was partly her fault. I just wished she had told me rather than taking the easy way out. But perhaps she thought I would never be able to forgive her if I knew the whole truth. And perhaps she was right.

I jumped when my mobile bleeped with a text.

Mum, don't be too sad. I'll ring you later. Tom XXX

I had the phone pressed to my chest, rubbing the plastic and trying to hold back the tears when it rang.

'Tom?'

'No, it's Matt.'

The reception was terrible and I could hardly hear him, but I caught the words *Lorna* and *all right*.

'Yes, I'm fine. Look, Matt, you keep cutting out. I'm on the train, but I'll call you when I get home in about half an hour.'

The air was chill with the threat of storm and as I approached the flat it began to rain heavily. I was wet by the time I got into the hall and I stood shaking the rain from my hair and wriggling inside my damp T-shirt.

Heavy feet pounded up the path. A loud rap on the door. The stained glass at the top was darkened by the shadow of a man's head distorted by the curve of the window. The doorbell buzzed twice. I looked towards Nic's silent flat as the buzz came again, then a burst of knocking.

'Open up. It's raining out here.'

I put the chain on the door and opened it a crack.

Matt, only Matt.

'I thought you saw me running after you.' He was breathless and laughing.

My own laugh came on a wave of relief and I took off the chain as discreetly as I could. He shook himself like a friendly dog.

'I was sitting in the car waiting for you. It would pick now to start a downpour. Get the kettle on, will you.'

I was suddenly very glad he was here. I'd been dreading coming in to the flat on my own. 'It's great to see you again, but why?' I said.

He took over the tea making. 'Let me have a drink first. I've been waiting for ages. One of your neighbours came out and I asked her if you were in, but she looked at me as if I was the mad axe murderer and wouldn't say.'

I smiled. 'That must have been Nic. I was staying at Alice's.'

He added milk to the mugs and passed one to me, heading for the sofa. The springs twanged as he dropped onto it. 'I should have guessed. We heard about Lorna and that's why we decided I should tell you this face to face.'

A big gulp of tea, so hot it scalded my tongue. 'You've seen Downes?'

'Yeah. I found out where he lives and gave him some bullshit about trying to track down a mate of mine from his year at school.' Matt patted the sofa beside him and I perched on the edge. 'When I offered to take him to the pub to talk about it he couldn't get there fast enough and after a few drinks we were best pals. Pretty sorry for himself is our Jacob.'

'Did he say anything useful?'

'Once he was well lubricated, I started on about how some people have it easy. Rich bastards who think they can get away with anything. Not like the rest of us.'

I put my tea on the floor. 'So what did he tell you?'

'He was going on about how he'd made some money once because he happened to be in the right place at the right time and I decided to take a chance. Told him I'd just realised I recognised him from your trial. Made out I was on the jury. Said I'd always wondered if he knew more than he said, even though he'd done brilliantly on the stand and fooled everyone else.'

I twisted to face him. 'And?'

'I overplayed my hand. Have to admit I was enjoying it, but he's not quite as stupid as he looks and he's obviously scared to death. He said he had to go, but I'd just got another round in and I managed to calm him down. Said I'd guessed he was covering for someone else at the accident and hoped he was well paid for it.'

This was agony. 'Matt, please.'

A long drink of his tea. 'I think you need to hear this properly. Make your own mind up about what it means.'

I raised my palm to him. 'Sorry, go on.'

'Well, he ranted on, but in the midst of all the bluster he said something important.'

I wasn't breathing.

Matt tapped his lips with his fist. 'Hang on I want to get this right. He said, "It wasn't my fault. She said she had somewhere important to be and there was no need for us both to stay, but best not mention she was there. I never knew there'd be any trouble."' Matt swallowed the rest of his tea in a noisy gulp then put his mug on the coffee table.

My heart, after one huge thump, seemed to have stopped. '*She*? He said, *she*?'

Matt took off his glasses: his face looked strange and naked without them. He rubbed hard at the lenses with a tissue. 'He tried to cover it up, but yes, definitely *she*. I pretended I hadn't noticed, carried on supping my pint.'

'Did you get a description?'

He slipped his glasses on again. 'No, he clammed up after that, but clearly she paid him to keep quiet.'

So tired, I was so tired. A huge sigh burst out and I wanted to howl with misery. 'Lorna killed herself, Matt. Did Alice tell you?'

'Yes. That's why I had to see you myself.'

'So you think she was the woman?'

'If she was, and she knew you were getting close to the truth, I suppose suicide would make sense.'

He looked at me and held out his arms, 'Come here.'

I pressed my face into his soft sweater. 'She could have told me. Even now she could have told me. I loved her so much, Matt.'

His heavy hand soothed my back. 'I know.'

After a while I moved away and he pulled a tissue from the box on the coffee table and handed it to me. I blew my nose and scrubbed my eyes.

He went over to look out of the window, hands in his pockets. A sunbeam split the dark clouds. 'What worries me,' he said, 'is that he may have guessed I was there for you. I'd bought him a few drinks, dropped him a few quid, and I was his best mate for a while. But when he got careless, I lost him and he walked out on me. I went after him, still trying to be friendly, but the little shite came over all macho. Talking about Mr Hillier and, *that nosy bitch*, who I guess is you, and how you were trying to fit him up.'

'Did you tell him I don't want to cause him any trouble?'

He turned, the shaft of sun behind him blurring his face. 'I'm sorry, but the way he was talking about you really got me. So I grabbed him, pushed him against the wall, and told him in no uncertain terms what I'd do if he bothered you.'

I swallowed and something stumbled in my chest.

Matt sat next to me again, taking my hands. 'I know that's not how you wanted me to play it, but, honestly, I think going softly, softly, with a fucker like that has its limits.'

Maybe he was right. 'OK, but don't do anything more for now, will you.'

'Whatever you say. But don't worry, I should think he's used to being on the wrong end of a bit of rough stuff. He's the sort who asks for it. Doubt he'll even remember what happened if he sees me again. More likely to remember the money and the pints. So I could let him know the woman is out of the picture and the case closed as far as you're concerned, if that's what you want?'

I leaned forward, elbows on my knees. *Case closed.* Was it?

Matt was cleaning his glasses again, giving me time, and I tried a smile. 'No, just leave it, please. It's probably best if we keep away from him.'

He shook his head, 'I just can't believe all this.'

'I know. I keep thinking I should have left it alone. Maybe it would have been better not to know. Lorna might still be alive.'

'You can't blame yourself for that. She made her own choices.'

It was good to talk to him. 'Do you know, Matt, I think I'm close to getting my memory back, which is what I've been hoping for all these weeks, but now I'm so scared I might remember something even worse, something terrible.'

We sat for a while in silence until I became aware of him shifting on the sofa, anxious to get going, no doubt. I smiled at him. 'But thank you for seeing Jacob Downes and for coming all this way when Emily needs you so much.'

'After we heard about Lorna there was no question.' He stood, with a quick glance towards the door. 'But it's a fair old drive home and I can't leave them for too long.' His smile and the look in his eyes told me he was already back with them in his mind. With his wife and baby. His own happy life.

When he was gone, I washed the mugs and made a vague attempt to tidy the kitchen, and I thought about Matt's suggestion that we should tell Jacob Downes Lorna was dead. It was actually a good idea, but it might be better if Mr Hillier did it.

He answered his phone right away. 'Mrs Glazier, I'm glad you called because Jake turned up here last night. He was very agitated indeed and seemed convinced we are trying to fit him up, as he calls it. I gather someone has been to see him on your behalf.'

'Yes, I'm sorry. It was my cousin and I think he was a bit too forceful.'

'That's the impression I got and I must say, Mrs Glazier, I'm not happy about it. I did tell you Jake was vulnerable.'

'You did and I can only say I'm sorry. I quite understand you might want nothing more to do with me, but I've actually rung to ask another favour.' He didn't speak, but was obviously too polite to hang up on me, so I ploughed on. 'First of all could you apologise to Jake if my cousin upset him and tell him he has nothing at all to fear from me. No one else will bother him.'

A sound that might have been a snort came down the line. 'Ah, that's different and of course I'll be only too happy to reassure him.'

'But, Mr Hillier, could you also tell him we think we've discovered who the other driver was and she's recently died. So it would be immensely helpful if Jake could give me some kind of description of her, just to set my mind at rest.'

'You're saying the other driver was a woman?'

I shivered, moving from the gloomy kitchen to stand in a patch of sunlight near the windows. 'Yes, didn't Jake mention that to you?'

'No. In fact I could have sworn he referred to the person as *he*.' He was silent, obviously thinking. 'But perhaps he was trying to mislead me or more likely, in my old-fashioned way, I just assumed it was a man.' Another silence, then, 'Anyway, what's important is that I can tell Jake no one else will harass him.'

'Yes, please do that.'

'I will, and of course I'll ask if he can help you with a description, although I can't guarantee he'll be willing to do so.'

I knew he'd try and I thanked him for all his efforts, but I could tell he wasn't hopeful. I threw the phone down telling myself it didn't matter that much anyway. We knew everything important already. As Matt said, the case was closed.

I must have dozed on the sofa, lying awkwardly, because I opened my eyes, unsure where I was and with a pain in my neck. I'd been dreaming about the accident and fragments still floated in my consciousness. The fragments were bubbles that burst when I grabbed at them, but there were things that remained as the dream dissipated. I saw the very moment it happened: the dark, empty road and the blinding light from another car coming round the bend. Then the silence; a terrible silence after the noise and chaos of the crash.

Another fragment: fire blistering my face as I tried to get near the wreck, fighting the hard hands that pulled me back. They were a man's hands, so they must have belonged to Jacob Downes: and if so he had saved my life.

How long I sat there, grasping at those bubbles of memory, I had no idea, but at last I was aware enough to know that I was very cold. Outside the sea was grey, with soapsuds of foam churning on the top of each swift-moving wave. Above them the sky was grey too, ripples of cloud scudding fast across it. But inside everything was muffled and I could feel all the silent rooms around me.

I was afraid to move in case the remnants of memory dissolved again. But when I stood, although I felt shaky, the memories remained. That dream was a jolt from my subconscious, I felt sure. I'd been ready to agree with Matt and Mr Hillier and accept the idea that it was all over and I'd found out all I ever would. But that wasn't good enough for me and it certainly wouldn't be good enough for Tom. The memories were there, I knew it now, and I needed to stop waiting for them to surface and to work on reviving them.

I didn't have the DVD, but I had plenty of other stuff that could help. The photo albums were still in the bedroom drawer, along with Tom's flow chart and the folder with all his printouts, and I brought them to the kitchen table. I carried the laptop in too and loaded the CD with the hen night photos. Lorna's note was still in my pocket and I read it through several times; each time more confused.

When I'd gone through everything, my eyes and back were sore and I wanted just to crawl into bed. But I couldn't let myself do that. I opened Tom's folder of stuff from the internet. Even if it held nothing useful he'd be happy to know I'd studied it.

I put the newspaper reports of my trial to one side. I could ignore those for now because I remembered it all too clearly. Tom had printed out loads of stuff about Dad and Parnell Pharmaceuticals and I read through those quickly. The articles from before the scandal were just puff pieces about British success stories or advertising stuff put out by the firm. The reports of the scandal told me only what I already knew.

There was one article however, published a couple of years after the accident, that featured an interview with Dr Penrose. The writer claimed he'd had an exclusive interview in which Penrose made *some startling allegations.* I imagined they would need to be startling to interest anyone so long after the furore had died away.

I took the article to the sofa and leaned back to read it slowly. Penrose claimed at least one of the many trials they'd done with Briomab had thrown up some worrying results. And his original report had concluded that this trial should be repeated, but he said his comments had been deleted, along with the details of that particular trial. He didn't know who was responsible, but said Dad must have authorised it. Apparently Dad wanted to get Briomab on the market right away to beat a similar drug being developed by Global.

Penrose told the reporter that other people knew about the deletion and some had initially supported him, but had been got at. '*I didn't blame them,*' he said. '*They were mostly young men who couldn't risk their careers. Those few that remained loyal to me were only saved from personal disaster by Mr Frome's death.*'

In fact, he went on to say that Dad had been obsessed with keeping control of the firm and threatened to destroy it rather than let Global take over. *He was willing to let all those shareholders lose their money. That's what it was all about really, his ego, and keeping control of his firm.*

I sat for a while with the article on my lap wondering why I'd never looked at the details closely before. If I had, I might have given more credence to Tom's theory about someone wanting to hurt Dad. Lorna had shares in the business. If she'd known the way Dad was thinking, it would certainly have added to her anxiety at the time.

My mind was whirling with thoughts and with that feeling of being very close to the memories. When the phone rang, I jumped.

It was Emily. We talked about Lorna for a bit, but Alice had told her pretty much everything. I read the note out to her.

'That's a funny kind of suicide note, but I suppose she didn't want the police to understand what she was saying,' she said.

'Of course, I hadn't thought of that.'

We were quiet for a bit, then she said. 'Matt told you about his meeting with Jacob Downes and that Downes let slip the other driver was a woman?'

'Which more or less proves it was Lorna,' I said. 'But I've asked Mr Hillier to try and get a description. I need to be absolutely sure before I talk to Tom.'

'I'm sorry if Matt was a bit heavy-handed with Downes. Hope it doesn't frighten him off.'

'If it does I shall just have to try even harder to remember. I'm close, Em, very close. Had a moment today when I was almost there.'

'That's good, but don't rush it, you need to take care of yourself. Your health and sanity are more important for Tom than finding out the truth.'

I picked up the article about Mr Penrose. 'Before you go, is Matt back yet? I'd like to ask him something else.'

'No, can you believe it; he called in at the office on the way home and got caught up in a meeting. I'd be furious with him if I had the energy.'

'And all because he came here. I'm so sorry. But can I ask you this instead, just to clear my mind? Did Matt argue with Dad at the reception?'

I heard her sigh. 'I suppose it doesn't matter now because you probably don't have many illusions left about your father, but honestly, Clare, his behaviour towards everyone was really awful around that time. I suppose he was desperately afraid he'd lose the company, but … Anyway the short answer is, yes. They had a blazing row outside. Not the first, but a rip-roarer and Matt was so upset we left our own reception early.'

That explained the DVD. 'Do you know what was said?'

'Basically, your Dad told Matt he had destroyed Dr Penrose and would do the same to Matt: family or not. Kill his prospects of any kind of career if he didn't stop supporting Penrose. He said he was prepared to sabotage the firm rather than let Global get their hands on it. Accused Matt of spying for Global and warned him he'd be responsible for Parnell's shares crashing. That would have affected all of us: you and Alice, and my Dad too, of course.'

'So what did Matt decide to do?'

'What could he do? He had to agree to abandon Dr Penrose and keep his mouth shut.'

I couldn't think of anything to say, but Emily went on. 'Do you know, afterwards, when we heard about the crash, Matt and I thought at first your dad might have caused it deliberately. You hear about people killing themselves and taking their whole family with them, don't you?'

I managed, 'Yes.'

'Look, Clare, promise me you'll take it easy. You've had a series of horrible shocks. So let yourself get back to normal before you go on with this, please.'

I promised I would, but I doubted she believed me.

Next morning my mobile bleeped from the bedside table: a text from Kieran.

Are you OK? Give me a ring when you get this. Been up all night. XXX.

He answered right away sounding beaten. 'I've only just left the hospital. They've stabilised her as they're calling it and I don't think there's much more they can do, but they're talking about sending her home soon. She says she wants to die in her own bed. But she's a tough old bird, so it's likely to be a while.'

'I'm so sorry.'

'I'm driving back after I've had some sleep. Just need to check the flat and collect some work, so that I can stay with her for as long as it takes. Will you be there?'

'Yes.'

'Are you all right?' he asked. 'You sound strange.'

'I'm fine.'

'No, you're not. Please, Clare, tell me or you'll have me worrying even more.'

I told him I'd found Lorna dead.

A moment's pause, then, 'Oh, Clare, I'm sorry. Look, I'm going to have a sleep then stop off at the hospital and if there's no change with Mum, I'll start back home. See you then.'

At the shop, Stella said how sorry she was about Lorna. Then she looked hard at me. 'Are you sure you're all right to work today?' I forced a smile, saying I was, and she nodded and said no more. She was busy with orders and spent most of the morning in the back room or driving the van back and forth.

There was a white sea mist over the whole town and few customers, and I was writing out some cards for telephone orders, when the door clanged open and I looked up to see Alice.

She closed the door quickly with her foot, but still brought a swirl of fog in with her. 'I was over this way so I thought we might have lunch.' She was smiling, but was very pale, obviously worried about me.

We went to a little wine bar just down the street. It was busy, but we managed to find a table, the rickety chairs creaking as we shifted, both of us very aware of the couple on the next table.

'Alice, I'm OK,' I said. 'Don't worry about me.'

She sipped her lemon and lime and placed it carefully back on the waterproof tablecloth, the pale yellow of the drink clashing with the red and purple paisley design. I looked out onto the misty street and shivered. I'd made a mistake coming out without a sweater.

'I get it, you're strong now,' she said. 'But sometimes it's better to give in when awful things happen.' I went to speak, but she carried on. 'And what about me? I loved Lorna too, you know, and maybe I need you.' Her voice trembled and she looked into the glass she was sliding back and forth on the table.

I touched her hand to still it. 'I'm sorry. I'm being very selfish, I know, but I need some time alone. I'm so, so, close to remembering everything and I need to focus on that for a little while.'

'Just have a few hours off tonight, please. I can hang around here and take you back with me. Might even persuade Stella to let you go early. It'll help clear your mind and we can talk. Tom's anxious about you too.'

'I'll come tomorrow, but I can't tonight, I'm sorry.'

'What shall I tell Tom then? I said you'd be there.' Her voice rose and the couple at the next table glanced over at us.

'I'll ring him and explain. He'll understand.'

'Are you sure?'

I bit the inside of my cheek to stop myself from telling her to shut up and leave me alone. It wasn't just me who'd had to face a lot of shocks recently and she looked close to breaking point. 'What I do know is that he wants me to remember and I can't let this moment go.' I looked at my watch. 'I've got to get back.'

She didn't move, just gave a little nod and I left her sitting there, pretending an interest in the congealing food on her plate, as the girl on the next table looked over and nudged her boyfriend.

Standing behind the counter that afternoon watching rain spatter at the windows, and listening to the heavier drip, drip, of a blocked gutter, I tried to catch hold of more fragments of memory. There was a puddle near the shop door and I took the mop and bucket from the back room, swishing it to and fro, hoping the mindless rhythm would bring some clarity. I had so many parts of the puzzle but there was something else, something I knew I wasn't getting.

When I got home, Nic's flat was dark and her car wasn't in the parking bay; she must have gone shopping. Kieran's car wasn't back either and, although I'd been missing him, I was relieved: couldn't face seeing anyone, even him, just now. I pulled on a mac and a pair of trainers to go for a walk. As I closed the main door, the back of my neck tingled and I shivered again.

Back on the rainy streets, I walked like a zombie. Lorna's note was in my pocket and I held it tight: as if her hidden thoughts might seep through the paper into my mind. But nothing came and a fierce surge of anger struck me. It made me gasp and stand frozen under an old- fashioned street lamp, hypnotised, as thin feathers of rain floated in the beam. *You said you loved me, Lorna, so how could you leave me like this: with no answers?*

I walked home, huddled in my mac, anxious to call Tom before he went to bed. When I came close to the flat, a car swished by splashing me with cold rainwater and I had to stop and hold onto the gate because I remembered the car that nearly hit me the night I came back from Cumbria. And all the other things too. They were real, I knew that. Lorna warned me that trying to get my memory back could be painful. But, could she also have sent someone to scare me? It was a terrible thought, but I was beginning to wonder if I'd ever really known her.

I let myself into the flat, shrugging off my mac and throwing it on the sofa. Lorna's note was still in my hand and I scrunched it into the pocket of my jeans. I needed to keep it near me.

I walked over to the big sitting room windows. It was past midsummer, the darkness falling a little earlier each day. And this evening the rain made it gloomy, shrouding everything in a grey veil. I felt almost as I'd done on the first day here, wanting to cry, but knowing there was no point.

I wondered how long it would be before Kieran got back and all at once I didn't want to be alone. I'd noticed Nic's lights were on again as I came in, so maybe after I'd called Tom, I'd go over and see her.

The phone rang.

It was Alice and I started to say I was sorry for how I'd been in the wine bar, but she cut me off. 'Clare, something's happened.'

The quiver in her voice turned me cold. I sat down. 'What?'

'You've got to get over here.' She spoke as if reading a script. 'Come now and don't call the police, don't tell anyone.'

The room took on an unreal shimmer. 'What's happened?'

Her voice wobbled. 'Just hurry, please. Or he says he'll hurt Tom.' The room wavered again as the line clicked dead.

Chapter Twenty-Seven

Seconds later I was beating and calling at Nic's door. 'Please, there's an emergency. I need to borrow your car.'

She tried to usher me into her hall. 'Of course, babe, but come in and sit down for a minute.'

I pulled away. 'No I can't stop. It's my son. I've got to get to him.

She didn't answer, didn't ask any questions, just reached out to the little table next to her and took a key from the bunch. I tried to thank her, but couldn't speak, and she waved me away. 'Get going. Good luck, whatever it is.'

The rain was pouring down and by the time I reached Nic's car, and struggled to open it, I was soaked. It wasn't until I climbed into the driver's seat that I realised what I was doing and had to sit for a moment to catch the breath that had suddenly gone. It was so long since I'd driven I wasn't even sure I could anymore.

I turned on the engine and adjusted my seat. One part of my brain was shouting, *hurry up, hurry up,* while another part was telling me to take care. *Find the windscreen wiper switch. Don't forget the lights.* Finally, I managed to crank the gearstick into reverse and to turn the car round. It bounced on the kerb. But then I was away.

Although I was hardly breathing, crouched forward, my eyes straining into the empty darkness ahead, I was managing all right.

The car slowed at the top of the hill and threatened to stall, but after another brief struggle, and a clash of gears, I was onto the main road.

The rain was beating down and the road was busy, but I thought of Tom. *Just keep going.* Heading into the country, I tried to lean back; to loosen my hands on the wheel; to unclench my jaw.

The windscreen had turned white with mist and I couldn't locate the switch to clear it. I rubbed a patch clean with one hand then rolled down my window. Cold air and spits of rain struck me, but it didn't matter. I was sweating anyway and at least I could see. The lights of the cars coming towards me were very bright. *Keep going, keep going.*

When I turned, at last, onto a quieter road, I put my foot down. *Not long now. I'll be there soon, Tom.*

My headlights reflected off the trees at the roadside – moving fast. There was nothing between Tom and me, but this long stretch of shining road with dark clouds rushing above it. A dull rumble: thunder in the distance. A flash of lightening so brilliant I flinched and my eyes closed for an instant.

And it happened just like that.

As I opened my eyes, a car swept by, its headlights dazzling. And, in that split second of brilliant blindness, I was her again – the Clare of the moment when my life changed.

The memory was there, then gone again, and as I reached out to grasp it, the clouds shifted above, the road spooled away, and I clung on with desperate fingertips.

I parked the car a few yards before Beldon House, cut the lights, and killed the engine. My heart continued to race and I put my elbows on the steering wheel, my hands to my face, and tried to slow my breath.

It was the oddest feeling. As I came back to myself everything slotted into place and at last I knew the whole truth. I remembered everything from before and since the accident, yet it was as if the nightmare of prison and the turmoil of the past few weeks had happened to someone else. I was myself again, the real Clare.

I jerked back to some sense of where I was and what was happening here and now. My world had turned inside out, but I had no time to think about that. I had to get to Tom.

I left the car and walked towards the house. The rain had eased, but it felt cold after the heat of the car and I shivered in my damp clothes. The country road was dark, just a faint glow coming from Beldon House. My feet sounded loud as they crunched on the gravel drive and, when I got to the front door and took out my key, I was very aware of the silence inside.

The lower hall was dimly lit; everywhere else seemed to be dark. There was a strange smell, like petrol.

I ran up to Tom's bedroom and flung open the door. The room was empty, the bed still neatly made. I looked into each of the other rooms – all empty – then walked slowly downstairs.

'He's not here, Clare.' Alice's voice from the kitchen. She was sitting at the table with a mug in front of her, the only light coming from over the cooker. It was so strange seeing her with my new/old eyes.

The blood drummed in my ears, but I made myself stand still and talk quietly. 'Where is he?'

She smiled. 'Staying with Mark. There's no one else here.'

'So why the phone call?'

A little head shake; the light gleaming on her blonde hair. 'I needed to see you, Clare. I can't go on like this.'

I sat, trying to slow my breath. 'It was you, wasn't it, in the other car, not Lorna? I've remembered seeing you there.'

She stood and poured me a mug of coffee. Her hand shook as she pushed it across the table to me. 'Yes, and I'm so, so, sorry.' Tears filled her eyes before she looked down. 'I was drunk, didn't know what I was doing. At first I just thought I'd wait until you were well enough and then I'd tell you, but I'd lied to the police, you see, and I didn't know how to get out of it.

We might both have gone to prison and Tom needed one of us to look after him.'

A tear ran down her cheek and she pressed the back of her hand against her mouth. I waited and eventually she said, 'And I paid Downes to keep quiet.'

When she reached out for me I moved my hand back and she bit her lip, twisting her pale sweater between her hands. 'Clare, please, I'm sorry, what more can I say?'

'But why did you drive back?'

'Like you said, I realised some capsules were missing and remembered how you'd been behaving. Knew you couldn't be drunk so the only explanation was that you were high.'

I stirred my coffee. 'If Lorna had nothing to do with it, why kill herself?'

'I don't know.' It was a whisper.

I took Lorna's letter from my pocket and smoothed it out on the table, then looked into her eyes. 'I've read this over and over, because something never seemed right.' She was watching me steadily. 'I could never believe Lorna would do something like that, but this seemed to prove it.'

Her eyes were very bright, as if with fever.

'But it wasn't a suicide note, was it? Lorna was a letter writer of the old school, a trained secretary,' I said. 'She would never have begun a letter like that. Just *Clare* – no *Dear Clare,* or anything. And the word, Clare, was followed by a full stop, not a comma. A comma at the start of a letter would have been automatic for someone like her.'

'So what are you thinking?'

'That Clare wasn't the first word of the note, but the last word of a sentence from the page before; part of a longer letter.'

'One she didn't send you mean?'

'Oh she sent it all right.' It almost hurt to bring out those words. Her shining eyes widened. 'But you never saw it?'

'No.'

I could see her brain ticking over. 'So that must mean … '

265

'That someone saw how that section could be turned into a suicide note. And used it.'

Her eyes moved from my face to the shadows behind me and she spoke slowly. 'I don't understand.'

We looked at each other and my voice was there on a shuddering breath. 'This letter wasn't written to me. I assumed it was because she called Dad, *your father*. But it was written to you.'

She made no attempt to speak, her hands flat against the table, as I read Lorna's words. *"I can't keep this secret to myself any longer. Guilt is a corrosive emotion, I know that very well, and in the end the only solution is to face up to what you've done."*

'She's trying to tell you she understands how you must have been feeling all these years and she wants you to admit what you did, isn't she, Alice? And I think she was saying she would have to tell me herself if you didn't. That's what she means by: *"I hope you can accept that this is for the best."'*

Her eyes were closed, the lashes flickering on her cheeks.

My breath stalled; my throat on fire, but I knew I had to keep going. 'Lorna told me she would think about the night of the accident, and she must have worked out the truth and written to tell you.'

She was absolutely still.

'You were all drinking together at the hotel that night,' I said. 'But when Sylvia arrived, without Toby and Steve, you came back to try and stop me driving. Lorna must have realised you'd taken your car out. Perhaps she even saw you come in again, very late, but didn't make the connection at the time.'

I held up my mug. The coffee was nearly cold. I hadn't touched any of it. 'Did you put something in her coffee, like you did with me at the reception?'

She rubbed the back of her hand across her mouth, wiping away the tears. 'What do you remember?'

'Everything. I know it was your car I saw that night, and you standing there when I crawled out of the wreckage. That's what I couldn't bear to know all these years.'

'I'm so sorry.' It was a whisper.

'But I also know I didn't take the stuff from your bag or get it from anyone else. I didn't take anything willingly. I was happy that night. Dad had said nothing about being my real father. He must have been intending to do it next day. I was happy and I loved Steve and my boys so much.'

I was crying too. I had known somewhere deep inside that this moment would come, but now I wanted to run away. To pretend I didn't know. But I thought of Tom. 'But *you* weren't happy, were you? And it was easy to slip the stuff into my coffee.'

'Clare, I'm your sister.' I could hardly hear the words.

'And you've known that for a long time, haven't you?'

With a sudden movement that made me jump she stood and turned away, staring into the dark outside and shaking her head. 'Yes, he told me a couple of days before the wedding. He was going to tell you the morning after the reception, but he wanted me to know first. He expected me to be thrilled.'

I watched her standing there, her hair shining, her shoulders stiff. 'So you planned to humiliate me: show him his precious daughter was still a junkie,' I said. 'I saw you on the DVD, sitting with me. I bet you kept me talking so I wouldn't notice anything odd about my drink.'

When she turned her face looked almost ugly. 'You still don't see, do you? I didn't plan anything. It was just an impulse. You were so beautiful, so happy, you had everything and you hadn't worked for any of it. I just wanted to show Dad you hadn't really changed. I had the amphetamines with me because I needed them myself. I was working and studying day and night. Trying to be a brilliant doctor: to make him proud. And it was never enough. Because I wasn't you.'

'And you hated me for that.'

She laughed. 'Oh no, I adored you. Always have. I would have given anything when I was young to know you were my real sister. But you left me. With them. It was me who had to put up with the

267

arguments. With Mum telling me she was going to kill herself. I was scared every time I came home in case I found her dead. And all I wanted was someone to talk to, a big sister to share things with.'

She was pacing, her hands clenching and unclenching. 'And I was happy when you came back after she died and you promised to stay with us so we'd be a real family. But then there was Steve: the first man to come along. You didn't give me one moment's thought, did you? Didn't care how I felt.'

She came close, her eyes slivers of blue ice, every word clipped hard. 'You're so like Dad. He betrayed Mum and lied to everyone. Do you know he said I should never have kids because they might inherit Mum's instability? And when I told him how much I hated working at the hospital, he said I'd better get used to supporting myself, because he was going to destroy the firm and there'd be no money left. You both thought you could get away with hurting people. I just wanted you to know what it feels like to be hurt.'

'And you did hurt us,' I said. 'But what about the others? Steve? And Toby. Alice, what about Toby?' My voice broke, thinking of my little boy, hating her for what she'd done.

Her fist was in her mouth and she turned to press her face against the wall as a groan burst from her. Her shoulders shook in great spasms and when she spoke her voice was a strangled croak. 'I didn't want anyone to die. That's why I came back to stop you driving. I loved Toby so much and I've hated myself all these years. But I've tried to make it easier for Tom and to help you too. There was no more I could do.'

She looked back at me, her face so distorted it was like an old woman's. 'If only you'd left it alone, we could all have been happy again.'

I forced myself to go on. 'But you murdered Lorna.'

She groaned and turned away again. 'I begged her … Told her there was no point in raking it all up: it would spoil everything. But she wouldn't listen.' She leaned against the wall as if she couldn't stand without support. 'I didn't want to do it, you have to believe me.'

It was my turn to look away. I couldn't bear to see her. Our breathing was loud in the silence. *Keep going.* 'And when I started raking it up, you tried to frighten me. You had a key to the flat so it was easy enough for you to turn on the shower and the rest of it. I suppose you thought I might see something on the DVD too. Were you scared I'd remember, or did you just want to make me doubt my sanity so you could keep Tom?'

She faced me again and the silence vibrated between us as I looked into her clear eyes. And, in spite of everything, I felt a wave of pity for her: my beautiful little sister who should have had everything, but was going to be left with nothing at all.

I walked to the back door, but it was locked and when I got to the hall, the front door was bolted. She must have done it when I was upstairs.

I heard her come out of the kitchen and stop beside the little hall table at the bottom of the stairs. As if too weary to stand, she half sat on it, making Mum's big copper vase sway. The flowers were orange dahlias today.

Alice's hand curled slowly around the heavy frame of Mum and Dad's photograph. I swallowed, but forced myself, not to flinch. Forced myself to look away from her hand and into her eyes. 'It's no good, Alice.'

She shook her head, then, very carefully, placed the frame back on the table. I breathed again and bent to pull back the bolts. Something hit me hard on the side of the head. It must have been the photo frame and I grabbed at the door to stop myself falling, but my feet slipped and I went down onto my knees. Through the haze of pain I felt Alice grab my arm. She was holding something small and shiny – a syringe. I thrust her back and the syringe fell at our feet. I reached for it, but she kicked it out of the way.

I headed for the stairs to shut myself in one of the bedrooms. But, as I reached the landing, the fire alarm began to shrill and I remembered the petrol smell.

Alice must have started a blaze in the kitchen.

Chapter Twenty-Eight

I turned for the nearest bedroom, but as I reached for the door handle Alice was behind me. She grabbed a handful of my hair, yanking it so hard my head jerked back. I kicked out at her catching her shin, and when she let go of my hair, I lurched against the balustrade.

I was still dizzy and I swayed over the rail looking down at the tiled floor in the hall below. Smoke was pouring around the kitchen door and running like a dark river over the ceiling. The alarm shrieked on, but I could still hear the rasp of my own breathing and Alice's too, as she stood watching me. There was a smudge of dirt on her cheek and she looked like our mother in one of her cold rages.

Her hand was behind her back. Did she still have the syringe? She must have planned to leave me unconscious in the house; to make my death look like an accident. Then no one would ever know what she'd done.

I swallowed down a mouthful of acid. 'Don't do this, Alice. Think about Tom.'

She walked towards me. 'I am thinking of him. He'll be better off without you. You were never a proper sister to me and you've never been a proper mother.'

'I know I was selfish and I'm sorry. But we need to get out. Then we can talk. We'll find a way through this.' As I spoke I was moving along the balustrade, trying to get to the top of the stairs.

She saw what I was doing and snatched at my waist, but I kicked out at her and she stumbled to her knees, pulling me down with her. I kicked again and again, but she held tight and we were half sliding, half tumbling, downstairs.

At the bottom we crashed into the hall table sending the vase of orange flowers toppling onto the tiled floor. I scrambled to my feet and pushed Alice away.

The smoke was getting thicker and I was coughing hard, my chest tight. I had to get out. I skidded on the muddle of stems and water and slammed hard into the front door. Dark spots flashed in front of my eyes, but I managed to drag back the bolt. It still wouldn't open: the deadlock must be on, and without the key I had no chance. I pressed my face to the wood for a moment, hot tears stinging my eyes.

I could hear Alice behind me, scrabbling in the puddle of water and broken stems, and as I turned I saw her pick up the syringe. The alarm was still shrieking, I was choking for breath, my eyes streaming from the smoke, but I managed to shout at her, 'This is no good. Just unlock the door and let's go.'

She stood with her back against the newel post of the staircase and as I watched I saw her raise the syringe and, as if in slow motion, plunge it into her own arm.

By the time I got to her she was sitting on one of the bottom stairs. She looked up at me with a smile then closed her eyes and lay back. The alarm stopped shrieking and in the almost silence I could hear the roar of flames close by.

I got behind her and dragged at her but, although her eyes were closed, her hand was gripped tight around one of the spindles of the staircase, and I couldn't move her.

I crawled upstairs, lurching into the nearest bedroom – Tom's – and slamming the door behind me. It was clearer in here and I could breathe more easily, but that wouldn't last long. I dragged the pillows from the bed to block the gap under the door. Then ran to the windows. They were old sashes and I slid back the metal locks and tried to push one up. But it stuck fast. I tried the second. It wouldn't move.

I pulled Tom's little TV from its socket and hit the glass again and again. The pane cracked, but didn't shatter. I dragged out a drawer from the bedside table. The wood broke with the first blow, but the long piece of metal from the side came free and I stabbed it into the crack and made a hole.

As I punched at the splinters of glass, headlights appeared at the gate and a car swerved onto the driveway, kicking up gravel. It was Kieran. He leapt out, his headlights still blazing, and looked up at me, his face contorted. Then he disappeared.

I kicked and jabbed the shattered glass as a ladder banged onto the window ledge and I climbed through on quivering legs. Kieran came halfway up and clutched me to him.

'Clare, oh, Clare, thank God.'

At the bottom, we clung together, and he said, 'Nic told me where you'd gone. Where's Tom?'

A wail of sirens: the firemen jumping out before they came to a halt. I shouted over the clatter. 'My sister's in the downstairs hall. She's hurt,' then pressed into Kieran's solid warmth. 'It's all right, Tom's not here.'

'What happened?' he asked.

I couldn't answer.

One of the firemen told us to stand back and we watched as they used some kind of battering ram on the front door. The hose unrolled and, as the water roared out, more sirens sounded from the lane and a police car and ambulance crowded through the gates, their lights flashing.

From somewhere a silver sheet appeared and Kieran helped me wrap it around my shoulders. I leaned on the bonnet of his car. It was still warm. All I could see was the front door beginning to crack. *Please, please God.* Someone passed me a wad of lint to press against my face and it was only then that I realised I was shivering, my eyes and mouth throbbing.

They carried Alice out on a stretcher, her face covered by an oxygen mask. As they lifted her into the ambulance her eyes fluttered open and I moved towards her. We shared one look before I turned away.

'You need to come with us.' The voice came from a vast distance: I must have dozed or maybe passed out. I was sitting sideways on the driver's seat of Kieran's car, my shaking legs stretched in front of me on the gravel driveway. A paramedic was tugging my arm and Kieran's hand was on my other shoulder.

'No, I'm all right.'

'You can go in the ambulance with the other lady. She'll be OK, but we need to get you both to hospital.'

I shook my head. I couldn't go with her, couldn't bear to see her. 'I'm fine, but she injected herself with something; you need to check it. Take her now and my friend will drive me. I need to … ' I looked up at Kieran. *Help me. Make them leave me alone.* Although I hadn't said the words he seemed to understand and led the man away.

I sat watching Beldon House burn: the flames warming me and stopping my shivers. It was almost peaceful now, the sirens stilled, the banging and shouting silenced, only the soothing rush of water in the background: a fine mist of it cooling my sore face.

I leaned back. *Don't think, don't think, not yet, not yet.*

Something cannoned into my legs and then into my arms. Tom. He buried his face in my shoulder muttering all kinds of things I could only half hear.

'Heard the sirens, made Mark's dad bring me.'

Mark's dad was standing next to Kieran and gave me an awkward wave.

Tom looked at the ambulance pulling away. 'It's all right,' I said. 'We're OK.'

273

I moved back and the flames lit up Tom's face. They must have done the same for mine because he flinched and his hand came to his mouth. 'You're hurt.' He looked towards the house, then back at me, his eyes wide.

'Alice has gone to hospital, but they say she'll be all right. I'm just bruised.' My effort at a smile was so painful I felt a hot tear spill down my cheek.

I forced myself to my feet and we walked over to Mark's dad, arms around each other. 'Kieran's going to take me to have my face looked at,' I said. 'So you try to get some sleep and I'll see you tomorrow.' Tom was clinging to me like a much younger child and I kissed his forehead.

Mark's dad pulled him away. 'Come on, let's get you back to bed.' He nodded at me. 'Don't worry, we'll look after him.'

When they reached the gate I saw my son turn and stare back at the house and I threw the silver blanket aside and ran to him.

I held him tightly and said, 'I'll come for you as soon as I'm patched up. You can stay at the flat with me while we look for a new home. We'll be together all the time from now on.'

Today the pale November sun is no match for the brisk wind coming off the sea and I huddle into my coat. Here on the hills above the shore it's quiet at this time of year and, despite the cold, I prefer it this way. I wave at Tom as he runs back and forth across the wide expanse of grass, trying to get his kite to take off. His friend, Mark, is with us, and he's already managed to launch his kite. It dips and dives, a dark bird in the chill blue sky.

I haven't visited Alice, but her lawyer tells me she's admitted everything and is pleading guilty. She says this is to make things easier for me and especially for Tom. I've had enough of anger and bitterness so I'll try to believe her.

It became obvious right away that the fire had been set deliberately, and at first, I expected her to try and blame me. But she probably realised that Jacob Downes could identify her from the crash site. And that Emily and Matt knew she was using ampheta-mines at the time of the wedding. Once I'd raised suspicions about Lorna's death, they discovered she actually died from a massive dose of insulin. Lorna's neighbour saw Alice arrive at her house around the time she must have been killed.

There's talk that Alice may have a personality disorder and I suppose that's one way to explain what she did. But I remember what she told me that night and I think it started all those years ago when we were kids. It was so important to her that Mum and Dad saw her as the good girl: their own real child. The one who always behaved well – so different from me.

One thing I'll never know is when my little sister's love for me turned to hatred, but then I doubt she knows that herself.

I do believe she loves Tom and it's odd because in a way I'm still grateful to her for bringing him up so well, helping to make him the kind of young man Steve would have been proud to call his son.

It's been hard for Tom and it's going to get harder still for a while. I've told him most of the truth and the way he reacted makes me wonder if he had some instinctive understanding of the situation all along. There's been publicity, of course, and when the trial happens it could get worse. My solicitor says it should be easy enough after that to get my own conviction overturned, although that doesn't seem very important just now.

I'm in touch with Mr Hillier and he tells me Jacob Downes made a deal with the police. Because of his help in identifying Alice, and my evidence that he probably saved my life after the crash, he won't be charged with perjury. Mr Hillier is trying to find him work.

Beldon House is being demolished and I plan to use some of Dad's money to help released prisoners. Nic and I have become even greater friends and she's been helping Tom and me to look for somewhere to live. I think we may have found the cottage I always used to dream of. It's not far from the flat, so Molly and

Nic can visit all the time. Nic seems much happier these days and I can't help smiling when I think of her.

And then of course there's Kieran.

Even in the cold up here on the hill, a glow goes through me when he comes into my mind, although if I'm honest he's rarely out of it these days. Tom really likes him and keeps suggesting he should live with us when we move. But Kieran agrees it's too soon. He knows I need some time with my son: just the two of us.

I push my hands deep into my pockets and walk down towards the boys and, as his kite takes to the air, I hear Tom laughing.

Acknowledgements:

I owe grateful thanks to many people, but especially to Moira McDonnell and Bryan Taylor for cheering me on all the way.

To Allan Guthrie for great advice and support over the years. To Sheila Bugler: my constant inspiration on the journey. To Jo Reed, Claire Whatley, Karen Milner, Amanda Hodgkinson, JJ Marsh, Marlene Brown, Liza Perrat, Lorraine Mace, Tricia Gilbey, Barbara Scott Emmett, Justine Windsor, June Whitaker and all the talented folk at the Writing Asylum.

To my editor at HarperCollins, Kate Stephenson, for her wisdom and enthusiasm.

And, above all, thanks and love go to my sister, Sue Curran, and to my son, Jack Farmer.